T0271669

Sweet Vidalia

ALSO BY LISA SANDLIN

The Famous Thing About Death
Message to the Nurse of Dreams
In the River Province
You Who Make the Sky Bend
The Do-Right
The Bird Boys

Lisa Sandlin

Sweet Vidalia

abacus
·books·

ABACUS

First published in the United States in 2024 by Little, Brown and Company
First published in the United Kingdom in 2025 by Abacus

1 3 5 7 9 10 8 6 4 2

A CIP catalogue record for this book
is available from the British Library.

HB ISBN: 978-0-3491-4701-7
TPB ISBN: 978-0-3491-4700-0

Printed and bound in Great Britain by
Clays Ltd, Elcograf S.p.A.

Papers used by Abacus are from well-managed forests
and other responsible sources.

Abacus	The authorised representative
An imprint of	in the EEA is
Little, Brown Book Group	Hachette Ireland
Carmelite House	8 Castlecourt Centre
50 Victoria Embankment	Dublin 15, D15 XTP3, Ireland
London EC4Y 0DZ	(email: info@hbgi.ie)

An Hachette UK Company
www.hachette.co.uk

www.littlebrown.co.uk

Nannie B.

The most difficult character in comedy is that of the fool, and he must be no simpleton that plays that part.

—Miguel de Cervantes, *Don Quixote*

Sweet Vidalia

I

On the first of February, 1964, Eliza Kratke walked home in late afternoon from a neighbor's and found her husband, Robert, in the driveway beside the Fairlane, the door standing open, his hand on the top frame of it. It was one of his rare weekends off from the railroad. Eliza thought that maybe he was going down to Dinwiddie's to buy a hose for the Whirlpool or had been there and was just returning. Later she would find that he had not bought a hose, or anything, since there was no package in the car or the garage or any room of the house. Much later it would occur to her to wish she had noticed if the Fairlane had been cold or warm. But what woman would notice a detail like that while her husband of thirty years watched her walking toward him with such an anguished expression on his face?

Eliza knew she was about to hear it, this secret that he'd been on the verge of telling her. For months and months, Robert had been brooding. Not sharing the vivid little happenings from work that formerly had invited her into his day. His abrupt silences collapsed ordinary conversations. Suspense had returned to their life. Eliza disliked suspense. It made her anxious, and being anxious made her angry and impatient. She was a preparer. Holidays, she assigned dishes or accepted her own assignment; vacations, she packed from a penciled list; emerging from Hitchcock movies into the cool of night, she did not feel safely thrilled—she felt wrung out and disheveled. But look at him there—whatever thing Robert needed to say, she would hear now in their driveway, she was sure. Her rib cage contracted violently. The fear housed there slammed upward and spread jangling through her chest. She pulled her wool coat closer and held his gaze, her own inquiring, *What could you have to say that I couldn't stand?*

Just before she reached him, his knees buckled. He caught himself on the door, clung to it, drew almost upright again. Eliza ran the last two steps and seized him around the waist. "There's a hammer in my back," he told the top of her head, "and in my front."

She helped him heave himself into the car. He lurched over toward the passenger door. Eliza was scrambling out to call an ambulance but he shook his head, lifted his hand, thumb up, index finger pointing like a gun toward the Whelans' house. She clambered in, understanding there would be no discussion and that he was not really pointing at the Whelans' but beyond, where Maple Street led to Pershing Boulevard and the hospital, only two miles away. He meant they would be there faster than an ambulance could arrive, and as there was pain, they should go now. She grimaced in return, gave a half-shake of her head, put the car in gear.

They often communicated this way, expression and gesture accomplishing an agreement between them. This agreement was modified by her reservations, but the disapproving shake of her head had stated that for the record, and she didn't protest further. With a flick of a glance over her left shoulder, Eliza tapped the brakes for the corner stop sign, turned right onto Maple, and drove the several residential blocks at forty-five, twenty miles beyond the speed limit. She turned left onto Pershing, a six-lane boulevard. Robert bent restlessly forward, then into the seat back; he could settle in neither position. When she asked him how he was, his answer was a tightening of the lips. She drove with one hand on his thigh, holding him in place.

She slowed for a red light at Ivy. Robert was grunting as he exhaled, eyes narrowed, lips compressed. These small sounds, full of the effort of withstanding, made her unable to wait out the light; she simply couldn't. Eliza whipped her head to see that the street was clear and drove through the intersection, leaving three lanes of stopped cars behind. Scanning desperately ahead, clutching Robert's leg, she took Walnut and Oak on yellows at fifty-five. As they reached Spruce, he folded, vomiting onto his feet. Eliza began to murmur, "Hold on, honey, hold on," and in her sharply increased alarm passed a cement mixer grumbling toward Pine and got to the light just as it changed to red. A driver on the cross street to her right charging into an early green saw her and stood on his screaming brakes. Eliza stamped her brake and flung out an arm to protect Robert; his weight hyperextended her elbow, but she saw she'd clear the intersection if she gassed it, so she did, escaping past the driver's shocked face. She trailed her hand over Robert's neck, then grasped his arm; against her sweating palm, his skin was dry and very cold. She made the next two lights on green, tailgating every car in front of her until it surrendered the lane, laying on its horn as she accelerated past.

The police car caught them a block from the hospital. Because she hadn't looked back, Eliza had been oblivious to the whirling lights, so the bleat of a siren switched to high volume made her jump in the seat and let out the cry she'd been continuously swallowing. She semaphored in the rear-view mirror *No, no, no* without slowing down. Most of her life she'd been afraid of police, from the day she'd seen them wade swinging into a tussle of unemployed men, her father included, at the sawmill gates. It was the transformation that had scared her. The screech of a whistle—and the policemen's neutral faces contorted into masks of naked, personal ferocity. It would not have occurred to her to stop and ask for the policeman's assistance; besides, they were almost there. It was what she was begging Robert to believe: *Almost there, almost there, hold on, hold on.* She swerved to the left lane so she could make the turn ahead into the hospital lot; this abrupt maneuver cut off the police car, and he fell back, on her bumper now, siren blaring angrily. Red light pulsed over Robert, but he did not react to the violent red splashes. Anguish was gone from his face. Robert's eyes were open now, and he looked almost bemused, as though he were puzzling over some small issue, his fingers hooked into his shirt. The left-turn lane curved ahead of her, traffic steady in the oncoming lanes so that she had to brake. She thought she would nudge out into the traffic anyway, force the cars to let her through.

Before she could do this, a policeman was shouting from directly behind her window: "Turn off your car!"

Eliza rolled down the window and stabbed her finger toward the hospital. Surely he would understand, surely he'd seen emergencies before: There was the hospital, here was a man with frost in his skin.

"Turn off your car! Throw your keys out the window. Now!"

Robert patted her shoulder sloppily and spoke. He'd been so quiet that it startled her and scared her; his voice was casual, drunken. "You go on, baby," he muttered as if he were encouraging her to go on to bed, and he would come a little later.

The way was clear now; she could have spun the wheel and turned. Driven across the broad boulevard and up into the horseshoe drive of St. Mary's, past an ambulance parked there, right up to the double glass doors radiating light. Instead, like a cringing girl, like the law abider she was—she condemned herself later—Eliza obeyed the official voice. Her brain throbbing *Wrong-wrong-wrong,* she killed the engine. She withdrew the keys and dropped them out her window.

The policeman's voice commanded: "Now open your door from the outside and get out! Keep your hands where I can see 'em!"

Eliza fumbled opening the car door and began to get out. "Lay down on the ground, lay—" The policeman's legs were braced, both hands on the black gun that pointed at her face. They confronted each other with disbelief. From the jerk of his features, Eliza saw he'd expected some armed-holdup hood or belligerent drunkard, not her graying hair and gold bifocals; she'd expected the hardened sneer of a union-busting bull, not an outraged child. Sharp-creased, badge gleaming in the six o'clock sunburst, belt loaded with leather scabbards, the patrolman loomed over her like a blond boy swollen to breaking with some sandbox injustice. He holstered the gun and scooped up her keys. "Lady, that's the most reckless driving I ever seen!"

"Please, my husband—"

"You know how many wrecks you just about caused?"

"Listen, I think he's—"

Eliza edged back, but he came on, shouting, "I been chasing you for blocks. Don't you know what rearview mirrors are for?"

What could she do with someone like this? She glanced toward the traffic a lane away, drivers slowed, gawking. Looked up, stupidly, as *Deliberate disregard, alcohol, license, registration* rained down on her, to the pink light snared between bare, black branches of oak that lined the boulevard. Then back to the red patches suffusing the corded neck, the downy cheek.

"Doctor!" Eliza hollered up at the boy. "Doctor, doctor, doctor, doctor!"

Doctor penetrated the clenched angles of the young policeman by visible degrees, like a nail steadily driven into wood. His head twitched toward the hospital, and the muscles around his eyes sagged. He bent into the Fairlane's window. "Oh God," he said.

She was about to shoulder him aside, but he shoved the keys at her and sprinted away to his car. Eliza lunged through the window. A foam of vomit was sliding down Robert's chin. She threw open the door, thrust the keys into the ignition, and scrabbled, hands and knees on the vinyl seat, to her husband. She was calling his name in a stream, *Robert-Robert-Robert*. His head lolled toward her, his expression still mild, and his left hand reached out to her. Gratefully Eliza grasped it—cold, so cold—and then Robert snatched it away from her. He let out a throaty, gargling noise; air hissed through his teeth. His weight slumped onto her, pinning her to the seat. She gathered in his right elbow and looked down onto his nape and the wine birthmark there. Eliza began to rock, the movement so slight that she did not notice she was making it. She went on this way, being crushed by him, weaving, whispering.

In this calm she dared to press a hand to his clammy forehead to measure the fever that was not there. His strained face cleared. Robert looked at her mildly again. That look frightened her silent, the lazy expression that told her he was separate from the cars crawling by on the boulevard, from the car he sat in, from her, from what was happening to him.

"Move away, ma'am," a voice behind her commanded, "move out, please."

Eliza protested, but she was dragged out. She staggered; her feet did not know where they should meet the pavement. It was dark here where she was; dusk shredded over lines of gray cars, street, fading trees, until it obscured like a backdrop. Revolving red lights whirlpooled around her. She turned her back and looked up beyond their range; the ceiling of the sky was wide lit with the fleshy, sprawled light of February. The cold, still air searing her edges, freezing the sweat beneath her coat, told her she had not escaped, was not currently escaping, that this was occurring now, this moment, that she was standing on a street in a moment that was not ending but being, going on and on without seam or relief. The lanes of traffic she had not turned into, had not forced to stop, were stopped, of course not the same cars but other cars, stopped, the intersection blocked by an ambulance parked haphazardly, its driver craned out. Blocked by the young patrolman, legs planted, both arms rigidly outstretched. That she saw steadily; there could be no mistake about the meaning of that posture—any car that attempted to pass would be met by the palms of his hands. The huffing, white-coated man who must have dragged her out had scrambled past her, the cold metal of his stethoscope had grazed her hand. He crouched now on the seat beside Robert. "Go!" He dragged out the syllable, chopping with his arm, then slid behind the wheel of her car. The ambulance straightened and fishtailed away. Her car—hers and Robert's Fairlane—made the turn she should have made and glided across the boulevard and away, far up into the hospital's horseshoe drive. Its glass doors popped open.

Eliza was disoriented by the emptiness of the turn lane. The car was something large and fast that she had worn and now it was gone. Beyond the patrolman's red-flashing cruiser, a car door slammed; a woman's voice asked her if she needed help. Eliza angled to see a woman in a scarf hesitate, then stride forward, saw a white swarm emerging from a rounded mouth, but she tilted herself toward the hospital. As she neared the middle of the street and the patrolman's back, he turned so that their eyes met. The curved bill of the cap was pushed back; his eyes glittered. He was looking at Eliza with the exact expression Robert had had when she'd hurried up the driveway an age ago: pained, expecting blame. The young man's lips moved; by some inexplicable delay, a white wreath wafted and began to rise before she heard what he said: "I'm sorry."

That was how Robert's message was delivered to her. On the cold boulevard, and in a colder second, one that flared, then clipped off, finished, she knew with certainty: that was what Robert had meant to tell her.

She ran. Somewhere far back in the three lanes of traffic, one car flipped on its lights, then another and another and another. Eliza ran through a gauntlet of headlights, up the horseshoe drive, past the ambulance, past the empty Fairlane, and through the hospital's wide glass doors.

II

Eliza Brock had been the unmarried daughter of a farming couple who'd moved down to Bayard when they'd lost their North Texas farm. Brown-haired, pleasant-faced, slim and shy, that was her. Living with her parents at age twenty-six, she helped her mother with a seamstress business. Her own dresses were old but ironed, rips made into designs with clever threadwork. Her shoes shined with a bit of biscuit. She also worked down at the courthouse for almost nothing, giving out sacks of rice and pintos to those who needed them. In those days, many did, including her folks. The worst part of that tedious job was picking out the weevils.

Robert Kratke—though Eliza didn't know his name

when she first caught sight of him in the Methodist hall—had been dark-haired and approaching handsome, not tall but even-featured. His lips were so beautifully cut, they were like the lips of the elegant-lady faces in the newspaper's sale ads. This young man was no stick, no stand-in-the-corner silent type. His face and hands were mobile, exaggeratedly so. Eliza could follow from maybe five feet away the conversation he was having with a friend: Something unexpected had happened, he hadn't known what to do, he had decided on a course, rushed into it full steam ahead until he'd come bang up against an obstacle and been stymied again. Then an idea had come to him—and he'd acted on it. Success! Other young men's faces and hands did not move like that. Eliza Brock studied him in her contained way, which she did not know was flattering because it was so deliberate and curious, and interpreted his mobility as the expression of an overflowing spirit.

What marvels we see when we want to.

It hadn't been an overflowing spirit at all. She'd learned that when she met his family. Robert had informed her that his family was deaf, but she was still unprepared. Dinner was quiet but active. Hands flew, drew down cheeks and sped to foreheads, produced lightning finger combinations. Faces stretched beyond normal contortion. They exaggerated silent laughter, shook with it, mother and father and brothers and wives, or stretched with surprise, contracted with sadness, disgust. They acted out what the hands were saying. She could tell what they were feeling about what they were saying, just not what they were saying. Eliza found herself tilting along with a silent recital, found her own face responding with an echo of the speaker's expression, but could not join in. It was the opposite of conversations she was used to, where you knew what you were hearing but did not necessarily know how the teller felt about it, especially if the teller meant to hide that part from you.

Still, they were kind enough, passing the potatoes and the chicken, urging her with graceful hands to eat. It was just that, engaged in their own stories or news, they soon forgot about her. For a while, Robert had translated, and then, as it's tiresome and isolating always to wait for the laggard, he'd just begun to follow along with the hands and the faces, joining in the conversation occasionally. Robert, the only hearing and speaking one, Eliza slowly realized, was the outer rim of the family's circle.

"They sent me to live with my aunt and uncle when I was two," he told her. "When they knew I could hear. They knew I should learn how to talk. I guess I'd picked up sign already." He'd lived with relatives until he was six and started school, not the same school his siblings attended, which was a special one for deaf children, but the school right up the street. He walked there by himself while his brothers waited for a bus, and he walked home alone too. His parents did not come to his teacher conferences or, later, to his baseball games, though they attended his brothers' at the deaf school, where they felt comfortable. Robert didn't ask them more than twice. He understood.

"I didn't want to see them so nervous," he said. "That made me nervous."

Eliza had taken out a book on signing from the library, and over the years, visiting, she had learned enough sign to convey messages about baby Hugh and to ask questions, give greetings. Robert's parents did not intentionally slight her and Hugh and, later, Ellen, who learned to sign from her cousins, forgot, then learned again next time. But it seemed to her mother's eye that the Kratkes delighted more fully in their deaf grandchildren, held them closer, longer. Had Robert felt that for himself when he was a boy? Eliza had always felt a tender pain for her husband when she pictured that.

Two of his brothers had gone to Gallaudet on scholarship; Robert had gone to the oil fields near Bayard, the town where they met. That was work he could get; the railroads were not hiring then, in 1934. She could keep children for women who had to work, widows and the like, he told Eliza, but he could provide, he could take care of her. To prove it, he'd found a house in a neighborhood he was sure would be nice once all its construction was complete. When he'd beguiled a banker into giving them a mortgage for the house, Robert Kratke was a proud man.

And Eliza a bride, scrubbing plaster smears and handprints from new windows, planting saplings she and Robert dug up in the woods, and, whenever some extra money came their way, painting walls: Ivory Cream, Celery, Pink Velvet. The hardware store sold soft colors back then, during those hard times.

III

Eliza called the kids from a pay phone and then stationed herself in the hospital's waiting room. She felt
the speed of the Fairlane still, the wrenching from one lane
to another, the horns, the red traffic lights, the pulsing
police lights. If she closed her eyes, it was all there again.
Opening her eyes on this square, pale green room jarred
her. Eliza noticed but did not wonder about the family
who, after the continuous snapping of elevator doors, kept
gaining members, taking all the chairs. Two small boys,
ignored, tussled over a G.I. Joe. One of them kicked her
ankle; she pulled it back beneath her chair. Voices from
the PA system arrived distant and garbled. She had been
forbidden to go where they took Robert.

More than an hour later, she was summoned to listen to a solemn doctor. They had done their best, Mrs....
Kratke—he read her name from a clipboard—but they could not save her husband. She should rest assured that, truly, the medical team here had done everything in its power. He was sorry.

This short speech was no surprise; neither did it feel real.

They let her go in then. The floor of the room was scattered with gauze and tape, bits of paper, a black plug, a latex glove. There was no blood but the sheet was twisted. Robert lay on a gurney, one bare knee cocked like he'd tried to escape. His chin was sunken into his neck and his head turned to the side, as if he could not bear to see her. His eyes were open. She skirted the bed. Wherever she stood, he wasn't looking at her. Wouldn't look at her. Even when she leaned over him, he gazed somewhere beyond her.

She was crying, and they were alone, him with mussed hair, his face turned away. No one bothered her. Eliza cupped his jaw. She had a sensation of having been crushed, of having just sustained a heavy blow to her body.

She pushed away a hanging tube and laid her head some long time on his silent chest. "Oh, Robert," she murmured to him, many times.

She assured him: "You were loved, honey, you were loved."

She pulled back to touch his unshaven cheek. He still looked like the man she'd married, hair mostly dark, just a few gray strands, chin furred in gray. Stockier. That clear, fair skin of his now weathered and creased. He'd loved the railroad, and he'd taken the longer, out-of-town runs his boss George Mull assigned him to make more money. Had they really needed it? Why hadn't she urged him to give up those runs, to tell George no? Stay home? Stay. She'd been so wrong not to do that. Wrong. This judgment on herself added to the weight pressing against her.

She clasped his veined arm, mashing down the wiry hair. His skin was warm. To leave this hospital room was to leave him behind. Leave her marriage behind. On the other side of its threshold, she was a widow. She wanted these last precious moments with Robert. With her husband. The ordinary times lived over and over. Rise, tend to meals, house, errands, husband, go to bed again. Stand in the doorway watching Robert walk from the car in a chilling wind, spring's wet thaw, the spread green heat of summer, through leaves skidding and scraping across the dry concrete of the driveway. A pair of compasses, her fixed at the door, Robert drawing nearer, the background of yard and neighborhood dialed through the quarters of the year into the next year and the next.

But it was of no real use, acting like he was still hers. Her favorite thing about Robert, why she'd fallen in love with him—the mobility of his face, his lightning changes of expression, his wide gestures, his smiles—that had gone.

A nurse knocked, brought her a sheet of notepaper

on which was written funeral home names and numbers. Mrs. Kratke should call one and they would send their employees to transport Mr. Kratke's body back there for preparation.

Not ten minutes later her daughter, Ellen, pushed through the door, cried, "Daddy!" She laid herself against Eliza's back and hugged her arms around her. Eliza pulled away to let Ellen nearer Robert, but her sobbing daughter didn't want to go closer.

"We got... we've got to..." Eliza held out the paper, gestured toward the door. Ellen went back into the hall while her mother, holding to the doorjamb, gazed hard into the room for a minute more.

Then she stepped out and made the phone call to the funeral home. Eventually her son, Hugh, and his wife, Pam, burst from an elevator. Hugh's tears started when he saw her. They huddled together in the greenish waiting room with another family whose hands knotted together, hope written on their faces. But not their family, not the Kratkes, their pained eyes meeting to confirm that today marked a day with an ending; the ending was here.

The funeral people arrived with their own gurney. At Eliza's suggestion, they all left to go back to her house, Eliza the first to reach the elevator. She didn't want to see Robert in a bag, covered, anonymous.

The crushed feeling stayed with her, moved with her. When she got home, in her doorway, Percy stood sentry, his rear end managing a wag or two. He'd always been more her dog than Robert's. Eliza bent down and scooped up the old white terrier with brown ears. It was a comfort to hug his stout little body, to receive a lick on her face.

A problem, worrisome, came up after Eliza had written the funeral home a $720 check for a plot and the casket. Mr. Warburton, its director, phoned two days before the funeral to tell her with a slight cough that the bank had returned her check.

"Oh, no, that's a mistake." Eliza's voice was raised. She explained the problem to Hugh, and he heaved himself up from the couch to untangle the misunderstanding, to get out of the gloom of the house. He went alone, and that was fine with Eliza. If she'd gone with him, she knew Mr. Warburton would have talked to Hugh anyway. That's what men did. In the meantime, Ellen and Pam took Pam's kids, Betsy and John, down to the park. There'd be another child soon; Pam was showing.

They were still at the park when Hugh came back, earlier than expected and looking as though someone had hit him. "Ma," he said, and fell back onto the living-room couch. "It's not a mistake. I took the check to the bank, and it's not a mistake."

Alarmed, Eliza sat down in the chair next to him. "I don't understand, Hugh. It has to be."

"Your checking account doesn't have enough, and

neither does your savings. You spent all this? On what? I mean, it's pretty late in the day to just go—"

"No, we didn't spend any savings." Running through the heat of her surprise and indignation was a flash of unease. "You know we wouldn't do that. I'm fifty-seven years old. Your dad was fifty-three—why would we spend money we need for later? It has to be a mistake."

"It's not. It's not a mistake. That banker showed me."

"Charlie Dillon, heavy man, black glasses?"

"I guess so. He showed me it all. And the last—" Hugh wrenched himself upright, shaking his head, not looking at her.

"What? What, Hugh?" Eliza's indignation washed away. A cold fear began to creep into her throat, up her arms.

"First I thought maybe y'all meant to remodel the house or something, but then I remembered we repainted two, three years ago. Listen, did Dad move your savings to some kind of stock market account, maybe? I thought of other stuff... but then this just barged right into my head: *Does Ma know? About this mortgage?* I don't know, something about how he looked at me. The banker. Did you know?"

"We just paid off the mortgage, Hugh. You remember."

"Yeah, I do. But there's a new one. Not a huge amount, but... it was Dad's signature on the papers. I can't make sense of it. Did y'all buy an investment property? I thought you'd have told us if you did."

"No, we didn't buy any—"

"And then I thought, *Jesus*...Ma, did Dad gamble? Last couple years, the railroad's always sending him on the run to Louisiana, right? Right? They have gambling boats right there. For all your money to—"

"I'm sure he didn't. I'd have known." But now the idea of Robert's secret throbbed in her head. "Wait a minute."

In their bedroom, Eliza unclasped the metal box where Robert kept their documents and banking records and riffled through the checkbook. She expected to find close to eleven hundred dollars, what they'd agreed to keep in the account in case of emergencies. Instead the final figure, in her husband's scribble, was $471.56. She could not locate the deposit slips for his paychecks. Panic flared in her. Back in the living room, trying to tamp down the panic, she told Hugh, "I think I better go see."

"You don't need to," her son said dully. Hugh looked a lot like Robert, brown-haired, compactly built, same clean profile. Ever since he was about twenty, lines in his forehead had begun to show. Now they looked set. Eliza felt sick to her stomach.

She had to speak to Charlie Dillon at the bank.

The banker went over it all again, pity clear on his close-shaven face. When she stood abruptly, he lumbered forward to take her elbow, asked Eliza could he do anything for her.

"Nothing. Thank you, Charlie."

Nothing unless you can explain what my husband has done here.

On the way out of his office, she bumped the doorway painfully with her hip. The bank she'd known for twenty years was unfamiliar; the walls retracted, and the station with deposit and withdrawal slips in slots, its two pens on chains, receded into shadow. This was because she was separated from the other people here—they were having a regular day. Eliza passed people conducting their business, a woman herding a child, a man in overalls smoking. They appeared to her as blurs. Her path was private, unlit. She went down two steps, clutching the handrail for dear life, and out of the bank into a slap of cold air. She slid onto the chilled vinyl seat of the Fairlane, behind its wheel. And sat there, not moving, short of breath. Lost. For a second she wished she could still believe there had been a mistake. But that was not Eliza, that was not her, that was a stupid, harmful thought. What is, is. She let it go and, beginning to be truly afraid, wondered what she would do now. She wanted to lie down, to flick off her bedroom light and lie down. One task remained—discussing payment with the funeral home—but that could wait until tomorrow.

She turned the Fairlane toward home. Eliza was not the sort of woman who fooled herself; at least, she hoped she was not. Their years had not all been happy or peaceful, she could admit that. The kids knew that. In recent times, she'd keenly felt a distance. Robert kept to himself. She could have pried, she could have insisted he talk to her. But Eliza had believed it a phase that would pass and they'd come back toward each other, as had happened on occasions in the past. Cycles, circles, they'd had those. She made herself see Robert with the kids, telling stories of crafty talking rabbits and determined turtles, his face bright with meanings, with silliness. Made herself see the two of them laughing together in bed; they had done that. That was true. Through the years, they'd had happiness and closeness. They had.

IV

She drove the Fairlane to the funeral home several hours before the public visitation to settle somehow the matter of the burial fee. Monthly payments? She'd also decided to notify Mr. Warburton, the funeral director, that she might skip the viewing. She meant to skip it, she was too unnerved, though she would say *might*. A widow might skip the visitation, she reasoned, being unable to...well, just unable. Surely that had happened before. Her absence would be easily explained with a somber head shake. The children would be there to speak to the neighbors, to their uncles, to others.

Eliza spoke to Mr. Warburton, assured him that the funeral would be paid for, mentioned installments. His customary seriousness became more serious, even wary. She promised and, as a gesture of goodwill, wrote him a check for three hundred dollars. She tore it from her checkbook, the checkbook that should have been able to cover it all. She told him she might not attend the viewing.

Mr. Warburton nodded.

As Eliza reached the door, the funeral director's secretary appeared on the lush beige carpet of the entryway. He must have sent her after Eliza almost immediately. A blond lady in a shirtwaist dress, her hair pinned up in a flat French twist. The woman's fingers closed gently around Eliza's wrist, and she led her to a soft wing chair, saying, "You need to know this..." Maintaining the light touch, making sympathetic eye contact, the secretary completed the destruction of Eliza's life.

A woman claiming to be Mrs. Kratke, a very upset woman, had made a scene earlier, she said. In the morning. The secretary hadn't recognized her; she hadn't been the same woman who had made the funeral arrangements. Eliza was that woman, Mr. Robert Kratke's wife. But this other woman had also claimed to be Mrs. Robert Kratke.

Mr. Warburton had persuaded that woman to leave. In case she should return, though, the secretary wanted Eliza to have this information. She searched Eliza's face, maybe to determine if Eliza understood the situation. The secretary got her answer to that question immediately from Eliza's "Wha-at?" From her staring, bewildered expression that, once she was assured that she had heard correctly, changed to one of sinking, drowning.

The secretary walked her to her car, and Eliza drove home in a haze, one-handed. The other hand, the one with the ring, the gold ring she didn't want to see, she held against a wound in her stomach, as though she had been crushed or shot. Ellen and Pam knew at once that something was badly wrong. Hugh entered the living room with a cup of coffee and stopped where he was. Ellen hovered, asking a flurry of questions. Eliza briefly grasped her daughter's arm, mouthing, *Wait,* then let her purse drop onto the end table with the drawer. She sat, squeezed into the arm of the couch.

"There's...the secretary at Warburton's said..." Eliza took some breaths. "That a woman came and made a scene. She said...she was Robert's wife." She glanced up at their blank expressions. None of them understood yet, except maybe Hugh. Hugh began to look as if a hard wind were blowing in his face.

"Your father had another wife. That's...that's what the secretary wanted to tell me. Like a...a warning."

Shouted exclamations from Ellen and Pam drew both grandchildren to the living room, John wielding a wooden gavel from his toy workbench. Betsy surveyed the adults and stationed herself under her mother's arm.

"Bullshit! That's just bullshit! I don't believe that!" Ellen spat this in Eliza's direction. Eliza could manage no reply. Ellen and Pam talked over each other, throwing out questions Eliza couldn't answer. Who was the woman? Had Eliza known about her? Not known? Why would she show up at the funeral home? Did she have any kind of identification? Any proof?

John snuffled, then wailed. "Pam," Hugh said, lifting his chin toward the toddler.

"Right, me," Pam said, but she picked up John and left the room, Betsy shadowing her.

Hugh sat down in a chair, both hands wrapped around his cup. "Give Ma a break, Nell."

Ellen barked back at him, "I'm not mad at her."

"You shouldn't be. This is it, isn't it?" His tone was sharp, bitter. "This is where the money went. Jesus Christ, the son of a bitch."

In the tense silence, they could hear a voice rise and fall in the bedroom where Pam must have been reading to the kids. Hugh stood abruptly and walked into the kitchen. A crash followed. Ellen ran after him and they had a raucous whisper-fight Eliza didn't try to overhear—the open wound took her attention. She bent forward over it. She hadn't questioned the secretary. After the first shock, she'd believed her.

Now another shock, from a thought so unwelcome she held her stomach with both hands. Would this woman show up at the funeral? Would she do something like that? Would she announce herself to Eliza, to her friends and neighbors?

Eliza groaned and staggered to her feet. She went and

lay down in her bed, not bothering to get under the covers, just gathering the chenille bedspread around herself. Gripping the bedspread in her fists, her elbows hugged to her body. It was a long time before she slept, and once she did, the talk outside her room—plaintive, angry, questioning, arguing—rumbled on and on in her dreams, endless.

In the morning, Ellen brought her coffee and hugged her. The others sat around the breakfast table with cereal boxes. Eliza kissed John and Betsy on the tops of their heads. But she had nothing to say, and her family must have said everything last night.

The next day was bright, with a stinging breeze. Eliza wore a black suit beneath her gray wool coat. She nodded to concerned neighbors, hugged Robert's two brothers and their wives—the oldest brother, Burton, had passed—and didn't linger with those who tried to keep her. Except for George Mull, a tall, bony, sunburned man, Robert's boss on the crew. He'd insisted on speaking to her as she was entering the chapel. Had uncharacteristically taken her hand to hold it, which Eliza was in no condition to appreciate, just wanting to get to a seat.

"My sincere condolences, Eliza," he'd said in his sober voice, and paused as if he might say more but didn't. The look on his long face was dour, stern.

"Mull's a self-righteous bastard," Robert used to say. "Company man, hand fulla *Gimme* and a mouth fulla

Much obliged," that was Robert's opinion. At company picnics he would touch his Dixie cup of lemonade to Eliza's and ask after her children; he was quick with advice and judgment. Courteous, not charming. She'd always thought that he was one of those people whose natural instinct was to say no rather than yes.

She retracted her hand from his and turned, but her step arrested. Her vision lost its focus. She'd blamed George for saddling Robert with extra weekends away on three-day runs for the railroad, midweek stints down at the yard. Now she saw that was wrong. It hadn't been his fault. The severe look he'd given her—he hadn't meant it for Eliza. It came to her that he'd meant it for Robert.

George Mull must have known.

She managed to walk on.

Directly after the service in the funeral home's chapel, a black car drove her family to the nearby cemetery. She took her seat in a folding chair beneath the green tent. Her children also belonged in this reserved first row, her shattered children. Eliza could still feel Mr. Warburton's secretary's grasp. *You need to know this.* Hugh put his arm around her, clutched her shoulder. His eyes were hollow. But Ellen could not be made to sit. She'd stationed herself just outside the far edge of the tent with a view of all the mourners. The old minister, Mr. Olsen, with the new, young minister, Mr. Henney, behind him, was about to leave the sideline and place himself up front to begin this final part of the service.

Eliza turned when she heard a strident voice to see Ellen confronting a woman supported between two large, fair-haired men. She couldn't make out Ellen's words but she heard the response, a shrill "I've got my marriage papers" from the woman. A little square-faced woman, clinging to the men, who practically dragged her into a chair in the back row.

Heads were turning. Eliza cringed.

That was her, there, Robert's other wife? Younger than Eliza for sure, probably in her forties. Early forties. Not really pretty, at least not with her brow squeezed like that and the wild look in her eyes. Who were the men with her? Eliza couldn't envision this little woman side by side with Robert, couldn't see them embrace, see her up on tiptoes kissing him. She couldn't form that incongruous, impossible picture. But just thinking it shrank her. Her neighbors were there, she'd nodded to them, and couples from their church, men who worked at the railroad with Robert, his brothers. They were all looking at the back row now. A face jumped out at her: Gloria, her neighbor Gloria, staring at her with confusion. Was everybody taking in this sight? Eliza thought yes, yes, they were, everybody who knew her.

Ellen did not claim her own place in the family's row. She stood at tent edge, blood in her cheeks.

Mr. Olsen welcomed the mourners, said Robert's name a number of times. Each time a stab to Eliza, who shrank farther inside her wool coat. Every bit of her was unwilling to absorb the sound of Robert's name, the amplified voice of the minister—"Come unto me, all ye that labor and are heavy laden"—her trapped presence here, her very balance. She felt herself a heap in the folding chair; a thing acted on.

Two soldiers appeared, one bearing a triangular bundle. They paused, formal uniforms smooth, spotless. Hugh stiffened beside her. Her son craned his head back, muttering, "Man, they better not..." Then he shot up, strode to the soldiers, and said something into the ear of the startled young man holding the bundle. It took a moment or two, but Eliza understood Hugh believed the soldier might not know to whom the flag correctly belonged... might even bestow the flag on *her,* the other wife.

Could this happen? Would Eliza live through that... mistake?

Hugh returned and slumped into his seat beside her again. The minister finished his verse about a yoke, and Jesus being meek and lowly in heart—*Yes,* Eliza thought, *that I understand, that I can feel, lowly in heart*—and promised the mourners that they would find rest in their souls. That part she could not believe. Her soul was stricken and battered. The crushing sensation she had, it came from there.

The minister assumed a respectful stance, and one soldier began a slow march. Eliza's breathing faded away. She shut her eyes but heard his steps.

When she opened her eyes, a tall young soldier, nose

reddened with cold, had stopped in front of her. He pivoted and set the bundled flag in her hands. Eliza folded herself over it. Maybe it would appear that she'd kissed the flag to honor her husband. The truth was that she could not stay upright anymore.

The coffin was lowered; the minister spoke on. Mr. Warburton materialized to usher the family to the black limousine that would take them to the reception in Faith Methodist's church utility room. In the car, without a word of discussion, Ellen gave the driver the address of Eliza's house, and the Kratkes were delivered home.

V

Eliza Kratke had not known, as she had not known anything else true about her life, that the Ford Fairlane was bought on a payment plan. When, two months after the funeral, someone knocked sturdily on Eliza's door, her fist closed on the covers. Not until the knocking became angry did she roll over and get herself out of bed, shove her feet into terry-cloth slippers. She was stiff and out of breath, achy from hibernation.

The man shoved the bill under her nose as though she owed him personally, not Walt Walker Ford. She had to gather her woolly brain. "Mr....?"

The not-so-young man, his heavy shoe planted across the threshold in what appeared to Eliza to be an unbalanced way of standing, seemed unused to being asked his name. The space between them bristled with awkwardness as he hesitated. "Red," he said, his bass rising like a question.

Eliza failed to take in the man's faded ginger hair and beige eyelashes; what she was taking in was that here was another deep and ugly cut after she'd thought she'd collected all the cruelty she could stand. "Mr. Red," she murmured, "come in." Eliza bent slightly as the breath went out of her. She clutched her housedress to her.

The man stared as though some woman somewhere had once clutched her dress like that, then gestured to another person in his car, an awful car, Eliza saw, with dents and scrapes and a smash in the windshield. He brandished a finger and then brushed his pants free of foam-rubber crumbs. Those, she knew, came from split upholstery. It seemed contradictory to her that a man representing Walt Walker Ford would drive such a junker but she was now living in a world of contradiction.

Mr. Red crossed the threshold and sat.

It was suddenly necessary to change her clothes. Not for modesty's sake; the housedress was flimsy, all right, but it covered her to the middle of her calves. The thing was, she'd slept in it. It was sour and wrinkled and in it she felt like she was back in the Depression again, living in the post office. She was about to lose the Fairlane. She didn't care about the car for itself; she could ride a bus. But she'd counted on selling it. Counted on the Fairlane to feed her and keep the lights on until she could find some kind of job. Eliza felt a need for thicker clothes, and more of them. "If you could give me a minute?" she said, wrapping the housedress closer.

Arthritis had distorted her knuckles and weakened her hands; getting dressed was something of an effort, and Eliza was not used to making it in a hurry. She searched out an old suit whose skirt had elastic around the waist and could be pulled on. When it was on, she knew, it would bell wide of her hips and stouten her further. She once would have cared about that. She didn't now. The suit's jacket was free of lapels and fastenings. The blouse, with its two streamers to be tied in a bow, was the problem. Robert had done this for her, tied the bow. She'd leave that till last. Eliza managed to button the blouse's three crucial chest buttons—she was heavy-breasted. She pulled the skirt over her head and down, eliminating the need for tucking. She struggled into the jacket. From her top drawer, she picked out a pair of hose and sat down on the bed. She drew them up before she realized she had nothing to make them stay up. Her forehead tightened. At this stage in the process, a girdle was out of the question. Her old garter belts had long ago been thrown out, gone with the wind. She recalled her mother rolling her stockings and tried this. When she stood, the hose unrolled over her knees.

What was the trick? She used to know. Had her mother knotted them? Her lack of dexterity rendered knotting also out of the question. Finally, she sorted through the miscellaneous box on her dresser, picking out from the hairpins and safety pins and straight pins and clip-on earrings two fat rubber bands. She treated these as garters and rolled again. She walked to her closet—the hose, thank the Lord, did not fall down on the way—stepped into a pair of black pumps. A twinge jabbed her, an inkling frilled and subsided, she didn't know about what. It was like she'd almost remembered something she hadn't been trying to remember. She held on to the post of the bed.

Pride. And dignity. Eliza, you remember those.

She tied the bow, followed by a check in the mirror. One loop of the bow was huge, drooping, while the other poked up in an ugly little tuft. She grasped the tuft and tugged gently, as if it were a baby's fist. The bow collapsed. Tears leaped to her eyes.

From the living room came a deep "Miz Kracky? We ain't got all day."

Eliza abandoned the two streamers to trail over her chest.

Forget lipstick or powder. The man was waiting. She smoothed her hair and returned to Mr. Red in the living room.

He sat there on the sofa, his elbow propped on its flowered arm, his cheek mashed on his palm. His mouth was slack, consternation on his face. He didn't turn as she came in; it was as though Mr. Red were daydreaming a sad dream, maybe of a home or a family long gone. He was not alone. A younger man with longish black hair that might actually have been brown if it were not so greasy and blue jeans rolled at the hems like a farmer's sat at the far end of the sofa, leaning forward to tap the ashes from his cigarette into his cupped hand.

"Stuffy in the car," he said.

"I'm sorry, let me get you an ashtray." Eliza turned to her breakfront, saw the bare shelves, and remembered. "Oh. I've thrown them all away."

Actually, several days after the funeral, once the children had returned to their own lives, she had smashed them. Along with every china figurine Robert had ever given her—shepherd and shepherdess, strolling fisherman, sleeping children, rabbit and spotted fawn—smashed them individually on her brick patio out back. Eliza had done it methodically, with force, like it was the most natural act in the world. Like it had to be done. She'd smashed the figurines because they'd been Robert's gifts to her and thus were clearly lies.

Eliza hurried to the kitchen. She didn't want a cigarette dropped onto the floor. She opened the icebox and retrieved from a corner an almost empty jar of Miracle Whip, which Robert had liked and she did not. She tried to twist off the lid, almost cried out from the pain in her thumb joint. Oh, that thumb! Eliza carried the jar into the living room. Held it out to the young man, who glanced toward Mr. Red with raised eyebrows. Mr. Red was still daydreaming.

"The cap." She lifted her chin. "Unscrew it and use that."

"I wasn't going to ash your sofa none."

"No, but you're like to burn a hole in that hand."

The young man's hair was too long but it would look all right if he washed it, Eliza thought. Better, anyway. While he squinted at her with his heavy-lidded eyes, Mr. Red woke up. His gaze fell on her hands, specifically the bulged knuckles, and the Miracle Whip jar. His brow wrinkled. He seized the jar and wrenched it open, shoved the cap at his partner, who shrugged and dumped the ashes in it.

"This's Widge," Mr. Red said.

Eliza sat in the chair across from them, from habit slipping her hands beneath the wings of her skirt. She nodded to Widge. She brought her feet in the black pumps together, glad for them and the hose and the suit. She knew very well what was about to happen.

"Miz..." Mr. Red was scanning the papers he'd brought.

"Kratke." Dully, Eliza supplied the name.

"Miz Kracky, your Ford's three months overdue," Mr. Red said. "Didn't you get the notices?"

Eliza took a breath. "Krat-ke," she said. "K-r-a-t-k-e." For thirty years she had hated this mispronunciation, "Kracky." It reminded her of *cracked,* crazy or broken; of *cracker barrel;* mostly of a phony movie grandpa whose lurching gait was as false as the *By cracky!* that came out of his mouth.

Making sure Mr. Red had caught her emphasis on the *t,* Eliza focused on his gingery hair and realized her mistake. Red—a nickname, of course. Dumb of her. She inclined her head to the end table butting against the couch, a low, one-drawered, rectangular affair meant to set cups or magazines on. Toward the back, its sides rose and narrowed into a platform for a lamp. "Pull out that drawer if you would, son."

Mr. Red—no, Red it must be—flinched at the request or at the *son*. Then reached out and pulled on the knob, but the drawer stuck because of all the envelopes jammed inside. He yanked. The drawer flew all the way out, banging against the wooden table. White envelopes scattered.

"Reckon they're in there somewhere. Oh Lord." She jumped up. "How do y'all take your coffee?"

Mr. Red—too late, the name had stuck; she could not stop thinking of him that way—was on his knees scooping envelopes. "No, Miz...lookit, you don't have to—"

"Sugar and cream," Widge said.

After another eternity in the kitchen and a lucky catch when she almost knocked over the percolator, Eliza crept back out with the tray and cups and saucers, the spoons and creamer and sugar bowl. She had cut a knuckle on the sharp edge of the Folgers can but tamped away most of the blood on a rag at the sink. Looking down at the neatly arrayed tray seemed to trip the muscles in her face; she smiled. *You damn fool,* she thought, *caring about a tray when they've come to take the car.* Then she realized—she almost staggered and had to stop and steady the tray—there was nothing more to be taken.

Shortly, she would put the house up for sale. She'd sold the television already, to her neighbor Gloria, who'd wanted a TV for her bedroom. Sold the freezer to Earl and Velma Fitzwalter. The furniture from the extra rooms, the scarred bunk beds in the garage, and the kids' old bikes she'd advertised in the *Green Sheet*. Hugh had refused her offer of Robert's fishing gear and his shotgun, so she'd advertised those too. She'd promised the Whirlpool to a young mother down the street whenever she sold her house.

Almost there. Eliza looked up from the tray to see that the envelopes had disappeared, the drawer had been replaced, there were two cigarette stubs in the jar cap, and the air of her living room, stale to begin with, was marbled with smoke. Mr. Red was rubbing his forehead, Widge grinning. She wondered if Widge was on hourly, Mr. Red on commission.

"Lookit, ma'am, when does your husband get home?"

Why didn't they know? What kind of backward company did they work for? The obituary had run for three days. Death records, even house listings, were more public than automobile contracts. Eliza found it easy to imagine that everyone in the state, not just her whole neighborhood and her church and her two children, knew that her husband was dead, that he'd cleaned out their savings and mortgaged their house, that he'd lived for some time with two wives.

"He doesn't," Eliza said.

Mr. Red was frowning at Widge, who'd ignored the

spoon, grasped the sugar bowl by its thin handles, and was pouring the sugar in.

"Doesn't what?" Mr. Red looked away from his partner.

"Get home." No need to be so prickly, she thought, but she was saying exactly what came to mind. Possibly, in his experience, her answer would mean that the husband had fled. She saw his face change as he got it.

Widge was waving around the china top of the sugar bowl by its tiny knob. "Like for dolls, Red," he said. "Cool."

Mr. Red slurped coffee and then twisted his watch around. "Lookit, Mrs. Crocker, uh, Mrs. Kratke, me and him have to be somewhere. I guess we could let you have the car a little while longer. Say we come day after tomorrow, how's that?"

"Well, all right."

At the door, out of long habit of standing at that door to see neighbors off, she thoughtlessly murmured, "Thank you for coming." Mr. Red and Widge pivoted and stared at her before finding their stride again.

Eliza'd meant to return to her bed, but she couldn't—she had the suit on. So she plopped down in a kitchen chair and stared out the window at the wide, leafing oak she had planted back when she had not been lowly in heart. The oak was in the spring stage she loved, when only some of its pale olive leaves were unfurled, so they appeared to be floating. What a spindly pole it had been thirty years ago. How unexpectedly deep she'd had to dig to set it in the ground.

Eliza picked up the papers the collectors had left and located the balance due on the car. A plan filtered into her head once she'd stared at the numbers then got hold of herself after a flash of flaming anger at Robert. At a quarter after five, when she judged Earl Fitzwalter would be home but not yet at the dinner table, she phoned and asked him how much her car was worth. He said he had to go find his Blue Book. He called her back with the information; next morning, Eliza called the *Green Sheet* and placed an ad, although it would not come out until Friday and today was Wednesday.

It felt unexpectedly good, energizing, to move; she'd forgotten that. She went out to the garage with a rag and Windex and polished the windows and chrome, wiped down the vinyl seats, the steering wheel, the horn, the dashboard. She filled a mixing bowl with hot water and dish soap and sponged off the dirt and bugs on the grille. The hot water soothed her hands.

On Thursday, the day Mr. Red was due to come back, she took the car and stayed away from home, leaving a note of apology on the door. She had to visit a sick friend, she wrote. And so, after going to the grocery store, where she doled out cash for the cheapest coffee and white bread, and the business college, where she picked up a pamphlet of courses, she visited Vivian Chester. She hadn't brought her anything, which felt wrong, but told Vivian she'd come to do whatever she needed. Eliza washed and hung a load of towels, underwear, and nightclothes; took a grocery list and did the meager shopping. To stretch the time out, she found herself vacuuming the rugs, washing the dishes, sweeping the kitchen linoleum. Under Vivian's direction, she filled her weekly pillbox with the right combination of pills for each day—this task a little trickier for her inefficient fingers, but she shook the pills out onto her palm, nudged them in the slots by color, and replaced the box on the bedside table. She made them both some Sanka and helped her friend to a chair so that she could lay on a pair of fresh sheets. She hadn't intended to do so much; she hadn't intended to do anything but avoid Mr. Red. These chores for her friend, though, begged to be done, and Eliza anticipated the pleasant lift she'd feel once she laid her eyes on a house in order.

When Vivian asked the inevitable questions about Robert, her dulled eyes brightening, Eliza answered them simply. She forestalled the expression of sympathetic condemnation she could see bunching in Vivian's face—her mouth was working peculiarly—and, feeling as if she'd swerved the Fairlane down another road just in time, she turned the subject to Vivian herself, to the doctors' tests and the hospital bills, which Vivian found fearsome, and Blue Cross, of all the thieving outfits...

For one day, she did not feel humiliated or bereft or as

angry or as gnawed with worry as usual. Vivian Chester could not thank her enough, and for the moment, the car was safe.

When Eliza got home, she plucked Mr. Red's card from the door. The card did not have Mr. Red's name on it, but she knew it was his. *Paley and Associates Collection Services*, it read, with an address and phone number, just like the card stapled to the top of the papers he'd left. On Friday she was relieved to locate her ad in the *Green Sheet*. A man came about the car on Saturday but left without making an offer. On Sunday, a couple came, the man liking it, the woman not. Then a pair of teenagers, who wanted a test drive. "Sure," said Eliza. She handed them the keys, then fixed herself square in the middle of the back seat. The drive was short. On Sunday evening, a young man came; he squatted and peered at the underside, raised the hood and asked about mileage. Eliza had forgotten to check, so he leaned into the driver's window and read it off himself. A good sign, she thought. Hip cocked, he jingled change in his khaki pocket.

"It's very reliable," she said.

"I'll give it some thought." He nodded to her.

"Someone else might want it." She astonished herself. Out of nowhere, the words had popped from her mouth. "A gentleman who was here this morning said he'd be back." The man tilted his head, said, "Oh, yeah?" She smiled as though to say she'd felt it only fair to inform him. He looked more interested.

"Your ad said you wanted—"

"I'll take a hundred less," Eliza said. "But that's bottom dollar. I told the other man that too. He thought the price was fair."

"Yeah? Tell you what. Get paid on Thursday. Lemme stop by after work then. 'Less I find something else'll do better."

"All right."

With hope and regret and hope, Eliza watched him climb into an old pickup and grind the starter. A slow, choking *ah-hoo-ah-hoo-ah-ah-hoo* and it caught. A puff of black smoke trailed him. That was a good sign too.

On Tuesday, a round week from his first visit, Mr. Red came again. She wasn't there, but when she drove back that evening, she knew what his mood had been from the three cards pounded into the doorframe with outsize, rusted nails. Eliza retrieved a hammer from the garage and painfully pried them out. Yes, he was only doing his job, and yes, she was hindering that job, but she was angered by the nails. The resulting holes marred the doorframe; not a good thing if she planned to sell the house. She had been visiting Vivian Chester's aunt Eula, whose vision was so bad she couldn't read the paper or *Reader's Digest* or see to mop up the chocolate pudding drips in her kitchen. Eliza had scrubbed away the drips and the marching line of sugar ants feasting on them, read the older woman some true-life articles, "Humor in Uniform," "Laughter, the Best Medicine," and the jokes at the bottoms of the pages until her throat was dry, then asked Aunt Eula if she had a friend under the weather. Aunt Eula had a number of them. She gave Eliza their names, along with each one's complaint: diabetes and a tumor of the pituitary gland and a faintly beating heart.

Eliza's heart was beating more steadily than it had.

She did not feel that her feet had found purchase, exactly; it was more like she had inserted herself into some kind of beneficial momentum. She didn't feel guilty about hiding from the collectors, nor did she curl up on the bed as before and try to plan the rest of her life. She thought about Thursday, when her potential car buyer might come back, and she went out and polished the chrome all over again.

On Wednesday morning, in case the collectors came, she taped a note to her door and drove the Fairlane off to Mrs. Galloway's house, where she found Mrs. Galloway's daughter with a spoon, whirling round Campbell's soup on the stove. When Eliza mentioned Aunt Eula's name, the daughter seemed to assume Eliza was from their church. Eliza did not tell her differently. "Oh, how sweet of you," the woman said, pushing back her limp hair; she sure did have errands to run. Eliza sat on the bed, squeezed out ointment from a tube, and massaged Mrs. Galloway's spongy legs. She did it lightly because the pressure hurt her own hands. The ointment, though, whatever it was — she tried and failed to read the tiny print on the tube — tingled and warmed them. "Hadn't you got the patience,"

Mrs. Galloway remarked, "and not rough and in a rush."
Yes, Eliza thought, *it's Wednesday and I've got patience.*

By Thursday evening, though, her patience had become a churning in her stomach. She kept bending the blinds, looking out the window. She had a hundred and eighty-seven dollars left to her name, and a telephone bill, a gas bill, a light bill. She'd had to make a mortgage payment, and her checking account was closed out. She was strictly cash now; she operated from her pocketbook. Three hundred and some dollars still owed to Warburton Mortuary—she had been sending them only thirty a month—and their latest letter, jammed into the end-table drawer, was regretful but stern.

Stop, she told herself, *it's Thursday.* She wished for the hullabaloo of television, but *If wishes were horses,* as her mother used to say. She got up and switched on the radio—no one was interested in buying a plain radio—and twirled the dial absently until a husky female voice stopped her. A ripe voice, mellow as a windfall pear, not at all in a hurry, sliding inside the rhythm:

"Mama may have, Papa may have, but God bless the child that's got his own..."

The bitterness, if you could call it that, came in something crackling at the ends of the lines, but her voice only implied it. It was embedded, somehow, in all the voice knew. Eliza leaned toward the radio and, as she'd never done when she was young and used to sing along with her favorite songs, tracked the luscious restraint in each word. *Pitiless,* she thought. *It's Billie Holiday.* The woman in sequins at a microphone, gardenia drooping, her gaze deadly matter-of-fact, irony escaping in the arch of a penciled eyebrow. The sad truth, that's what the song was. It sobered her. Surveying her own living room, Eliza found the flowered sofa, the lamps, the breakfront, the picture frames, drained of sentimental familiarity. They sat, hard-edged, inanimate, wood and cloth and metal that anyone might accumulate or leave behind.

She missed the sound of the old pickup turning into her driveway but heard the *scree* of brakes as it stopped, and she peered through the blinds in time to see it shake itself. The man who'd come on Sunday climbed out. Eliza rose from the sofa, smoothly, as though floating up to the top of deep water, and met him with the car keys.

"Take her out for a spin," she said, and she did not go with him. After he'd coasted back into the driveway, the young man again squatted and peered beneath the car like the underside might have rusted in the four days since he'd scrutinized it. Again he lifted the hood, hooking it in one swift movement as Eliza could never do, and inspected. He got back into the car, seemed to be trying on the driver's seat as a woman would try on a sheath dress; he tapped the horn and fiddled with the dashboard. Eliza stood back, shading her eyes from the harsh yellow rays of the six o'clock sun, her hopes swelling.

Then another old car, one with dents and a cracked windshield she recognized, pulled in behind the car shopper's pickup. A strange man in a suit slid out of the passenger seat and brushed at his shiny trousers. The driver, Mr. Red—it must be Mr. Red, though she could not see his face behind the enormous glass spiderweb glittering in the sinking sun—took longer. He was kicking at his door.

She was so intent on the young man in her car that she ignored the strange man and held up her palm to Mr. Red when he stridently called her name—*Mrs. Kracky* again. The mispronunciation transferred his agitation to her. Still a few paces away, Mr. Red started: "Lookit, Mrs. Kracky—" Eliza glared and stalked to the men to hold them off.

"Lookit yourself, Mr. Red," she muttered. "I'm doing business here." She extended her glare to the stranger, who looked amused, at what she couldn't imagine. He was amusing enough himself. He looked like Charlie the Tuna in the TV commercial, a sleek tube ascending with no neck to a chubby-cheeked, goggle-eyed face and a fringe of fine black hair, middle-parted. He looked like his bulk had been squeezed into the shiny gray suit, ballooning upward from small, neat feet and inflating the jacket to capacity.

The tuna held out a plump hand. "Ray Paley," he said. "I hear you been running my no-count boys around." Eliza glanced over to Mr. Red, who looked off miserably toward the street.

She wrung the soft hand. "Eliza Kratke," she said, emphasizing the *t*. "I've got some sick friends."

"I guess you do." Ray Paley's large, wide-set eyes were still amused but Eliza saw clearly that the amusement was draped over a wall of confidence, an authority built of bricks and mortar, one brick at a time. He carried himself like many men she had known. Like a sheriff. The Fairlane's door was shut, carefully; the car shopper headed for them.

"And I sure hope, Miz Kracky"—Paley winked—"that the bus runs by your friends' houses."

Eliza stiffened. A spark sizzled the length of her body and shot from her head into the air. A spot at the crown of her head burned.

It was not just the threat, a poor joke at her expense, or the wink with which he had delivered it. It was that he said her name wrong when he knew better. That was the straw. The humiliating scene that was sure to follow—Ray Paley seizing the Fairlane in front of her prospective buyer—could only be puny compared to those that had come before.

This car shopper in khakis, she didn't know him from Adam. He had no claim on her pride. At that moment, a course of its own making set hard in her, its two contradictory paths the only way open to her. *So be it,* she thought, and resolved to gamble the five or six hundred dollars she stood to gain, that she'd washed and vacuumed and read and massaged for. She threw the desire for the money away and went straight toward it in the same motion. She challenged Ray Paley's sardonic gaze and raised her voice:

"I'm glad you brought cash, Mr. Paley, because I'd rather not take a check, no offense intended."

"Hold up there, hold up a minute." The man in khakis hurried over. "I'm real innerested in your car here, ma'am." He slid a fist in his pocket, surveying the three of them. Eliza turned to him, clenching her hands so that the inflammation in her fingers throbbed.

"Then I'd have to get full asking price, son. Unless this gentleman wants to come up a hundred. Since he was first." She forced herself to turn back to Ray Paley. Mr. Red might not even have been there. Her business was with the boss. His sleek face was lit by sunset now, a sheen of pink across both smooth cheeks. His mouth was open. He knew exactly what she was doing, and he seemed to be calculating—not the situation in front of him, but her. Eliza Kratke.

A horn tooted *da-da-da-daaa* and Eliza, startled, saw Earl Fitzwalter grinning out the window of his late-model Chevrolet. "Hey, neighbor! Don't you sell off that fine machine. I might buy it myself!" Earl slapped the Chevy's door in salute and cruised on.

The car shopper might have taken Ray Paley's calculating stare for a bargaining ploy and upped the ante with a stare of his own, but with Earl's interruption, he'd apparently had time to squint at the sorry car his competition had arrived in. He pulled a roll of bills from an inside jacket pocket, slipped his wallet from a back one, and topped the roll with a bill. "Full price, ma'am," he said, "cash on the barrelhead." He cocked his hip, and he cocked his jaw at the other two men, and they all stood there in the twilight. Birds twittered to beat the band; it seemed to Eliza she'd never heard them so loud, or never heard birds at all.

Prickling all over with the knowledge that at any second Ray Paley could crush this deal, she asked, "What's your name, son?" While the man was telling her his name, she was drawing a pen and a small square of paper from her pocket. She scrawled *Larry James* across the title. She'd already signed it.

Larry James glanced at Mr. Paley and Mr. Red, said, "No hard feelings, gents," and handed her the money. He smiled at her. "Missus and me'll be right back. 'Scuse me, sir, gotta ask you to move your car."

Without looking at his boss, Mr. Red trudged off to their car, got in, threw an arm over the seat, looked back, and gunned out of the driveway.

Eliza counted out the hundred-dollar bills. Most went to Ray Paley for the delinquent payments and the balance due on the car, but five of them she tucked into her shirtwaist pocket. "Make out the receipt to Eliza Kratke," she said, and she spelled it for him. "I thank you kindly for waiting on me while I did for my friends that can't do for themselves."

"Lady, you are..." Ray Paley's head raised about a quarter inch and settled curtly back into its former position. He looked as though he might be about to say a number of things but could not decide which to say first. "Red," he called finally, "got a receipt pad on you?"

Mr. Red trotted up with the pad, ballpoint pen clipped to it, gave these to his boss, and stepped back. While Ray Paley scribbled a receipt, Mr. Red contemplated Eliza from a distance. He took in her Keds and bare ankles, her loose print dress with the big round buttons, the gold eyeglasses on her plain, lined face as curiously as if he were looking at a zoo animal with no plaque to identify it.

Eliza took the receipt, folded it, and returned Ray Paley's nod. She did not wait for them to reach their junker car. She went into her house, locked the door, put the receipt and four bills into the drawer of her empty breakfront and one bill into the change purse in her pocketbook. Without switching on a lamp, she eased herself down on the sofa, dusk in her window and the buzz of a single musical note in her heart.

VI

A conference over selling the house drew her children home together for the first time since the funeral. Until they came, until they walked through the front door carrying the fresh air along with them, the idea of the house sale was a thing like a real estate sign or the weather. It existed—Eliza knew of its existence—but she did not have to interact with it. Not until her family sat in the living room by the tall breakfront—Ellen in a navy sweatshirt with her long auburn hair windblown, Hugh in a pale blue work shirt with the sleeves rolled up, and Pam, his wife. They'd left Betsy and John with Pam's mother. Pam, short and shapely, athletically made even after the kids, shed a windbreaker to reveal her round middle covered by a T-shirt that depicted a white dog with a large black spot circling one eye. The real estate lady was due to arrive in an hour and a half with the contract.

"I wish you didn't have to do this, Ma. I wish...me and Pam'd take on that second mortgage, but with the new baby coming, we spend ever red cent we have. Maybe you could take in some little ones, babysit like you used to, I don't know." Pam nodded and Hugh said this again as he rubbed his forehead, which looked like it had been rubbed plenty already.

Her children's distress would be eased if she sold the house, and that was enough to make Eliza's limp pen hand twitch, although signing the sale contract went against everything she was built of. Selling the house instead of leaving it to them when it had once been paid off, square foot by square foot, until it was free and clear?

Losing a home had proved a grave injury to her parents. They'd once owned a small plot of land not too far south of Lubbock, a house and a barn for the cows. A garden Eliza worked, cows she milked. She liked to stand up in the hayloft and look out on the tall panhandle sky, on a road running through the fields. A black car had chugged up the road. She knew who it was because it had a shield painted on its side, and she climbed down the ladder and ran from the barn to tell her mother. Her father should have been in the fields but was hunched at the table with her mother. They were not talking. But they had been talking for weeks, arguing, planning, hoping, hopeless.

Eliza ran into the middle of the bad feeling in the kitchen. It was thick; both of them had it. Her little brother, Roy, sat on the floor, knees up to his chin, watching them. When a knock sounded at the door, her father's shoulders straightened. He lifted the shotgun that had been lying on the floor beside him.

Her mother stayed where she was. With great force, she said, "Don't, Jake." Her father laid down the gun, got up, and met the sheriff at the door. There was a rumbling that was them speaking, and then her father came back to the kitchen with papers. "Gimme the key, Frannie," he said. Her mother took the house key from her pocketbook and gave it to him. When she sat back down at the table, her breath left out of her.

The family bundled up and moved south to Bayard, a midsize city in piney East Texas where Jake's brother lived. Months after their move, they managed to find a ramshackle rental house. Even after the war, when money and credit were flowing again, even then her parents rented. Never bought another home that could call a sheriff's black automobile to their door, that could make them lay a key in the sheriff's hand.

To Eliza, the plan to live off the proceeds of her own house sale was appalling. To spend it away. Robert had not yet qualified to receive a railroad pension when he died. Neither could she draw on his Social Security. The man at the Social Security office had put on a regretful face as he informed Eliza that she fell into the "blackout period." Her kids were older than sixteen and she herself wasn't sixty. Eliza, holding her empty purse on her lap, didn't know which urge was strongest: to cry or laugh or scream in frustration. *Blackout period.*

Here was Ellen, insisting she didn't need any inheritance from Eliza, she just needed her mother to be all right. Hugh worked for a large trucking company; Ellen worked part-time and attended a college in Nacogdoches, was studying science so she could be a dental assistant. Maybe even a dentist, she said, rolling her eyes.

At that, Hugh's wife, Pam, who had been grim, seemingly determined to be mute during this meeting, startled them all by breaking into cheers and applause.

Their conference turned for a while to Ellen, lightened while she stammered about classes, a pre-dental program, a scholarship and whether they'd award it to a girl, how long it might all take. If she could do it. If. Her long hair, parted in the middle, draped so that she let them see just a section of pinkened forehead, mobile eyebrows, and lips. Eliza, clutching Ellen's hand, could have listened until morning. Finally, though, Hugh looked at his watch and dragged the house issue back on the table.

Focused only on the hundreds of monthly mortgage checks filled out, the balance as it shrank year by year toward that bountiful zero, Eliza fought Ellen's idea. To use up a paid-for house! To eat it in bits—in egg cartons, bread, hamburger patties, electricity, and gas. "It'd be like setting fire to thirty years."

Hugh's face crumpled. Pam's flamed. Ellen jumped up, yelling, "Daddy already did that!" She stomped from the living room.

Eliza managed to stifle the ragged scream in her mind: *Robert, if you could see the hurt in Hugh's face, in Ellen's. Look at the damage you've done—are doing—to your children's hearts. Deep, permanent. Did you think of the kids when you were running off to your woman? How could you not think of them? You left them too. You left them, and they know that. Just as bad, you changed me from their mother into their burden.*

Eliza trailed Ellen down the hall, past framed photos of her kids and grandkids, past blank spaces where pictures of her and Robert had hung. She sank down beside her on the scuffed wood floor of her childhood room. The posters of Ricky Nelson and *Life* magazine covers of a pregnant Jacqueline Kennedy and Caroline on a pony were gone. Ellen had taken them with her to college. Eliza put an arm around her daughter's hunched shoulders.

Ellen aimed a flurry of batting at Eliza's hand, little slaps that were physically painless. "If they planted a tree on my grave and it grew up and then it died and rotted and the sticks and branches blew away," she said thickly, "that's how long I'll hate him."

Eliza endured the slaps to keep her arm around her daughter. She had no answer for her, only the arm, and she kept it around Ellen only by main force.

Eventually the doorbell rang. Hugh stuck his head in

Ellen's room. "She's out there," he said. Eliza didn't move. Ellen twisted around to her brother. "Make that person leave the papers. If you don't think I'll sign Ma's name, you got a million thinks coming."

"Okay, so maybe she can find a smaller...cheaper place—"

"She can find *another* place."

Hugh squatted down, groaning. "Just...just back off for one minute, Nellie." He spoke over his sister to Eliza. "Ma. Say what you wanna do."

Ellen grabbed a fistful of Hugh's long-sleeved shirt, a part over his biceps. "I would cheer"—she pulled at the sleeve, repeatedly yanking his arm with it—"while this house burned to the dirt."

Eliza took hold of her daughter's wrist, forcing her to release Hugh, forcing her to take back the willful hand, which Eliza then smoothed onto Ellen's blue-jeaned knee. This movement, automatic, abnormal because it had once been normal in a way that had passed, tapped at a spot in Eliza's head. It reminded her of someone. Her. Herself, wasn't it—this was what she'd often done a dozen or so years back. When Hugh was going out and she wanted him to stay, Nell used to clamp onto her big brother.

She was doing that now, again, only he was clamping onto her too and their shoulders were shaking.

These arms. All these arms.

Eliza raised herself. She greeted the real estate lady in the red plaid suit with the straight skirt and nicely spread white collar, laid the papers on the dining-room table, and signed the contract in four places, pushing hard on the triplicate form. After the kids left, Eliza's public self, patched together for their sakes, departed, leaving no forwarding address. She kicked off her dress shoes and sat down on her bed.

She couldn't make herself feel sleepy, though. She had slept and slept after the funeral. The Fairlane's departure—more specifically, the style in which it departed—had routed Eliza from hibernation.

Now she was awake.

Consequently, she saw she should come to an authentic agreement with the house, with its already-planted For Sale sign. The bereft fumbler who had signed a real estate contract had to emigrate to a new geography, as though heaving away one suitcase, one cardboard box at a time. Eliza had to make the shift happen. Ignorant of any beginning point, she fell back on the example of her parents. She made the change into work.

Her family had packed up and moved down south to Bayard, a city to the northeast of Houston, where one of her dad's brothers lived. The brother sorted mail for the post office and also tapped out telegrams at the Western Union office beside it. Bayard was not the farming life they knew. Farmers were working oil rigs. Tall pines shut out the sky. Trucks piled with huge logs ran the two-lane roads. Her dad went to a sawmill or anywhere else he'd heard might be hiring for the day. He was always gone during the day, working or looking.

This, her parents had understood; work, Eliza understood. This change would be a kind of work. Like exercise, like the lifting and setting down of barbells. She said aloud to herself in the kitchen, to her tense face reflected in a living-room window, even to her old dog, Percy: "I'm leaving this house. I am selling this house. I will find a new place to live. Life will go on. My children are healthy. They will be part of my life always. I am not selling my children." It was not this house that had caused them to exist or love her or caused her to love them. It was just the place where the love began and where it had been carried along until now.

She told the mailman she would probably be moving soon. He nodded, advised her to fill out a change-of-address card. Regarded her with a twist of kindness. He knew her story. To her neighbor Gloria, who knocked one day with a loaf of banana bread and a brightly strained manner, she said, "Guess you saw I put my house up for sale."

Gloria, wrapped in a scarf and car coat, sighed open-mouthed. Maybe because she now had a subject she could state opinions on, a topic that would probably not cause her neighbor to withdraw into a condition that rendered her dumb, Gloria did not hand off the gift and hurry away. She shed her wrappings, sat down at Eliza's table, removed the foil, and gestured with a slice of banana bread. "I saw the sign. Oh, Eliza, now you're talking! Thank God. You wanna know the truth, I've been scared to death I'd come over here some day and find you...you know. Lord, I've been worried. Here, Percy." Percy, drawn to Gloria as to the harp of an angel, gobbled up a pinch of the bread.

There must have been a grinding of forces, there must have been, Eliza reasoned, a falling away, the thud of a bottom, a settling. These she did not feel. She was the same pierced creature she had been since the funeral, only ambulatory now. But the release, when it arrived, was visceral. A release of the body. Harshly willed, spoken into being, muscled into being, but still so alien that she went and studied her face in the bathroom mirror. Yes, that was Eliza Kratke looking back at her, and she could do this. It was just a house. *Just a house, just a house.* Not the law. Not the bill of rights, not water or salvation or an infant child.

The shift that she constructed forwarded a motion begun by the unfathomable woman who was able to sell the Fairlane not only out from under Ray Paley but with his amused collusion. This different woman now sat down at a dining-room table that would be the next item to go.

All right. Three years away from a widow's Social Security. She would have pawned her gold wedding ring—she'd yanked at it, but her arthritis prevented its sliding off her finger. Daily expenses were eked out from the stash in the breakfront. Babysitting paid fifty cents the hour. Her week evading the car collectors had taught her she might find a place taking care of the old, some elderly people who had more money than the ones she'd visited. But it was one thing to do for someone for free, for surprised and grateful thanks, another to do for obligation. To hear the same complaints every day, smell the same medications, be shut in the same house, as full of outdated furniture as her own, see daily the undusted photographs of graduates and brides and young parents, their arms clamped around wiggly toddlers now grown. Then, inevitably, the empty bed and another house with the windows permanently closed against drafts. She shuddered. She said to herself, *No.*

I want my own.

She heard the articulation of this desire as clearly as if it had come from her mouth, which it had not. It had traveled upward from her spine through other bones, through and around organs, through blood, through skin, and then that desire had voiced itself in the vicinity of her neck, halfway between her heart and her ear. A voice without voice! And she heard it. Clearer than a school bell, than a siren. Closer. Inside her, outside her but intimately near. She wanted her own, whatever that meant. Billie Holiday had known. Singing that song, well before she sang that song, Billie Holiday had known. Eliza knew and she didn't know. But she wanted it. How dare she not take any meager opportunity that was flung at her? Her father had. Her mother had. And that's where Robert had left her, like she'd not deserved anything else.

Eliza shook her head no until she rattled her brains.

She got up and pushed an opened window to the top. Sun lay on a patch of overgrown grass beyond the trees, blue shadow beneath them. The breeze was sweet on this early morning, and she let it play over her face for some long time.

She forced herself to sit down at the table again, to unfold the brochure. The business college offered two-semester programs that would prepare the student for employment as, depending on the classes chosen, a book-keeper, secretary, stenographer, draftsman, legal assistant, court reporter, or "business owner." Eliza pushed back her hair, added and subtracted. She could afford one semester. She would just have to buy the books for the second semester and learn as much as she could from them. Eliza laid down the pencil and threw her hands over her face. Daunting, to master so much by Christmas. Whether she could succeed—she shouldn't dwell on that. Stranger things had happened, and they had happened to her.

VII

"How are you, Mrs. Kratke?" The real estate lady said her name correctly and Eliza was lifted just hearing her professional trill on the phone; maybe she had corralled a buyer. The lady's next words were "I'm afraid there's a problem."

Eliza did not say, *Oh, really?* or ask *What is it?* Her lips pressed together; stillness like cellophane wrapped around her. Loss had trained her to know its appearance needed no encouragement. Despite her triumph with the Fairlane, her new plan, she felt thrown back into the role of a subordinate, subject to whatever was going to happen next. She waited, stretching the curly phone cord. She did not sit down; she kept her feet. Her fingertips chilled.

The real estate agent told her that she had discovered a lien filed against the house by a person named June Kratke. Mid-March, it was filed; she'd read it on the county books. Was this Mr. Kratke's sister? Of course she wouldn't pry into family business; she had a family too, and when her mother died...The woman coughed. However, Mrs. Kratke would know that a lien hindered any sale. It would need to be removed, for without a clear title, the company could not issue the necessary insurance required by the state and the buyer. Could Mrs. Kratke straighten this out?

Eliza murmured that she would look into it and call the lady back. Only then did a little of the pep that identified the real estate saleswoman inject itself into her voice. She'd just leave the For Sale sign right where it was for now. They'd talk again soon.

Eliza found herself in the garage, roomy now with the car gone. The tremor begun inside of her had now swum through to her hands and jaw. There was a five-gallon can of gasoline somewhere in here. Not up on the shelf with the pegboard, hammer, screwdrivers and wrenches, the drill, the cans of nails and jars of screws. Not behind the box of Christmas ornaments or with the haphazardly piled garden hose and sprinkler. There it was, in the north corner by the lawn mower. She picked it up by its greasy handle, putting her shoulder into it, expecting heft, and ended up snatching it off the concrete floor. Tilted it; the gas trickled to one side. Not enough to soak the living room, let alone the whole place. She regripped the handle and swung the tin can into the garage's frame wall, over and over and over again until it mashed in and her right hand was screaming.

After an unsteady while, she trudged back into the house, bringing the can, and ran hot water over her hand. Then she dug out all the threat letters from the little drawer in her living-room end table. She took them into the backyard and splashed the gasoline on them. Went back into the house for matches, returned, set the white pile—*whoomf!*—ablaze. Her neighbor Gloria stepped out and waved. Eliza waved back. Gloria pulled her washing off the line, settling for a smile and a hesitant thumbs-up in lieu of conversation. Smoke drifted across Gloria's yard; good thing she had taken her clothes in.

In the meantime, since the last smash of the can against the garage wall, some small device that seemed independent of her bored through the rage so she could think. She picked up Percy, pacing and hugging him. Then sat down on a kitchen chair and installed the old dog on her lap.

After seeing the confrontation with the other wife at the graveside, Mr. Olsen, the stooped minister of her church, had suggested Eliza come and talk with him privately, but the day she'd arrived, he was sick with a cold. She was left looking up to young Mr. Henney, the new minister, whose wavy bangs defied his Brylcreem. Mr. Henney flipped through a three-ring binder and, stuttering a little, said he believed Mr. Olsen had meant to advise her on anger.

"I'm so sorry he couldn't be here today, Mrs. Kratke. Reverend Olsen of course has many more years of

experience than I do. But I believe he'd have you understand that anger...even natural, even though you have a
genuine right to it, is an acid that will c-corrode. C-corrode
you. Not the object of your anger. You might feel your
anger would reach that person, Mrs. Kratke. That your
anger would reach that person and punish them. But it's
not so. The anger will corrode *you*."

As an authority, Mr. Henney sounded ill at ease, like
he was reciting from the binder. He must have taken note
of her skeptical face.

"I know that's not fair, Mrs. Kratke. But there is a way
to avoid it." Mr. Henney gazed down into his own lap for
a moment, then stalwartly raised his head and plunged
onward. "That is forgiveness. That's what Reverend Olsen
would advise. You really have to forgive whoever has hurt
you. For your own sake, Mrs. Kratke, your own sake."

Eliza's skeptical face must have become blank. Because
it felt blank. Mr. Henney launched into an example then
that was not in the manual.

"Think about Mrs. Kennedy after the horrible tragedy last year. Remember how she stood there in that black
veil? And how she'd taught little John-John to salute when
the coffin of his father passed? I don't think I'll ever forget
that. Ever. But my point is, remember how silent and still
she was? Not a hint of anger when certainly she had a reason for it."

Eliza, whose eyes felt gritty from weeping, who'd wept
over the young president's death, choked out, "What?

But...but excuse me, Mr. Henney, you didn't see Jackie Kennedy once she was by herself, did you? You can't know how she felt or how she feels now! She's a young woman who's lost her husband. Her children have no father to raise them. Oh, she's mad. You bet she's mad!"

Mr. Henney, who'd been inclining sympathetically toward Eliza, twitched back as though she'd pushed him. He swallowed, but he stuck to his script. "Of course Mrs. Kennedy stood strong for the sake of the public—yes, certainly, I agree with you there. But I believe, and I know Reverend Olsen believes, that silence and stillness are a recipe to c-calm the soul."

Eliza had heard him. Nevertheless, being under the funeral tent with that woman, Robert's other wife, resisted any recipe that young man had to offer.

Now she became aware of the smell of gasoline. She turned in the chair, looking around the dining room. Ah, the oily stuff was on her hand. She'd stroked Percy's head and now he smelled like gasoline.

Being under the tent with that woman had been torture enough for Eliza's present lifetime. She hadn't even known her name. She would not be in her presence; she would not speak to her. But someone would have to.

Abruptly Eliza stood up, cutting off this thought, dumping Percy. Then she had to stand him up and pet him back to himself again.

VIII

Her neighbor Earl Fitzwalter was a lawyer. Steeling herself for her friend Velma's pitying expression, she walked to their house. Eliza asked him to negotiate obstacles with the other "wife" — notably, to fix the lien. Not for free. In return, she would give Velma the large mahogany breakfront she had always admired.

Earl Fitzwalter looked down. "You one hundred percent sure he didn't leave a will somewhere?"

"We looked everywhere."

"Of course he'll fix that lien!" Velma clenched her small Baptist hands. "The dirty witch."

Earl's eyes rolled to his wife and back to Eliza. He nodded and then gave Eliza some advice. In order to have some income—that's what she needed, right, income?—"Rent out the house and go live somewhere cheap. With one of your kids, maybe."

She did as Earl Fitzwalter suggested, him being a lawyer, though the kind that kept a walk-up office and drove around more than some others. She rented out her house and moved. But not to Hugh's place in Houston, as she'd told the Fitzwalters and other neighbors she would. She stayed in Bayard. Moved far across town into number 2 at the Sweet Vidalia Residence Inn, a motel offering a bedroom/living room, shower bath, kitchenette, a walking-distance-away grocery store. That it accepted pets had sent the Vidalia to the top of her list. She couldn't in good conscience have Percy put down, and she couldn't imagine some father taking the old terrier home to totter out, tongue draped over his gums, to an energetic ten-year-old looking for a pal to play with. Besides, she loved him.

Eliza had her budget figured close. The Fairlane would pay for the business school's tuition. The house's rent, less Robert's mortgage, would be her only income. One hundred and seventy-eight dollars a month. It was not enough. She knew it was not enough, but she hadn't told that to her children. She'd told them she was selling off belongings—the lawn mower, the bedroom suites, the dining table and chairs, the couch, that infernal end table that had collected the creditors' dunning letters. She'd exaggerated the proceeds of these sales to both her children.

Eliza took the cheapest room at the Vidalia and did not

ask why it was less than the others. She'd peeked in and seen just a motel room with tiny kitchenette. No problem; she could clean and fix it up. That took seventy-two dollars a month, ninety on five-Friday months. Food, hers and Percy's, was thirty-five to forty-five; bus, ten. Forget about a telephone; she would use the Vidalia's pay phone outside the office. That'd be maybe six dollars a month. She'd wash her clothes by hand in the big sinks in the Vidalia's laundry room rather than paying for the machines. Drape or hang the wet clothes to dry. There would be, as there always were, predictable extras like birthday presents and postage, and sneaking ones, like a bad tooth and shoes that should have lasted longer.

"Ellen and I don't like you living in a motel, Ma," Hugh said when she called him from the pay phone outside the office her first night there. "Why don't you live with me and Pam?" She would share a room with Betsy; Betsy would like that, Hugh said.

For Eliza, this was excruciating to hear. The forced loft in her son's voice. The strain. She knew well enough he didn't mean the first word of it, that pride and self-regard had driven him to make the offer. She didn't think less of him for it, though she wished he could be honest with her. But her son needed the pride, didn't he? Eliza pressed into the motel's wall to stay out of the drizzle. Cupping a hand over her ear to shut out Sixth Street's traffic, tires sizzling in the rain, she pictured the little ranch-style house they lived in, in a Houston neighborhood where the houses were built close together. Three tight bedrooms and one bath.

"Hugh," she said, "the baby'll be here soon. Where are y'all putting the bassinet?"

"Well. In with us, for now."

She refused Hugh's offer. He became mock growly then, saying, well, if she didn't want to … and then reported on his job, how Pam was frazzled from the pregnancy and from tending Betsy and John, and added a remark about the weather over there. She didn't hear his relief, exactly; it was more how quickly he gave up on the idea.

A dream she'd had as a little girl suddenly floated up whole before Eliza's eyes — a rainy day, her parents arguing, and her very own playhouse with a door she could close.

Pam got on the line. "Eliza?"

"Hi, honey."

"John! Take that out … Hugh, get that thing out of his mouth before he swallows it! Eliza, are you really doing okay in that motel?"

She'd just arrived that afternoon; how could she know if she was doing okay or not? Mist was soaking into her face and hair, and the drips from the overhang were starting to puddle by her damp Keds. "I'm all right, Pam. Those kids running you ragged?"

"Ever damn day, I—" A yelp and an angry wail drowned her out. The phone knocked against something, and Eliza heard Pam holler, "Jesus God, Hugh, just take it away from him and go in the other room, will you? Can't hear myself talk. I'm sorry, Eliza." Her voice became close again. "What'd you say?"

"Nothing. I'll see y'all in a couple months at Thanksgiving. And my new grandbaby! He'll be here by then."

"Or she," Pam said. "And yeah, she better be."

"Or she," Eliza agreed. "Listen, I want to bring you a damask tablecloth I don't have room for here. I s'pose I kept it because my mother gave it to me as a wedding gift. How's your mama?"

"Still complaining. If it's not her diabetes, it's her high blood pressure. I swear, they take turns."

"Well, bless her heart, I understand that."

"Yeah, but you're not always telling it. Say, Eliza—" Pam lowered her voice.

Eliza almost shuddered, standing there outside the Vidalia's office, growing damper by the minute. She couldn't bear to hear the same false offer again in Pam's voice. She told herself their motive was kind even if the invitation to live with them in their crowded little house was not sincere. But the dishonest way of talking with her own family embarrassed her, made her impatient.

"Pam, I realize I could help you with the young'uns. But your mama would feel awful left out, and I'd have to sleep in Betsy's room right up next to yours and Hugh's, and we'd be squeezed in like sardines at the supper table, and, Pam, you'd lose your mind."

The line was quiet. "You know I love you, Eliza," Pam said.

"Thank you, honey, I love you too."

Eliza hung up, on balance happier than sad with this exchange. Shielding her head with her hands, she hurried back down to her room. She sat down on her chair and dried her face with a towel.

That playhouse Hugh had made her recall, how dearly she'd wished for it as a child. It could have been in a tree, like one boy's she'd seen, but it could also have been on the ground, a little house to walk into, a little table to share with Becca, her doll. A door to shut out grown people. A window that blue showed through. Filmy curtain riffling in a breeze, and all the time in the green world. With sudden force, it hit Eliza as she untied the wet Keds that she'd gotten exactly what she'd wished for fifty-odd years ago: a house scaled small.

She had a little half-moon table designed to fit against a wall, flat on one side, round on the other, a vinyl-covered chair snugged up to it. There should have been two chairs—maybe the manager had retrieved one before she moved in. But at least Eliza did not have to sit across the table from an empty chair, reminded daily of Robert. One chair belonged at this table, and Eliza sat on it. The stove and refrigerator were maybe three-quarters of normal size. Little four-burner electric, barely space on it to set down a stirring spoon; a fridge that was shorter than she was; a single sink; a patch of cupboard; a twin bed and a low ceiling. A bathroom she could hardly turn around in, the shower partitioned off from the toilet by a hard plastic divider that accordioned open and closed. The second time she used it, its plastic handle broke off.

She had a window with curtains, not filmy but plastic, and behind those were clanky, yellowed venetian blinds. She'd seen right away that she had the no-choice situation of keeping her blinds closed and living dim-lit or letting the other residents look in on her like a TV show. Dim-lit it was; she cast 40-watt shadows on kitchen linoleum. It was as well she had the blinds, for her door opened onto the Vidalia's parking lot, and that ended abruptly in Sixth Street.

She would not have told Hugh or Ellen how she dry-heaved the first night after she set down Percy in room number 2, went back for her suitcases and boxes, set them down, and closed the door. How from room number 1 came barking and a steady whacking, like faint movie-machine-gun fire. Poor old Percy had wearied himself tottering back and forth, puzzled by her muffled sounds, spine hair ridged at the barking wall. The barking soon stopped, and he was left with only Eliza to focus his dumb, expectant eyes on.

Water pressure had been mounting behind her eyes since the taxi driver had refused Percy that afternoon.

"No, ma'am, no animals in my car," he'd said, his finger wagging sideways.

"He won't go. I already walked him," Eliza told him.

"Ain't my rule. Company rule." The driver, a young Black man, his hair flaring from a shaved-in part, dipped his head. "I take you. Cain't take the dog."

It was late in the afternoon, the summer sun angling so that leafy shadows fluttered over the yellow car, a breath of breeze beginning. Eliza looked around foolishly, as though surveying other, invisible modes of transportation. "But . . . but I don't have any other way to get him there."

"Call you up a friend, have him bring him." He eyed the pile of things beside her in the driveway. "Where all that stuff going?"

Eliza could not think of a friend she would want to call. Her friends had been her neighbors. They thought she was going to live with Hugh, and she had not told them differently.

"Sweet Vidalia Residence Inn, over on Sixth."

"That's a piece." He put the car in gear. "That dog leak, I got to answer to the boss." He looked at her pile again.

Eliza quickly raised a hand to her chin to hide its quivering.

A wrinkle came in his smooth young forehead. "I'm sorry, ma'am." He backed slowly from her driveway.

Eliza hurried in and called another taxi company. The telephone was due to be shut off; she did not know when. Maybe at the end of the workday, five o'clock, which was four minutes away, or maybe, she hoped, not until night when some man or woman with a stack of orders got around to her number. She came back out and made herself wave at Earl Fitzwalter when he drove by and greeted her.

The next driver arrived in a white car a nervous twenty minutes later and curtly said the same: No dogs in the taxi. He cited not his boss but city ordinance. He backed away. Eliza went in again, located in the open phone book the last taxi company's number. She did not ask them about dogs in advance because it was easier for them to say no on the phone. She took a precious ten-dollar bill from her change purse, tucked it in a pocket, and went outside again. It was coming evening now, people in to supper, except for the Hooks kids down the block, hollering and running through a sprinkler.

The third taxi was green with black-and-white checks. The driver slowed to see her hand holding Percy's leash, looked down at Percy, drool-mouthed and panting, and cruised on by.

Eliza's knees gave out; she sat down on a suitcase. She'd brought everything off, everything: sold the living-room and dining-room furniture and the tools in the garage through the *Green Sheet;* gave Velma Fitzwalter the mahogany breakfront she'd admired in return for Earl's future straightening out of Eliza's house lien; called the Salvation Army to pick up assorted boxes of linens and clothes and whatnots. Besides her two suitcases, she had two boxes packed with plates, cups, utensils, pot, kettle, frying pan, radio, and clock. Also her pillow, and Percy. She was exhausted from all the getting-rid-of and the being-afraid-she-would-not-get-rid-of. Up until now, she'd thought she'd done well. She supposed she could drag it all back in, sleep on the floor, and make several bus trips tomorrow. But there was still Percy. They would not let him on the bus for certain.

Her eyes smarting with tears, she carried Percy back in. He seemed glad to be inside, walked to the spot where the couch used to be, stood awhile, then folded his legs under him. She steeled herself to call Earl Fitzwalter for a ride, reached for the phone, drew back, reached again, and snatched it off the hook. A smooth silence met her ear. She listened harder. Flat quiet; no clicks, no echoes, no hums. Somewhere the man with the work orders ran his finger down to the next number.

Eliza went back out and lifted a suitcase, hauled it in, strode out to get the other, panting like Percy.

A yellow taxi coasted into her driveway. The same young driver stuck his head out the window. "Put him in a bag," he called.

She approached the taxi, pushing back her hair; she didn't think she'd heard him correctly. "What?"

His forehead was truly wrinkled now. "Put a bag over his butt and I take you. If you don't go calling Yellow Cab for no more dog rides, hear?"

"I hear." Eliza took the folded ten from her pocket and handed it into the car. "I'll be right back," she said.

She toted out the suitcase. When she returned with Percy half stuffed into a paper grocery bag, the driver had the suitcases in the back seat and was slamming his trunk.

It was a fast ride to the Sweet Vidalia, him asking her twice how the dog was holding up. After her belongings had been stacked by the office, she touched the young man's elbow. He turned.

"I will remember your kindness," Eliza said.

"You 'member my craziness," he said. "That dog like five hundred years old?"

Eliza inspected Percy, with his bland dog grin, tongue lolling from the side of his toothless mouth, his cloudy black eyes peering up pertly as though he were taking in his new surroundings. He didn't seem to be bothered by the paper sack. "Pretty near," she said, "but I couldn't just leave him by the side of the road."

"No'm," the young man said, "cain't do that."

Then he was gone, and Eliza, no time to think about the life she'd left behind, stood before a white office door festooned with plastic onions. More onions framed a placard with *The Sweet Vidalia Residence Inn* written in red and black cursive. She pushed in, paid a week's rent, and received her key. She'd carried Percy, squeezing him as she fiddled her door open, set him down in the room, and folded up the dry paper sack. She went back and forth for the rest of her things, hauling them in, and shut the door. Then she could cry.

Her chest heaved, her eyes burned, but nothing fell. Somewhere in the momentum of rushing in and out, phoning taxis, holding the dead receiver, finding a paper sack, the crying had shuffled back inside her. She had almost burst into tears the second she climbed into the yellow taxi's solid, broad seat; it took a fierce effort to hold back. Now the impulse was gone, and she was too tired to go searching for it. She'd finally lain down, still dressed, on the bed, covering herself to the neck with its limp chenille spread. Percy whined until she reached down and dragged up his hairy hide. His jumping days were over. He'd circled, stumbling, toenails snagging the chenille, collapsed on a plain, and began a slow slide down the slope and into the indentation of her waist.

Then she'd gotten up to call Hugh and Pam. She'd told them none of this.

Back in her room now, after drying herself off, Eliza started toward the tiny bathroom, then stopped, realizing that she had not walked through her old rooms, giving them a goodbye look. Not a glance at the brick or the window trim or the yard. She'd been too grateful to be in the taxi. Too concerned with the state of Percy's bladder. Well, she thought, this was something. She'd needed the house, yes, but she didn't need to cling to it.

In the metal-edged mirror of the medicine cabinet, she saw how far past due her permanent wave was. She needed a haircut, some loft and curl. She ran her brush through the brown hair, silvery at the temples. It fanned for a second, lion-like, around her face. Her hair hadn't been this long since before Hugh's birth. No beauty parlors until she was ready to apply for jobs.

Well, as Miss Scarlett would say, *Tomorrow is another day.*

Eliza frowned as she got in bed. That might be true but it was also true that Scarlett O'Hara was Vivien Leigh, whose tomorrow held a slew of features unavailable to Eliza Kratke's tomorrow. She switched off the light.

IX

Except for the big Safeway, as starkly carved out of the Vidalia's neighborhood as a landing zone in a thicket, the real estate in this humble part of Bayard had long been spoken for, divided into middling-size storefronts, cafés, and offices and whittled again into two-customers-at-a-time shops and street-level doors that opened onto sharply vertical stairs. Here cars streamed by all day and there were enough at night to keep her awake when her neighbors didn't. Her neighbors, on either side and the floor above her, were mostly young. Some were students attending the business college. More were working at jobs they disdained, thumb-twiddling, waiting for something to hit them, a windfall or a friend with a gimmick.

That was how Eliza got along with them in those first few weeks before the school year. She did not judge them aimless. From her passing conversations with them, she suspected that all but the most dedicated partyer had some secret dream stowed behind his eyes. Nothing for public consumption because that would invite ridicule. But sometimes, hints would fall out of the sides of mouths; hopes, downplayed by sleepy eyes, would seep out in her presence. That had to do with her age, she knew, the threads of gray in her hair, her dresses that weight loss had made roomy now, her Keds, but also with her neutrality. Everybody wants a mama with a listening ear, not quick to call them down or boss them. To Eliza, what they did was what they did. These were not her children. Besides, she shared an aim with them: having a roof overhead. They sweated the rent, and she did too until her tenants' check arrived—most of which was consumed by the Vidalia, some by Robert's mortgage, leaving her a small amount of cash she could change into singles and dole out. It was true she was the only tenant of the Vidalia who had rent money coming in and did not care for beer-drinking parties. But it was also true she worried she'd fall short every month, and her neighbors had been twinkles in heaven when she was marking a ballot for Franklin D. Roosevelt.

The business college was up on Tenth. On her first day, she was ready at six fifteen for her eight o'clock class and sitting at the half-moon table, towel draped over her lap so that her skirt would not get stained if her shaky hands spilled the coffee. It was hard to draw a clear breath. Her breath caught somewhere shallow and shoved down again.

When had she felt like this? Eliza could not dredge up a time. Her first day of grade school had been a proud, new-shoe day, and later she loved school because it took her away from some of the farm chores. She was not scared on her wedding day despite her mother's red-faced mumblings because she and Robert had already made love several times in a field far from the road, on a quilt he'd taken from his mother's house. She was scared with Hugh, her first baby, but the fear had been overpowered by the entirety of pain and, behind that, the inextinguishable notion that she was just about to have the most exciting birthday party of her life. After she discovered Robert's deception, the paltry passbook savings at the bank, she'd certainly been afraid, but that had been a sick fear, spreading, numbing her stomach and her limbs. This fear was different. This fear was solid. It filled her body like cold metal in a mold.

At twenty-five to eight, dressed in her pull-on skirt and suit jacket and a blouse buttoned at the neck, no bow, she stepped down from the safety of the bus. She walked past a Maytag appliance store and a florist's and stopped before a brick arch of majestic proportions. Curlicued letters above the arch spelled out *Carlton Business College*. Eliza's life had never allowed her to consider college, but here she was now, at a kind of college. Strong forces were propelling her in opposite directions—into the maroon-brick building, and back down the street to the bus stop—so she weaved awhile with the morning mist clinging to her worried face. Then, stiffly, she mounted the broad steps, her pumps scratching against the concrete; she felt as if brick columns were pushing down on her shoulders. A bespectacled woman at a glassed-in desk directed her to room 122. Eliza trudged down an empty hall and fit herself into a desk in the back row of that room. She was almost surprised she could bend. She was the first one there; the lights weren't even on yet.

Room 122, Eliza bet, was older than she was. Its high ceiling was dull, patterned tin. The high transom windows had not been cleaned in some time, so their dingy glass filtered out the mild gold of September. Rectangles of whitish sky slanted down into the classroom in visible shafts. Old-fashioned lamps hung down on cords. There were scuffs in the green paint on the walls, a sour, olive color, and the two charts that hung there—a replica of a typewriter's keys, and a bunch of symbols that Eliza supposed were shorthand—curled at their edges. The teacher's desk anchored the classroom, as she remembered, a big wooden ship for the captain in front of a stretch of smeary blackboard.

Her own slim desk was familiarly carved and marked on. Gone, though, was the top that hinged up to offer a drawer for pencils and paper, ruler, pink eraser, the kind of desk that Eliza had studied at when she was in school. It had a simple tray to write on, a blond, polished surface that it seemed books would slip off of. Experimentally, she rested her forearms on its cool slickness. Her damp palms stuck, and she sheltered one hand with the other.

If she failed these bookkeeping courses, what would she do? What other work could she get? Running a cash register at the 7-Eleven, on her feet all day, fumbling with sacks? Babysitting. Tending to old folks. She was probably dead wrong to try for something she considered better.

And how clumsy would she feel here, amid a crowd of rosy, chirruping girls? Like a rough-coated mule in a herd of ponies. Not understanding the teacher's questions, being called on by name and not knowing the lesson, sitting there dumb-mouthed, dumb-brained. *Oh, please, no.* Eliza was not loose enough to shudder; instead, she contracted further into the little blond desk.

"Is this your first day?" a thin voice ventured. Startled, Eliza heaved her whole body backward in its direction.

"Oh, that's stupid, it's everybody's first day. I meant, have you not been here before? One more class and I am out of here. Business Math. Flunked."

In the shadowy corner, a girl sat half folded on a stool, holding out a cigarette, flicking a match against its cover. She appeared to have a black shawl draped over her head. The only thing Eliza could see clearly was the flame when it caught and then the orange tip of the cigarette as she sucked in.

"What I really wanna do?" The girl went on as if Eliza had asked her. "Is go to Europe, probably London or maybe Germany, and go to an art school or a printing school, learn true engraving like my grandpa used to do. I know a lot already." She blew out smoke.

Eliza could not find anything to say to this. A young girl wrapped in an old lady's shawl and puffing on a cigarette was new to her, but she was relieved to hear the girl's voice, glad that someone was talking to her.

"Over there, they treat you serious. You can learn all sorts of printing, like lino-printing—that's when you make a picture on linoleum. You know, like you probably have on your kitchen floor—oh, shut up, Louise!"

Eliza craned around farther. She could not see Louise anywhere. "Pardon?" she said.

The girl tinkled out a pretty laugh. "I'm always doing that."

"What?"

"Oh, I'm Louise. People tell me my mouth is like the Mississippi, wide and fast. I'm here because a relative gave me five hundred dollars to graduate business school. But I don't wanna do business. Never, never, never, no way. I wanna make pictures. I can draw like you wouldn't believe."

"That so?"

"Wanna see?" Louise hopped off the tall stool and bobbed over, the black shawl not slipping off her head but swinging like a sheet with her uneven walk. Eliza peered down to see one built-up shoe and up again to notice her stoop. The shawl covered her back, Eliza guessed, for a reason. Maybe a curve, maybe a hump; she could not tell. When Louise was close enough that smoke drifted into Eliza's face, Eliza saw that the shawl was her hair, center-parted, black and straight and slide-y as rayon. She took the writing tablet Louise offered. It was a Big Chief with pale blue lines, a pencil tucked into the middle of its thickness, up by the seam. The girl had turned the tablet sideways to sketch the room, making it very like Eliza saw it: antiquated, deserted, dark. The shafts of light were there but they ended without illuminating darkened lumps of desks, a tangled forest floor too far from treetops. There was a crosshatched figure in the rear of the drawing, huddled, all rounded back and no neck, light hair drooping on a line of collar. The figure gave the room its scale and, by the way it slumped in on itself, a loneliness that made the place seem emptier than if no one at all had been there.

"I look that scared?" Eliza said.

"I may be taking a little…artistic license." Louise pronounced the last two words with relish.

Her eyes were light; Eliza thought blue, but maybe gray. They were almost as heavily lashed as a doll baby's, and her eyebrows winged gracefully in a way tweezing aimed for but seldom accomplished. That they extended a little farther than usual above her nose made her prettier, Eliza thought, like a fairy-tale girl before anything magic happens to her.

Eliza told Louise her name and that, yes, it was her first day, and that—she couldn't help saying it—she felt just exactly like this clever drawing showed her, scared. It felt better to say it.

Louise's eyes lit at *clever*. "But you're so old," she said cheerfully. "The oldest person at Carlton, I bet. How can you be scared?"

Because if I can't make good with this schoolwork, Eliza thought, *I don't know what I'll do.* But this was too naked a statement, and it would be said with too short a breath, so she kept it to herself. "I need to do good," she said.

Louise looked delighted. "Your problems are over," she declared, turning her head away to blow out smoke. "I've got something that'll help you." She tamped her cigarette on an oblong, enameled box she was carrying and thumped its lid, which snapped down by itself. "My grand-daddy kept his cigarettes in this. He had a snuffbox that matched it."

Eliza let herself sit back in the seat, just a little. "My mama dipped snuff."

"Yeah?" After extracting her pencil, Louise placed her tablet in a workmanlike manner beneath her arm and sat down in the next desk. "Ouch." She swept the fall of hair from under her bottom. "Did your husband leave you for some secretary slut? We've got some like that. Doris and Hilda and...Maxine. You're even older than them. No, Doris graduated, I think. The rest of them"—Louise waved her pencil at the empty desks—"they're just out of high school and studying to be secretary sluts themselves.

Oh, and Terry. He raised his hand once and asked could they guarantee he'd get a secretary job, since he's a man. The teacher told him in the French government, the secretaries are men, but they have a better name. They're *aides*. Carlton's got an answer for everything that'll take your money."

"What about you?"

"Me? I'm just passing through. After I redo the math class, I get my certificate."

"And then you get the five hundred dollars?"

"Oh." Louise looked down. "I got that when I signed up for this last class. And it, uh…it just…" She fluttered her hands like birds flying away. "You know?" she asked, with more fluttering.

"Yes, I do," Eliza said.

Two girls entered, glanced at Eliza and Louise, chose distant seats, and whispered to each other.

"Hey," Louise said.

Eliza turned her attention back to Louise, who was tapping her knee. "I'm going to give you my notes. For every damn class." She flipped over her hands so that her palms showed — *Ta-da!* — and tilted her head, clearly waiting to be thanked.

Or acclaimed. Eliza smiled at the girl's pose, the shine in her eyes and her pursed lips; she took Eliza's mind off herself. "Thank you. Don't guess you'll need 'em off in London."

Louise drew herself up. "Damn straight."

Another girl walked in, then a boy who wafted across the room and disappeared into the gloom of the opposite corner, then, as a crowd of girls tumbled in all at once, chirruping just as Eliza had imagined, the dozen hanging lamps ignited. Cones of harsh white light poured down. It felt to Eliza as if the walls had jumped back and a bucket of water had been splashed in her face. Blinking, she saw a short, round woman in a saggy cardigan sweater planted behind the captain's desk. The teacher had a red notebook in one hand and a pen in the other.

"Welcome to Business Math. I'm your teacher, Miss Dewitt. Please listen for your name. If you do not hear it, speak to me after class. Anderson, Cathy," she boomed.

"Here."

"Baker, Mary Ann."

"Here."

The names rolled on. A slim girl with a bubble hairdo twisted around to Eliza and said, "Hi." She caught sight of Louise and turned around again. "Unh," she grunted.

Louise leaned toward the girl's back, hissing, "Eat shit and die."

"Kratke, Eliza."

Eliza forced her hand up and answered, not, as she had learned in school, *Present,* but, like the others, "Here." Louise answered to the last name *Molineaux,* the girl on Eliza's left to *Ruffin, Jeannie.* Eliza thought she'd seen the tall, red-haired girl before but maybe the familiarity came from the way she gripped the desk edge and swiveled back and forth in her seat like any four-year-old. How freely she moved, angling away from and around to Eliza. Jeannie wore an orange dress hiked so far up her meager thighs, Eliza was obliged to view France.

"You don't have long to live," Jeannie said, staring at Eliza meaningfully.

The lift Eliza had felt from her conversation with Louise and the casual greeting of the bubble-haired girl evaporated. What a mean thing to say. She had been right, she was too old for school, but she'd imagined she would be ignored or condescended to, not taunted.

Jeannie said, "Your name's Eliza? Hi." She rolled her eyes. "You're about to be bored to death."

There was not room to be both bored to death and scared to death, Eliza found. She was not fooling around here. Every problem posed in every class, she took as real and not an example, knowing she could encounter it on the outside, in a job she would need to keep. During her family's first months in Bayard, when Eliza's dad's brother had secretly let them sleep in the post office, her mother used to talk about "the wolf at the door." After finishing some lady's nice dress, she would heat the flat iron on their hot plate and press down the dress seams, the bodice pleats, protecting her work with dampened brown paper so as not to scorch. "Reckon this'll keep the wolf from the door another day," she'd say, and fold the dress breast-side out, for carrying. Eliza's brother, Roy, almost a teenager, thought it was funny. He'd pretend to scan the dirt path behind the post office and the cornfield nearby for the wolf. "Okay," he'd say with a wink, "he's gone."

"Told you, baby." Mama would snap her fingers and pick up the folded dress.

Louise prodded Eliza's arm on the third day of school. "Hey, wanna eat your sandwich with me?"

Why not? Louise wasn't the only one who was friendless.

They ate outside the school on a concrete table at the edge of a little park that filled at lunchtime with business-school girls, packed in on the benches like birds on a line. No one sat with Louise and Eliza. "They're jealous of me." Louise hooked her head toward the others, her black hair brilliantly slinky in the sunshine.

Eliza took out her cheese sandwich. "Couldn't be because you're not very nice to them?" she asked. She'd noticed two women who were older than the rest taking notes as steadily as she did, and she'd have liked to talk with them, hear their stories.

Louise swelled. "I'm nice. They're not nice back. And when somebody's not nice back to you, you don't tolerate that shit. Sorry, Eliza, you probably don't like hearing bad words." She had brought Cheetos, and her mouth and fingers were orange.

Thinking of her own kids and her babysitting, the sick people she used to tend, Eliza sighed. "That particular bad word's been underneath my fingernails more than once. Why're they so jealous of you?"

Louise tossed her head, lifted a forearm so that a skein of hair slid over it. "Well, my long hair. And then..." She plunged her hand into the Cheetos bag. "I drew some of their pictures. They didn't like them."

"Why not? You got mine sure enough."

"That's it! See, you didn't mind because you're *mature*. They're not." Louise's head went back; she broke into a merry laugh, hugely self-satisfied. She drummed her feet beneath the table. "The pictures were too perfect."

"Uh-huh, and why was that?"

"Because my pictures were really and truly them. See Beverly?" Louise's right hand pointed; the left was buried in the Cheetos bag. Beverly was the bubble-haired girl who had spoken to Eliza. "She acts so stuck up. I put all that haughty in her picture. And you know Jeannie Ruffin? Birdbrain—that's how I drew her." Louise's stoop increased; her eyes narrowed with injustice. "They got mad."

Eliza smiled, folded up the wax paper, and dropped it in her sack. She brought out a sheet of Kleenex and wiped her fingers. "You want a Kleenex?"

"In a minute. I'm not done."

"Don't know how you got that in their pictures, Louise, but I know this. You make fun of people, they feel bad, and then they're not going to like you."

Louise's narrowed eyes did not change. "I know," she

said. "Price I pay for art." But the glance from underneath the doll-baby eyelashes surprised Eliza with a self-mocking awareness, and the girl came out again with her contrary laugh, made up of malice and merriness. "Wanna see something?"

Eliza wanted to go in and study for Business English — letter-writing, proposals, queries, and so on. "For a minute," she said.

Louise sucked her finger and thumb tips, took the Kleenex Eliza offered, and ran it around her orange lips. She flipped open the tablet she always carried with her to the page the pencil was stuck in and scribbled some words with that curled-hand posture left-handed people used. "Oh, wait." She made a tsking sound with her tongue and block-printed a heading. She turned the tablet and pushed it over. *Our Founding Fathers,* it read.

Abraham Lincoln stared out at Eliza in as fine a detail as a number-two pencil could make on chalky tablet paper. She studied the face. Louise must have copied it from a photograph Eliza had never seen in books, a photograph taken perhaps before the one chosen for official purposes. It was personal, revealing, as though Lincoln had not yet transferred his attention from recalcitrant generals and corpse-strewn battlefields to the black-draped photographer set up on the carpet before him. The distant formality conveyed by the set of the head was belied by a depth in the eyes, a loneliness stubbornly withheld from the beholder. Below that, darker grief was sunken in. A knowledge contained, again stubbornly, within the eyes and the line of the lips, that the done was done, the undone bitter, and none to answer for it but himself.

"Sad, isn't he? I read, Eliza, I do. When I'm interested. And I study pictures down at the public library. You didn't think that, did you? Put the pictures and the words together and that's what you get."

Shaken, Eliza flipped the page. Benjamin Franklin peered out above the famous bifocals, the curvy lips not yet flattened into decorous reserve. He looked sly and amused and at home with himself, a man ready to joke equally with drinkers and kings. There were other statesmen, too, on the following pages, stately heads in keen detail, their eyes eerily alive.

Eliza looked up. Louise was not watching her avidly, as she had before, for a response. Chin in hand, she was gazing out at the cars stopped at Tenth and Chestnut. Unwillingly, Eliza found herself choosing the girl's own word.

"Why, Louise, these are … perfect."

Louise reached for the tablet, shrugging. "Told you. What am I s'posed to do? Draw bad so they'll like me?" She disentangled herself from the bench. "Gotta go. Oh, wait, I brought these for you." Louise dug in her flimsy bag and handed her old notebooks over with an air of benevolence. "I made good Bs with these," she said. "Use a mirror." She strode away with her bobbing gait before Eliza could ask what she meant.

Eliza settled into Business Math and figured weekly

payroll on a ten-employee business, according to the hour-
lies and salaries given, and then calculated the taxes due.
At afternoon break, Maxine and Hilda, the older business students, drifted over and spoke to her. They talked
about their children. Hilda's boy was a senior in high
school and on the football team. She crossed her fingers,
saying, "Scholarship." Maxine could not even imagine her
kids that old. They were four and seven; years of maca-
roni stretched before them, as Maxine saw it. She was a
pinch-lipped woman who hugged her elbow to her ribs and
held her burning cigarette in two rigid fingers by her jaw.
Neither woman asked Eliza if she had kids. Neither woman
asked Eliza anything about herself. She decided that sitting
with Louise and listening to Jeannie Ruffin cheerfully run
on about nothing was not so bad.

X

Eliza didn't mind walking the blocks home from the bus stop. It was still warm, and even before Carlton's classes began, she'd occasionally visit with Mary, who sold vegetables out of a pickup in the Vidalia's lot. Mary was neighborly, talkative. Today she shooed her son out of the second lawn chair, asking how Eliza was liking the school. She invited her to sit.

"School seems all right, far as I can tell." Eliza set her books, her notebook, and Louise's stack of notebooks on the concrete. She asked after Mary's husband, who was trying to get on at one of the plants, and her teenage daughter, who all of a sudden didn't want to be seen anymore selling tomatoes and cucumbers and squash on Sixth

Street. "Debbie used to like it," Mary said, "sharp at making change. Now that's all beneath her."

"How they are at that age," Eliza said. She slipped her feet partway out of the shoes and rested her heels on the backs of them.

"Sometimes I just want to rattle her bones. How'd you stand it?"

"Can't give 'em away."

Mary laughed. "I might try."

"How's your husband coming with his job-hunting?"

Mary shook her head for a while. She was a nice-looking woman; in her straw hat and sunglasses and braids, Eliza thought, Mary could almost be a teenager herself.

A car pulled in and a Black woman about Eliza's age got out to examine the tomatoes. She squeezed and then chose four, and Mary put them in a paper sack. "Them in the stores," the woman complained, "ain't nowhere near ripe. Look like it, then you go to pick 'em up and they's hard as rocks."

"Taste like rocks too," Eliza offered.

"Ain't that the truth. Lemme see your squash there." Mary held out a bucket, and the woman picked two. "Not but me and the old man now. Naw, just put 'em in with the tomatoes," she said when Mary reached for another sack. "No use in running through your sacks there."

"Thank you, ma'am," Mary said, taking the dollar and a quarter.

The woman nodded and walked away.

"Bob," Mary said, dropping back into her lawn chair, "he's not swift at finding him a job. Picky. Bob's one picky man. Not like my first husband, Mike. Mike'd work at whatever there was, God bless his soul. I tell you, Eliza, I think I went backward. Why'd I think one man would act just like another? Faron, you get down from there!"

Her barefoot son, Faron, was doing a little dance on the roof of the cab. "Hot," he said.

"Well, get back down then, genius." Mary pointed sharply, and the boy slid down the windshield onto the hood. "I'm bored," he called.

"You rather be bored or hungry?" his mother barked. "Take your pick." Faron slouched away from the truck.

"And don't wander off nowhere neither."

Faron poked out his bottom lip and waggled his head from side to side.

"Well, I better be going in." Eliza gathered her books. "I got homework to figure."

"Don't you miss him sometimes?" Mary hunched in the chair, both hands on the arms of her sunglasses. "Sometimes I miss Mike so much, I can't barely breathe. I thought someday the kids'd be grown and it'd be like...like that woman said, just me and the old man. Felt good when I thought that."

Eliza gazed down on the stubborn ring she hadn't been able to wrench over her swollen knuckle. She didn't know how to answer. Did she miss Robert? How could you miss someone who'd beaten you all over and left you bleeding?

Somebody who'd destroyed you? Could she miss the Robert she married, the one who'd held their babies—could she draw that line? No. If she ever quit being angry at him, would she miss him? Would that be her reward for getting over her anger? Wouldn't that be the booby prize.

"I mean, when the kids are at school and Bob's deigned to go out job-hunting and I'm out by myself in the garden, I swear I can hear Mike's voice telling me to come on in before all my freckles run together... and I stand up, gonna smart back to him, you know, and then I...I miss him so much, my back teeth ache."

Eliza patted her knee.

Mary rubbed beneath the sunglasses. "Am I nuts? You ever miss your husband that way?"

Eliza stalled by opening the top one on the stack of Louise's notebooks; Mary would probably go on in a second without her answering. The pages were dense with a back-slanting handwriting from which Eliza could not decipher one English word; it looked like Egyptian to her. She let the cover drop and looked off to the street, where a convertible drove by, blaring music, a white-shirted man at the wheel and a blond woman in the passenger seat, their hair blowing.

Mary's question made Eliza shrink. She wouldn't tell her story, not even to this young woman she liked. It would disarrange her, scatter her forces, let bad things out into the air. She could not. "I guess," she said, "I'm not ready to talk about my husband."

Mary jerked off the sunglasses. "Oh my God, and I'm pushing you. I'm sorry—" Her reddened eyes glimmered, and her freckled nose wrinkled in concern.

Eliza had run a mile from her neighbors' and friends' strained silences and mumbled condolences, from Mr. Henney's earnest one. Poor Mr. Henney. He'd been trying to be helpful, but she'd challenged him and left the church office without the usual parting courtesies. All these people knew; they talked about it among themselves. Oh, Eliza must have been quite the popular topic for a while. She could have told Mary what Robert had done as a kind of a practice, she supposed. Just to hear herself say it. Would that take out any of the sting? It was the truth. She couldn't change it. But she was glad she'd kept it to herself.

Now she could go on feeling easy sitting here with Mary and her baskets of tomatoes. She hadn't spoiled that small pleasure, and she needed any small pleasures she could accumulate. She had avoided creating one more person in the world who pitied her. Eliza shoved her feet back in her shoes, patted Mary on her blue-jeaned knee. She would go in now, while she was ahead.

Eliza tossed in the bed, then got up and filled the kettle. Turned on the plastic fan. She leafed through Louise's notes. Gibberish, every line. Page after page of it. All she could understand were the numbers. The pencil or ink pictures that adorned almost every page explained Louise's general unpopularity.

They were caricatures, as there was distortion: Miss Dewitt, the Business Math teacher, her face squashed and nose tip blackened, jowls hanging so that she looked like a suspicious bulldog. Terry, the sole boy in their class, drawn with headscarf and upthrust shoulder, the black-ringed eyes of a silent-screen star. Beverly, her long face horsey, nostrils flaring, lip twitched with disdain. Maxine with tiny, wild eyes, deep inside an arch of smoke, like a mouse furious in a hole. There were other faces: a young man whose full-lipped smile was dimmed by an accusing chin; another whose squinting demeanor brought to mind a mole, his tipped head shaped like a teardrop. Eliza did not recognize them. But she would bet that, even with their fanciful embellishments, someone somewhere would. Louise, she thought, was a girl who yahooed the wolf to her door.

XI

All Eliza could do about her own wolf was live with him. She wrote down all she could manage of what the teacher said, making stars by what she didn't understand and would have to find in the book and read again later. Once she'd read it again, if she understood then, she'd give her own head a pat. It was awfully silly, and she'd never do that in front of anyone but Percy. Alone in her room it was okay, though. It helped her keep plowing ahead. Her notebook grew fat with writing, and when it filled up, she set it on the night table in the spot her telephone would have gone if she'd had one and bought another in a new color at the Safeway. She figured her homework in the notebook, ripped out the pages, and scissored off the torn hole side, for neatness. Then she copied over the homework on the next fresh pages, so example problems followed notes in the proper place, and she had a record of what she'd written once she handed in her homework.

In August she had gotten the good news about her new grandchild, a healthy baby girl they named Lucinda, and the wolf stayed outside. In both September and October, her tenants were many days late with the rent, and the wolf barged through the door; Eliza ate cornflakes for breakfast, salted-tomato sandwiches for lunch, and for supper she laced her hands across a growly stomach and listened to the radio. She strung out a plump tomato for three days and brushed her teeth with baking soda. What she could do, she did. What she couldn't, she held at bay by saying prayers for her kids, then she branched out to the truly misfortunate, those whose tragedies surpassed a husband's cruelty and a light pocketbook. Nights when that backfired and she got stuck in worry, she walked the dog.

She usually walked him morning and evening but in October, she and Percy took many a chill turn. They stayed away from Sixth and walked the more residential streets behind, past close-built, screened-porch houses with runners for driveways and big-wheeled tricycles abandoned by the steps. Percy snuffled in the wet leaves. Eliza was not used to being out at midnight; she had not known how streetlights would glitter the leaves in the gutters. Many were browned already, but on Greavey and here and there on Sutter, the wet black streets were margined with gold.

Once, she saw a man stumble from an alley, and she and Percy veered to the opposite side of the road; twice they passed a man walking three dogs himself, the man tilted backward to counterbalance the force of the taut leashes. On the third occasion, the man spoke to Percy. "Say there, old fellow." He squatted and extended a hand, and his tall, sniffing dogs disappeared Percy from Eliza's view. "*They* won't hurt you. No, they *won't*. Don't mind *them*," the man crooned. "Got some miles on *you*, don't you, fellow?"

"Percy's fourteen," Eliza said. A light wave of wind rustled what leaves were left on the trees, and she pulled her coat around her.

The tall dogs lost interest, milling, so Eliza could see Percy again, his throat strained toward the man's scratching hand. "That right? Don't look a *day* past thirteen and a half. *You* live next door to us, don't you, Percy? We hear you sometimes."

"You live at number one?"

"Yes, we *do*," he said, replying as if the question had come from Percy. "Not so *many* places glad to have us. Guess *you* know about that, huh, boy?"

"Called four of them," Eliza said, " 'fore the Vidalia said I could bring him."

"*We* know how it is. Yes, we *do*. *We* been tossed out. All a dog wants is to love a person, and people throw 'em out like garbage. We never figured that out, huh, Percy? Huh, Caesar? Sit, boy." At the mention of his name, a big white dog with a blunted face stopped his digging. One bound and he sat by the squatting man. "*We* just keep our distance is best. That's what *we* do."

What Eliza could see by streetlight was a hooded sweatshirt and thick, chopped hair. She felt awkward introducing herself to the top of his head, but she did. "Knew I heard barking over in number one," she said. "Glad to meet you."

"Likewise us," he said. "This is Caesar and Toby and Mrs. Hudson and Morton." The other two dogs loped over and sat.

Toby or Morton; Eliza took a guess. "You walk every night, Mr. Morton?"

"We do. Nice out here then. Morton's the first name." A hand slipped into the sweatshirt pocket, brought out a bone-shaped biscuit.

"He don't have teeth," Eliza warned, but he was already snapping off the end of it. He fed the chip to Percy, who braced his legs and gobbled. The dogs, alert to the biscuit, sat like three well-mannered children, licking their lips with long tongues.

"We saw *that*, didn't we, fellow? Not a *tooth* in your old head." Percy, mannerless, was beside himself, dancing stiff-legged, tail beating the air.

Morton stood and distributed biscuits all around. Three snaps and they were gone. He was tall and unshaven, lean as the dogs. He stepped toward Eliza but looked off to the side of her. His eyes were so deep set and shadowed that, had his head not moved, following the dogs, she would have taken him for a blind man.

"Well, we got to get on," she said. "Cold out here." She gave the leash a tug. "Night, Morton."

"Night, Percy," he said. "*Come* on, Caesar, Mrs. Hudson. Step it up, Toby. Park's waiting. Can run then." The dogs sprang up, and, with a heave, they all started off together. Eliza had the odd sensation of a sleigh leaving.

Behind her she heard, "Night, Eliza."

XII

Friday was rent day, and Friday evening there were open doors at the Vidalia, many of the young people free of work, drifting in and out of one another's rooms. The rock and roll music was loud, as were the laughter and talking. Though Eliza smiled in at them as she passed, home from school, she did not leave her door open. She did her homework for Monday, and she fixed herself something to eat, meat loaf with saltines and canned peas or a baked potato with margarine and plenty of salt and pepper. She ate supper at the half-moon table and then washed up the plate and the knife and fork and put them back into their slots in the drawer. She sponged down the counter. She swept the little plot of kitchen linoleum. She reopened a textbook

and studied another advanced chapter. That was enough—
then she sat. Though the Vidalia provided a twelve-inch
black-and-white with rabbit ears for a deposit and a dollar a week, she'd gotten out of the habit of television after
she'd sold her own. Television was too jumpy, too much of
a contrast with herself. Eliza turned the dial on the radio
instead.

She discovered the Staple Singers. Their blended voices,
mellow and surging, excited and serene, simply took her
away. She leaned against the headboard of her single bed,
her pillow behind her back, her bare feet crossed at the
ankles, and listened. A woman's voice would sweep out,
take hold of the song, and lead it on. What bends and turns
her voice made, what sad and exalted places it went. Following, Eliza's body was both clenched and flowing. She
hummed with the song, her eyes closed. At last the woman's voice stepped back into a man's bass and the others'
low crooning, and all the voices melted together into the
end. Opening her eyes, Eliza felt as though she had been
somewhere. Maybe a place she had really been and not
properly noticed before, or maybe a place she had never
been.

It was odd to open her eyes on the Vidalia's chipped
three-drawer dresser and find how still she had sat while
traveling. Her whole life now was odd, she thought,
unrecognizable to her former self. After so many years
of talking to and sleeping with one man, keeping up the
house, raising her own children, babysitting for grocery

money, knowing the same neighbors, she now spent her days with rooms of other people's children. She lived in a kind of set of houses with an array of strangers. People came and went. You knew them how you could. Even if they were signed onto the slow boat, they were all en route to somewhere, and since she happened to be sharing with them the same place or ambition, she found everyday chance meetings more vibrant than before. Eliza decided this was because people here were getting from one another little pieces of something big and whole they used to get somewhere else or had never gotten and dreamed of.

She was part of that. A conversation with this kid or that one often yielded something new. The free nature of their friendliness perked her up, carried her along even after she'd gone into her silent room.

Beware, though; she'd caught herself comparing past conversations with Gloria or Velma to discussions with young people she wasn't destined to know well. That wasn't fair, was it? Were these conversations lesser because she was alone now? Well, truthfully, Eliza thought they were. For a while. But what she had was what she had, and she'd better take it. Find some value. Because belittling this new life wouldn't help her.

She had unexpectedly run into her former neighbor Gloria on the street near Carlton. Gloria, driving by, had seen her and pulled her car to the curb. "Eliza! Eliza! What are you doing back in Bayard? I thought you were a Houston lady now!"

A half-truth was better than none. "I'll spend Thanksgiving with Hugh and Pam," she told Gloria. "But I'm taking a few courses at the business college before I go back."

"My goodness, really? Then you're going back to Houston?"

Eliza managed a sympathetic expression. "Gloria. Do you still have that awful pain in your lower back?"

"God, yes. I've talked to three doctors so far! And you know what they all said? That I need to..."

Gloria went on. Eliza listened intently, murmuring and nodding.

It turned out Jeannie Ruffin lived up in number 32, and she and Eliza often waved to each other. A surprise, though, was that the boy Louise had drawn wearing eyeliner, a tall young man who was excelling at the business school, tapped on her door one afternoon, late. "Hi, I live down the street, on Greavey. I just saw you come in here. It's Eliza, right? I'm Terry. From Carlton." He offered his hand. Eliza invited him in for coffee and of course for talking about Carlton, which transformed effortlessly into gossiping. She was taken aback at how thoroughly she enjoyed his company. He wasn't aloof, like he was at school. Terry was warm. He was funny; he made her laugh. He talked to her so easily in spite of their differences, almost intimately. Terry lifted her spirits, even if after he left she felt the quiet more acutely. Could it be that he was a little lonesome too?

She didn't count on seeing him at her door again. He hadn't enjoyed her coffee, she could tell. Yet Terry stopped in two weeks later, bringing a sack with his own coffee to brew.

On Sunday she went to a new church she could walk to, and after that she knew that school was just the next day. But Saturdays were dreary. She took to doing her washing, small though it was, on Thursday nights in the big sinks in the Vidalia's laundry room. She hung it through Fridays. Saturdays, she lugged in the ironing board from the manager's office and ironed the three dresses, the skirt, and the blouses she wore to school. This she kept her door open for, for the steam iron heated up the room. Malcolm Bettcher from number 17, plastic bag with coat hangers hooked in the hand over his shoulder, caught sight of her over the board.

"Got a promotion to assistant manager, Miz Kratke," he announced. Malcolm was older than many of the other residents, a quiet single man around thirty with hair you could see through already.

Eliza nosed the wrinkles out of a collar. "Well, that's nice," she said. She stretched the blouse and pressed the front, nipping around the buttons.

"Yep, shirt-and-tie man now."

"Guess you'll be moving out of the Vidalia."

"Not yet. I'ma buy me a GTO."

Eliza nodded, flipped the blouse over, and swiveled the iron up to the gathering at the back of the shoulder placket. "That's a Pontiac, isn't it?"

"Yeah, boy," Malcolm said, "got a three-eighty-nine V-eight under her hood."

She looked up. His pleasurable flush extended to his scalp. "Be sure you make the payments, Malcolm. You don't, they come and get your car."

Malcolm waved away that possibility. "Speaking of money, Miz Kratke, dry cleaners're gonna eat me alive. I don't suppose you'd wanna take on some laundry and ironing little cheaper than what they do?"

"Oh Lord, no, my arthritis…" Eliza set down the iron, held up the blouse by its collar, slipped it on a hanger, and hung it on the pole with her other clothes.

Malcolm was still filling up her doorway.

"Lemme see your bag," she said. She counted the shirts inside—men's white, long-sleeved cotton—and read the slip with the price on it. "Malcolm, you can get you some polyester and just whip 'em out of the dryer soon as they's done. Don't need to iron a thing." She handed him back the shirts.

"Won't be sharp-looking. And now I'm on salary, I'm working some pitiful long hours."

"Well, I don't think I can do it, I'd have to tote—"

"I'll go get the board for you and bring it here." Malcolm gave her a crooked-tooth smile. "Buy you some spray starch too. I like starch in my shirts."

Eliza pondered. It wasn't much money, about the same as a few hours' babysitting. Shortfall money. But she could do it here in her room, and she was used to working in the house.

"Get a big can of starch," she said.

Malcolm did, and he got number 22, Danny Pearson, to bring his shirts too. Danny was on at a plant and wore mostly blue work shirts, but his pants were grease-spotted and had to be soaked in the sink. He was a peacock who liked the ladies; Eliza could tell that from the lock of dark blond hair drooped artfully on his forehead and the snap in his blue eyes. He had money to burn and no inclination to waste a night staring at the tumbling of a dryer. Eliza washed and ironed, hung and folded, added to her labor the machines' cost, and collected her accounts receivable. When her canoe threatened to spring a leak, a force in her body took over. The one day Danny picked up his clothes and said he was short and he'd catch her later, her arm, working contrary to her mind, which told her to say, *Well, all right,* reined in the coat hangers. Her right arm understood before she did that it was not fine; she replied that his clothes would be ready when his payment was ready. Leaning in the doorway, one elbow propped up high on the jamb, one hand on his hip like James Dean, Danny tried his blue eyes on her. Eliza countered with a smile of plain brown resistance.

The bills and quarters she kept in an empty Smucker's jar. When the jar held ten dollars, she walked to the store and bought a sack of groceries with ironing money. Saturday had a reason then.

XIII

Another surprise: Louise showed up at her door. "I put on more limp, Sandra'll tell me anything," she said simply, naming Carlton's gatekeeper secretary, which explained how Louise had found her at number 2 at the Sweet Vidalia. "Whoa, what is that?" She pointed to the white spotted lump of Percy on the bed.

"That's a dog, Louise."

"If you say so. I like your glasses, Eliza. They're so old-fashioned, they're kind of neat. Can I try them on?"

It was news to Eliza that her gold-rimmed glasses were so antique they could qualify as a type of fashion. There had been complaints from — she skipped over his name in her mind. *Those glasses make you look old, Eliza, they make you look like an old woman,* he'd said, and so she had suffered more current pairs. Either the heavy plastic or metal frames slipped down the bridge of her nose or the nosepieces mashed deep red ovals into her skin. These old frames, her mother's once, had no nosepieces, and they were weightless, springy, secure, hooking around her ears.

Eliza unhooked them and passed them over. Louise hunched to see herself in the mirror over the night table, scooping her black hair behind her ears. "What d'you think?" She whirled, long hair fanning. "I can't see shit but who cares!"

"Fetching," Eliza said, making out only the blissful smile on the blur of Louise's face.

"Can I borrow them sometime? There's this concert... can I? Can I wear them?" Louise preened, tilting her head this way and that, drawing her lips into a bud, wrapping the sides of her hair around her neck like silky scarves.

Eliza smiled, holding out her hand. "No," she said.

"What d'you mean, no? I wouldn't sit on them or anything or go off and leave them." Louise unhooked the glasses, dangled them over Eliza's hand.

"I mean no. I'm doing homework here, girl." The problem she was working on was a bookkeeping one, number 9 in chapter 10 of the level-one book, four chapters past where the class was studying.

"Okay." Louise dropped the glasses and, seemingly unfazed, sprawled on the bed by Eliza's chair. The book lying on the bed, its pages held open by one of Eliza's heavy black shoes, flipped closed and the shoe tipped over.

Louise's lip curled. "Eww," she said, thumping the black shoe. "But you mean no, you think I'd wreck them, or no, you don't wanna lend them out, or no, what?"

Either of those, Eliza thought. She blew out her breath. "My Lord, Louise, hadn't anybody ever told you no?"

"My...relative when he said he wouldn't pay for art school. He said no." At the word *relative*, Louise's face twisted into a goblin's. Then it cleared completely. "But people give me things, Eliza," she said. The girl's sharp chin canted. Now Louise didn't seem insulted or anxious; she was that dog in the old RCA Victor ads, puzzled by mysterious sounds emanating from a Victrola.

Arguing with Louise would get her nowhere. Eliza picked up the book. "'If your payables are four thousand,'" she started, "'and your accounts receivable only thirty-four hundred, and you owe a payroll of eight hundred, taxes of one hundred ninety, and you must account to each vendor in order to assure continued credit, make the following disbursement, according to the sums owed below.'" A list of debts to each vendor, divided into current and past due, strung down the page. Eliza rotated her stub of a pencil inside the tiny plastic sharpener; the shavings plopped neatly into a Vidalia ashtray.

"All right, now, first you subtract out the payroll because you got to pay people or they're not going to darken your door—"

"Pleassssse..." came a wheedling whisper.

Had Hugh and Ellen wheedled like this? They must have, but Eliza did not remember it, or if she remembered it, they'd wheedled to a different mother in another land.

She laid the book on the bed and replaced the shoe on the page with question number 9. "Know what? I need to learn this all by myself, without any help from you. I'm gonna have to take the test by myself, just me and my pencil. So I better get started learning now." She escorted an open-mouthed Louise to the door, ignoring her increasingly pitiful limp. "Come by and help me another time, hear?"

"Old drudge," Louise said.

Eliza folded her lips, pulled open the door. They both turned as a knapsacked boy with a bicycle hefted on his shoulder clanged up the metal stairs to the second floor.

She could have let Louise go but decided not to. No. No, she would not let her go.

"Come easy to you, saying that, didn't it. Who pays for your course at Carlton, that you?"

"I told you. A relative."

"You pay your own rent?"

"Solly pays most of it." Solly being the boyfriend. "But I pay some. I've got a job in a print shop." The friendly mien of her entrance had disappeared but so had her crooked posture; Louise stood near to level in the door, her blue gaze flat as a sheet of aluminum.

Eliza's voice was equally flat. "How many years you got

to draw? I mean, to make something of yourself, Louise, how many would that be—fifty? Sixty-five? And lemme tell you this, I believe you're gonna do it. I do."

They eyed each other.

"I may be a drudge, but drudging is the only thing between me and the deep blue sea."

Eliza was holding to the frayed rope of confidence much as the next person was, much as any kid at the Vidalia. She knew, they both knew, that Louise Molineaux was clever and mean enough to hone the specifics of Eliza's restricted life into a blade that would slide beneath the skin. Uncharacteristically, Louise stumped away before doing that.

Eliza shut the door ungently and latched it, sat back against the headboard with a sigh. *Drudge. Old drudge.* Louise had said that to a woman whose mother had taken on the keeping of her family. At a time they had only their old car to stay in. When her husband was regularly getting turned away from day work at the sawmill, and nights they all were huddled together in the back room of the post office. Her father's brother had let them sleep there on the sly for four long months. Their bundles, what her mother called their "kits, cats, sacks, and wives," stored up against a back wall during the day. Them creeping in after hours. Her mother had cleaned houses and run a seamstress business at night with Eliza as labor. She had gone to ladies' homes and tape-measured them for new dresses or turned out old ones, kneeling at the hemmer with a mouthful of straight pins. Late into the night she pedaled the Singer.

When Eliza wasn't doing the handwork, hems or buttons, trimming seam allowances, or pressing down seams, she went to sleep by that whirring song.

Before Eliza could consider what she'd said to Louise, she found herself halted by the memory of roses. Ridiculous. The smell rising from Sixth Street was of diesel exhaust and a fresh, cold rain; from the Vidalia, it was frying hamburger and cigarette smoke. But it was not a smell that ushered in the memory.

Satin roses. Strips of white and pink satin, ruched and folded into flower cups. The yellow circle of a kerosene lantern.

Her mother had agreed to outfit a whole wedding party on short notice. The mother of the bride, although not well off enough to purchase lace and seed pearls, had no taste for simplicity, and Eliza and her mother had sat up till gray light, sewing the specified adornment: satin roses. While Dad and Roy slept on their pallets, they'd formed a short, kerosene-lamp-lit assembly line, Mama cutting, Eliza shaping and stitching tight the cups of the roses, tacking the finished flowers to dress shoulders and waists while Mama set in the zippers. Pricked fingers could not take her from her place in their little line, and woe to her if she bled on a dress. As Eliza recalled, they'd done it fueled on syrup and cold corn bread. The sugar smell woke Roy, and he'd smacked his down half asleep and rolled over again, and in the morning when he awoke, his hair was spiked with syrup.

The vision walked her into the kitchen, where she made herself some coffee. Eliza sat down at her table to parse the matter out. To slack off on her doubled-up bookwork in order to get all she could from Carlton's courses, to fail to keep that plan, meant to her a fault in character. Meant she lacked her mother's toughness and drive, her resolve to set supper on the table. And to set supper on the table was not a simple catering to the belly, either, not a small aim. How intimately Eliza knew it went beyond that. To Jake and Frannie Brock, it had been a measure of backbone and a trust completed. It moved them in unison during the thirties, through the day and the world. She could see again, by a kerosene flicker, the underside of her mother's jaw, the lift as clear as the bowing of her head. Her father nodding as he took in the supper plates, as though counting up his worth. That was money during that time. It didn't stay in hands or pockets or purses; it went to stomachs. It went to stave off fear and string a family together.

On the other side of the teeter-totter was the fact that she was years older than her parents had been back during that time in the post office. They'd seemed old to the young woman she was, but now she knew just how young they were. She remembered a sensation of motion dislodging her in her sleep, as though the apparatus of dawn was racing in, panting to a stop. She had waked to a kaleidoscope of charcoal and pearl grays and a sound like two doves crooning in the eaves, a deep and a light. The relative prosperity of the war years and after had loosened her parents' bond rather than tightened it; Eliza had always attributed that to the loss of Roy. But it was true also that their common purpose, the need that had kept them moving in such prideful tandem, had come unfixed, and nothing else, certainly not Roy's death, had worked to bind them.

Pride goeth before a fall. That was the short version of Proverbs. *Pride goeth before destruction and a haughty spirit before a fall*—there was the genuine. What she heard clearest now was a line from a play by William Shakespeare read aloud by a tenth-grade teacher, young Miss Eames, who everybody knew had been jilted: "'My pride fell with my fortunes,'" Miss Eames read and stopped to swallow. The other sayings were surely true, but this last was Eliza's particular truth. It was whatever shards of pride Eliza gleaned amid the breakage that held her together. The vision that she could make a way for herself rather than have to take leavings. This made pride almost a tool, not a danger or a sin. As far as she could see, anyway.

If this time was not her own personal Depression, then what was? She was obliged, she decided uneasily, to be her own measure.

Eliza picked up her textbook, read the homework problem. "Okay, now." She understood what the problem was asking her to do, but she read it again because it was good to repeat the business terms aloud. "'If your payables are four thousand and your accounts receivable only thirty-four hundred, and you owe a payroll of eight hundred, taxes'..." *If you're paddling that canoe,* Eliza thought, *you've got a right smart leak already.*

The door knocked, two taps. She clicked her tongue and heaved up to open it.

Louise Molineaux filled the doorway, serious as a warrant. "I saw them on your nightstand," she said to a baffled Eliza as she strode past. "In case you didn't know what to do, do this." Louise picked up the top notebook, stretched it open in front of the mirror. Eliza peered over the girl's crooked shoulder, squinting. The writing was no longer Egyptian. It was slanting, close-packed English. Backward—she had written the notes backward.

"Had you figured that out?" There was no inflection at all in the girl's voice, no pique, no crow.

Eliza shook her head.

"Didn't think so." Louise exited again.

XIV

Nine or ten cotton shirts were a load of ironing, considering the arthritis. You didn't just skate over cotton; it had to be pushed on. She mulled making a doctor's appointment, but she needed rent and food and school-supply money more than pills. Besides, Dr. Bradley Fisk had known her and Robert for twenty-five years, and she did not want to see him.

One Saturday after Malcolm's ironing was done—it was only noon, too early for Danny to bring his yet—she climbed the metal stairs and knocked hesitantly on number 26. She was unaccustomed to knocking on her neighbors' doors, more used to them knocking on hers, asking for matches, then dawdling in the doorway. She had not even met Ike. Jeannie Ruffin had pointed him out to her, a wiry young man bicycling out of the parking lot with a pack on his back. He was the Vidalia's one college student. A real college student, enrolled at the university several miles away. Ike was a pharmacy major, Jeannie thought, or maybe even a med student; her eyes dazzled with respect at those three syllables: *med student*. She'd heard that Ike knew all about medicines.

Eliza waited some long time and knocked again.

A thud. After a while, footsteps. The door cracked open far enough for a little chain to snap taut behind it, and an eye, crusted with sleep, peered out. Blinked.

Eliza told him her name and stuck her hand through the slit in the door. A limp hand shook hers.

His room must harbor a powerful mess, like most of them she'd seen, even the girls': Scotch-taped posters peeling off the walls; clothes strewn all around, the dirty with the clean; beer cans in pyramids; full ashtrays on the table and floor, maybe even marijuana cigarettes—she knew about those now. Eliza supposed that, as a college student, he probably also had papers scattered all over the place and books in tippy piles.

"I'm down in number two," she said, "and I hear you know about medicines. I need to know what to do about arthritis I have in my hands." She held them out to the slit in the door.

More blinking from the crusted eye, then his palm hit the lights. The door closed again; Eliza heard locks shifting, and then it opened to reveal the young man Jeannie had pointed out, shirtless, his loose jeans unbuttoned at the waist. A double bed with a canopy that met the ceiling contained a tousle-haired girl lying back on pillows, sheets tucked under her bare arms. Eliza'd already taken a step in; embarrassed, she edged back.

"I'll come back another time."

The girl sat up, sheets shifting, and smiled.

"No, no problem." Ike nudged her elbow toward a chair, not vinyl like hers but a plain wood kitchen chair like she'd grown up with, painted green. Dangling from a back slat were two strands of thick thread, closely knotted at the top.

This was not the Vidalia. Not its decor, anyway. A maharajah might have slept in the bed. The canopy was wicker, flat where it met the ceiling but arched at its lower edges, curving down to attach to the posts. It was almost orange with lacquer and age, woven through at intervals with diamonds of a midnight blue. At its end, a bicycle hung from the ceiling on hooks, as if arrested in a ride through the air. Tall bookshelves of varying wood tones stood against the walls, which were painted the crimson red of a theater carpet; short bookcases ran under the window, packed with books and accordion files snugged by their rubber bands. On top of them sat old glass jars in assorted sizes, blue and green and clear, their labels turned evenly, directly front. They appeared to house dried grasses, in different shades of green and gray, and seeds.

Underneath everything lay an enormous rug showing pale birds on a branching tree in golds and greens and a milky sky blue, missing in some places where it was worn down to threads.

"Hold out your hands again."

Eliza set her pocketbook on a yellow bird and her hands, ringed and ringless, ten fingertips lined up, on the table.

Ike slid a hand under one of hers, elevating it so that her knuckles made a roof. He rotated his wrist so that her hand rocked gently, side to side. He drew her hand toward him, set his other hand lightly over it. He was looking somewhere over her shoulder as he did this, and he did not so much press as feel and seem to listen, as if his hand were reading hers. Dr. Fisk did not touch; he poked or thumped.

"How long?" Ike asked, and Eliza knew what he meant.

"Not so good for about a year or two, but worse the past year. The right one aches if I write too long."

Ike glanced at her. "You're a writer?"

That was a funny idea; Eliza smiled. "I go to the business college. Lotta writing to do. Sometimes at school, my hands hurt."

"Uh-huh. Why is the skin so chapped?"

"Been handling wet clothes, ironing for people."

Ike had gone back to staring over her shoulder. Nodding, he set down her hand. "What was your name, again?"

She told him, and he said, "Okay, Mrs. Kratke. Tell you straight. Think you're going to have to choose between

140

writing and ironing." When Eliza opened her mouth, he said, "I know, I know. That's up to you. For now, get some Vaseline. Rub it in after you finish everything. It's cheap and it works. If your hands stay this dry, the skin'll crack, and that's how infection gets in, through cracks in the skin, understand? Then, if you're serious—" He walked over to a bookshelf and pulled a plastic bag from a box there, unscrewed a bluish jar, and sifted out some grassy stuff into the bag. "Use this. Boil the herbs, drink some of it as a tea while it's hot, and soak your hands in it in the mornings." He visited three more jars around the room, talking, pinching herbs from each one into the plastic bag.

Eliza's nose was twitching at the smell, like dried grass cuttings with a whiff of perfume. She thought about Bradley Fisk's office, bleach-smelling and eye-blindingly white, the doctor's white coat and stethoscope, polished black brogans, bifocals slid down to his nose bridge, his jowly pile of a face and bald head. And here she sat with a half-naked boy whose long hair was as tousled as the naked girl's in the bed. Scanning the maharajah room, she didn't recognize herself in it, and she felt foolish, crazy.

"What medications are you taking?"

"Why, I don't take any. Should I be?"

"I just need to know for contraindications. Don't expect those knuckles to go back the way they were before, but this can reduce the inflammation. That's the culprit, the reason they hurt. How are the rest of your joints?"

"Not so bad as my hands."

"Do you exercise?"

"Well, I walk the dog. Other'n that, I take the bus."

The corners of his mouth turned up; he shook the bag. "Which room did you say you're in?"

"Two."

"Two. Western boundary of the Land of Arf."

"The what?"

"Just what I call it. Morton's too much, isn't he? That would be why old lady Poston gave you two. You won't complain since you have a dog too." Eliza cocked her head at that. Of course. Ike was right, that's why Eliza had gotten number 2. But also—old lady Poston, the Vidalia's manager, was a good ten years younger than she was.

Ike slid into the green chair. He tucked his brown hair behind an ear and hooked his bare feet on the rungs. He bent his index finger and extended it, slowly, then the middle one, then the ring finger. "Okay. Don't just jump into your mornings cold. Soak your hands, then warm them up. But gently. No harsh motion. Got it?"

Eliza imitated him, her knuckles aching.

"Right. Do you take aspirin?"

"Time to time. Saturdays for sure."

"Take one every day. Won't hurt you, and it could help with the inflammation." He set the bag on the table and tapped it. "Not cortisone, but better than a sharp stick in the eye."

"Well, thank you, Mr., uh..."

"Sinclair. But it's Ike. Listen, Mrs. Kratke, since you're

in business school, you can't avoid writing, but I'd advise against a whole lot of other handwork. And you need to be regular with the herbs. There's a cumulative effect. Possible, anyway, but that depends on you. Try this a month and get back to me."

Eliza nodded. She couldn't bring herself to "sir" him but she didn't feel inclined to "son" him either, like she had with that Widge or the young man who bought the Fairlane. She reached down for her pocketbook and brought out her change purse. "I understand. How much do I owe you?"

Ike eyed the plastic bag. "There's about two dollars there. Pay me when it works."

After a moment, Eliza said, "No, I don't give Malcolm and Danny their clothes without they pay me. I don't like owing anybody. And there's your time to boot." She pulled a dear five from her change purse, laid it on the table, put her hand back in the purse, and looked at him.

Ike pushed the bill back to her. "Practicing medicine without a license costs a lot more than five dollars. If it works, bring four next time for the herbs. And keep walking your dog. Walking's good for postmenopausal women."

Eliza returned the five to her change purse, took the bag, and stood up, her face warming. Her gaze dropped from Ike's eyes to his smooth chest, four or five hairs sprouting from the groove of his breastbone. She had never heard Bradley Fisk say such a thing. A woman her age, a man his age—Eliza's menopause had not been discussable. But Ike was young, and—she gazed around the preposterous room again—she was different now, maybe a tiny bit younger herself. She could take in this important information.

The girl in the bed waved at her. Eliza said, "Bye." Ike walked her to the door, three steps. She thanked him again; he shook her hand again. His grasp was not squeezing, the way most people's were.

Once she was outside on the landing, clear, cool air rushed at her, along with a leaf like a gold star. All around the Vidalia, oak and gum and elm were letting loose their leaves, a pretty sight.

Danny Pearson, holding to the rails, clumped up the steps, his hair twirled flat on one side and flapping out on the other. When he saw Eliza, he mumbled that he'd bring his clothes down; he plucked at the soiled shirt he was wearing, sniffed it, and wrinkled his nose. Passing her, he gawked at the bag of herbs she held. His reddened eyes lifted upward to number 26 and then focused, with difficulty, it seemed, on her face.

"Ike give me some herbs for my arthritis," Eliza said, pronouncing *herbs* without the *h,* the way Ike did.

Danny's slack mouth looked rope-burned along the bottom lip. He sighed, said, "Oh. Oh, whew," and blew out a beery breath she turned her head from.

Eliza went down, swimming through the autumn sunshine, gold and blue as Ike's old carpet but without the worn places, one endless scroll fresh this minute. Her favorite season. After the close room, the itchy, earthy smells, the jumble of color, now she felt dunked in openness.

What a sweet surprise, to feel this way.

As soon as she did, though, the ache—memories of Robert, his other woman, his lies—reverberated. She reached for the handrail. *Stop,* she ordered him. She would never forgive him, and that, maybe, was not the smallest part of the wound he'd inflicted on her.

XV

On the Saturday before Thanksgiving, she called Earl Fitzwalter in what she hoped was the interval between lunch and the afternoon football games. "Eliza. How you getting on?" he asked. "How's Hugh and his family?" Fine, she told him and then asked, "Have you talked to that woman yet? About canceling her lien? I sure do need to sell the house."

"Well, now, she could cancel the lien or sign a quit-claim, one or the other. I've been meaning to get around to it, Eliza, I sure have, but I've been busy-busy. Try to get to it real soon. I did find out that she lives over in the south part of town. June Rummidge is her name, though she calls herself—well, you know."

Eliza sagged against the Vidalia's wall, deeply disappointed. He did not sound confident. He rushed into telling her that it would be good if she didn't have to go to court over it. "Courts and judges, just getting on the docket…"

Eliza hardly listened to Earl's song and dance; she recognized the tune of the speech, one in which the speaker was singing his way out of bad news. She willed herself to be diverted by a dilapidated pickup with a load of brush and yard bags leading a parade down the street, the cars behind bleating their horns. Earl discoursed on timelines and municipal back-scratching while a wailing ambulance weaved down the middle of Sixth; the honkers abandoned their horns to dodge to the shoulder, but the pickup maintained its stately pace. Ambulances unsettled Eliza.

The ambulance driver's partner pulled himself half out the window to yell and gesture at the pickup. She wondered if the pickup driver could hear—deaf, maybe? It was enough of a show that she almost missed her cue to thank Earl.

"…let you know when I know something definite."

"I'd appreciate that."

"Sounds real lively in your part of the world," Earl said.

Certainly in comparison to Earl's conversation, Eliza was thinking. "Well, you know, Earl, the big city." She took a breath. "Thank you. You say hello to Velma for me."

* * *

Eliza got up at five in the morning, soaked her hands and exercised them, then drank a cup of herb tea. It tasted like weeds, pure and simple, so she'd make herself a cup of coffee as soon as she and Percy got in from their walk. She drew on gloves to protect her exercise work from the cold morning air. They were white church gloves with stitched-down pleats on the back; she had worn them only on Easters. She didn't know why she'd put them in her suitcase when she'd left out so much else, but they came in handy now. Come Christmas, when Pam started nagging her about what she wanted, she would say: *Gloves, warm ones.*

Sometimes, in the gray morning, the sodden leaves stewed in the gutters now, the sidewalks bare, they'd meet Morton with Caesar, Toby, and Mrs. Hudson in tow— he'd appear out of the fog like a charioteer. Percy, tongue hanging, would start his stiff-legged dance. The tall dogs would sniff him again. Morton would squat and produce the magic biscuit chip.

"Lord, you been out all night?" she asked him today.

"Now and again." He spoke, as before, to Percy. "We're *night* folk, aren't we? *We* don't like that old daytime. Opposite the *whole world, we* are, upside down and backwards."

"All folks don't have to be the same," Eliza said.

"That's *right.* That's what *we* say." Morton petted Percy, who tumped over on the damp sidewalk, crimping his paws. Morton scratched his belly. Percy wriggled. "Like that, *don't* you, old boy?"

"Listen, Morton." Eliza had an idea. "Thanksgiving's coming and—"

Morton stood, giving his leashes a hitch. The dogs snapped into line. He looked off to the side, where a car with its lights on was driving by.

Eliza persevered. "And I was wondering if you might look after Percy when I go see my son. I could leave you my key. They won't take him on the bus and you're right next door. I got plenty of food for him."

Morton's head followed the car down to the stop sign. "Oh," he said, and squatted again. "*We* could do that. Sure. *That's* not a problem, is it, Caesar?" The white dog, in lead position, showed his blunt face but did not bark.

Eliza jogged the leash. "Well, we thank you, then. Bye, now."

It was heading six thirty, so she moved off down Sutter. Morton and his bunch continued the other way, turning for Greavey. They all met again by doors number 1 and 2 at the Vidalia. "Eliza wears *nice gloves,* doesn't she, Mrs. Hudson?" she heard him say before he dropped the leashes and let the dogs rush inside.

Eliza put the kettle on to boil for instant. "We got to get moving," she said and then caught herself, talking like Morton.

Surroundings, she'd found, were catching. She no longer wore the suit to school. She'd gotten as casual as the girls, wearing her homemade shirtwaist dresses with the bias skirts. If she weren't as slim in the waist as she'd been at twenty, her skirts still had flutter. The rayon did that, and the bias cut. Rayon meant careful hand-washing, but if she used cold water in the laundry-room sinks and hung the dresses from the pole strung across the room, they didn't shrink. The young people at the Vidalia washed in hot and threw every stitch they had into a hot dryer. She'd burst out laughing at Jeannie Ruffin when the girl reached for a gauzy, embroidered cotton blouse— imported, she'd informed Eliza, from *Ind*-ya—and it came out the size of a baby's shirt.

First chance she got, Jeannie laughed back at her, pointing at Eliza's girdle clothespinned to a hanger. Eliza retired the girdle and switched to pantyhose, thanks to Jeannie.

Beholding the dangling slivers, she had not at first believed she could fit her legs in them, much less her rear end. But how they stretched. Now that it was cold, she wore them *and* socks, and let the girls snicker if they wanted.

XVI

Carlton held classes on the Wednesday before Thanksgiving, and not wanting to miss hers, Eliza would be obliged to catch the Greyhound to Houston late Wednesday night. The damask tablecloth she'd promised Pam was folded in a sack she'd tuck at her feet. Her suitcase was packed with fresh clothes and a bag of cranberries. They'd always had the canned before, a maroon jelly tube shivering on a saucer; Eliza felt like trying something different this year. The recipe on the bag was simple: wash, then boil for five minutes with a cup of sugar. Percy had divined her leaving. He had no interest in his usual nap but patrolled their room, toenails clicking against kitchen linoleum, a thump, then padding around the carpet, sniffing.

Lisa Sandlin

He collided with her ankles as she packed, and when she sat down, he collapsed his hind legs too and fixed her with his bulging eyes. "I'll *be back,*" she told him.

Mrs. Hudson had answered Morton's door and at once attached her snuffling black snout to Eliza's skirt, nosing for her crotch. Eliza inserted her hand between skirt and nose. Her palm was slicked. She nudged the door and leaned in, bumping against a wall of dog aroma. "My Lord." She breathed through her mouth. "Morton, where are you?"

"*Here* we are," he said, swinging out from behind the door. He was in sock feet and an undershirt, and his thick brown hair lay in bangs on his forehead above the shadowed eyes. "Sit, Toby, Caesar. Leave off Eliza's dress, Mrs. Hudson." The dogs retreated into a bulkhead around his knees, and Eliza stepped in.

Despite the smell, Morton's room was neat enough. Like Ike, he had books and notebooks, his shelves fashioned from cinder blocks and boards. His single bed was made, its blue corded spread scattered with black dog hairs; at its side were plaid doggy beds, well used. Instead of a table to eat off of, he had a homemade desk, a plain pine door supported by two two-drawer file cabinets, and an upright wooden chair. A typewriter sat on the desk, a sheet of paper rolled in the platen, by a stack of printed pages. On the counter next to the stove sat curious humps of various sizes—two of the large humps covered by little plastic coats—and small bottles with stoppers and labels.

"I've put Percy's food up on my kitchen counter. If I leave it on the floor, he'll knock it over and try to eat it all," she said. "You sure it's not too much trouble to walk him with your bunch?"

"We thought we'd just bring Percy over here while you're gone. If that's all right. He'll be safe here."

"Well, that's fine with me." Eliza couldn't think of anything else to say, though Morton seemed almost approachable. He stroked Caesar's head and smiled, his gaze nearer her face than before. He wasn't talking in his usual singsong. It was Morton who felt safe here, clearly. She brought Percy and his food over to number 1 and watched him be surrounded, a tiny old tanker nudged by giant, eager tugboats. She brought her hand up to wave at Morton, having decided that *Happy Thanksgiving* was too personal a comment.

Morton stuck a magazine in it. "Something to read on the bus," he said, and faded back behind the dogs.

"Why, thank you, Morton." She hesitated, then smiled and went to get her suitcase.

Louise's Volkswagen screeched into the Vidalia's parking lot at 10:42 p.m., little time to spare. Eliza hopped up from the suitcase and hauled it into the car's back seat, took the paper sack containing the tablecloth with her into the front.

"I got tied up with my boyfriend," Louise said. One

corner of her mouth crimped in a dismal half smile. "I mean, we've been working long nights. Getting ready to go to London. Soon." The little car shot off; Eliza was thrown back against its seat. Noisy as a Yazoo lawn mower, she thought, but Louise hollered over the engine's commotion. "Last night, though—we got broke into," she told Eliza. "They ripped off the people upstairs too. Sue had a bowl of candy left over from Halloween. Wrappers all over the floor. They must have hung around eating it, stupid junkies."

Louise growled and went into a dire recital of things stolen: Television, record player and speakers, money. It was the money that she seemed most upset about; Eliza could understand. There was worry in her face, and that worried Eliza—she advised the girl to buy another lock or two. They flew through a succession of yellow lights and a red, the tires squealing as Louise railed a corner. Shifting, she jerked her long hair, which was draped over the gearshift. The girl stuck her head out the window and yelled some prize curse words.

"Louise." Eliza gripped the door handle. "I need a ride, not a stroke."

Louise petted the air. "It's okay now, okay, okay. I've got it under control." She glanced down at Eliza's lap. "What's that magazine?"

"Just please look where we're going, honey."

"*American Dog?* Are you fixing to enter Percy in a contest?" Louise swerved around a car turning right into a supermarket parking lot, accelerating as she went to beat another red light.

"No, I'm fixing to keel over. Slow down, Louise."

"Almost there." Louise squinted down at her watch. Both of Eliza's feet were braking against the car's rubber mat. "Seven minutes. Piece of cake. Listen, Eliza, will you keep something for me? In case those shitty stealers come back?" Now Louise was staring sideways at her, her perturbed face yellow in passing streetlights, then flitting to gray, then yellow.

"Get your eyes on the road and I'll keep your firstborn, Louise."

"Damn, Eliza." Louise looked over at her again. "Danger may be good for you. I've never heard you make a joke before." She wrenched the wheel into the Greyhound lot, where two buses were breathing out diesel. Eliza threw her hands out to hold the dash when Louise stomped on the brakes. "Okay," she said, flipping back her hair. "I'll pick you up on Sunday afternoon. Give it back to me then, all right?" She reached across Eliza and popped the glove compartment, took out her grandfather's oblong case. The enamel box was wrapped with duct tape. Eliza was surprised at how heavy it was. Something was inside—not snuff or tobacco, because it rattled. Briefly she wondered what it was, but catching the bus was foremost in her mind.

"Don't want anybody getting my keepsake," Louise said. "You know how that is."

Eliza, from whom all keepsakes had been subtracted,

dropped the heavy box in her pocketbook and did not take time to snap her purse shut. She wanted to answer from solid ground. She climbed out with the sack and got her suitcase from the back seat. She reached to close the door but it slammed on its own; Louise had snaked herself over to the passenger seat. "Have a good time," she called. A whirl of black hair and the girl reversed, spun, waved over her shoulder as she spurted away.

Fretting about Louise and robbers, Eliza headed for the back of the bus for an irrational reason—it seemed more populated, and all the other seats and riders would serve as ballast to hold her down. Surely robbers who'd cleaned you out would not return. They'd be busy selling the stuff they stole and spending the money. Wouldn't they?

She passed single men and single women, couples, pairs of men, pairs of women. The times, they had changed, Eliza knew that, from a popular song and from the relief of white and Black riders sprinkled round in no particular concentration. She sat down in the seat before the bus's last, a bench seat, next to an older white woman. Across the aisle sat a drowsing Black lady and a girl of about twelve, the woman with her purse snugged to her chest and the girl curled against her.

Eliza tucked her pocketbook by her hip and settled the sack with the tablecloth on the floor. She was left with *American Dog*. Too dark to read. It came to her that this was the first traveling she'd done alone since she and Robert were married. Because Robert worked the railroads,

they'd had a pass and always traveled by train. Eliza
would take the window, watching the light change, hills
and towns sliding quietly by. Robert, who'd seen it all
before, would doze in his reclined seat to the train's lulling
chunk-a-chunk.

The bus wheezed, rolled, braked for a couple to clat-
ter up its metal steps, and wheezed off again. The couple
passed her, tossed their backpacks on the floor in front of
the broad back seat. They sat, and the bulky girl lay down,
resting her head in the boy's lap. Eliza heard her say, "I
think I might throw up."

Uh-oh, Eliza thought. She and her seatmate, a woman
maybe ten years her senior, exchanged a significant glance.
After this silent communion, the seatmate spoke up in
a friendly way. "How're you? I'm Winnie. Going all the
way to Reno." Eliza gave her own name and said she was
just going to see her kids in Houston. Winnie's dentures
gleamed a startling white in the bus's gloom. "I'm going to
see my grandmother."

"She must be quite an elderly lady," Eliza said.

"Oh, she was. Dead now, but she won't leave the house.
People I sold it to are threatening to sue me."

Lively, Eliza thought. *My life is lively.*

She was pleased with this insight. Pleased with the picture of a lively life rather than hibernation or sitting in her
clean old house alone or even sitting in that house waiting for Robert who hadn't had a lot to say in recent times.
Determinedly, she blocked Robert from ruining this little

pleasure. Oh, he was there, all right, the ache was there, but she made desperate shooing motions in her mind, scattering the bad memories as if with a broom. It didn't mean they weren't there, just that right now the memories weren't allowed in.

It was pure dark outside the bus window. Eliza asked Winnie to tell her why her grandmother was so stubborn.

Wide awake, Eliza saw Hugh as she got off the bus; he was slouched on a bench outside the station, his head lolled back in sleep. She touched his shoulder. As his eyes fluttered open, he smiled, saying, "Hey, Ma." He reached out his arms. Eliza sat down and hugged him, for a minute oblivious to diesel fumes and stained concrete, riders shuffling with their suitcases, a chill that moistened her face. She just embraced her son, whom she would love always. Whatever her life was now, there was this reason that existed apart from all else.

"Didn't you tell me twelve forty-five?" Hugh rubbed his eyes and stretched.

"Yeah, but we got delayed. A…startling event." Hugh turned his head to her. "Not now—I'll tell you and Pam all about it tomorrow. Sorry you had to wait on me." It was two o'clock and still velvet dark.

Hugh hefted her suitcase, loaded it in the car, and navigated Houston's freeways, which had more traffic than Eliza had expected at this hour and on Thanksgiving Day.

The city. The big city. This was where her old neighbors thought she lived now. They sailed over a bridge near the port; down below sat countless rows of small cars and the stacked freight cartons painted in every color. They landed finally in a neighborhood of little ranch houses, each on its green plot, made individual by siding color and landscaping and, in Hugh's case, by his daughter in the doorway bundled in a pink sleeping bag, trying to walk in it. She wriggled out of the sleeping-bag cocoon and came running, threw her arms around Eliza's waist. Eliza set her cheek on Betsy's head and breathed the girl in. "My goodness, what are you doing up in the middle of the night?"

Betsy tipped her head back and Eliza kissed her forehead.

"I used Dad's alarm clock! Where's Percy?"

"Percy's got him a reservation at the Ritz hotel. He's going to dine on pheasant and wine. You didn't sleep right behind the door, did you?"

"Noooo." Betsy's hair swung as she shook her head. "Percy doesn't have any teeth. How can he chew his dinner?"

"They have a waiter at the Ritz," Eliza said as Hugh pushed open the door and stood back, "who feeds him bites on a fork."

Precious, her granddaughter's smile, like rays from Eliza's own personal sun. She was a precious child. They went inside, and, quiet as she could, Eliza peeked in at the sleeping baby. *Cindy,* she said in her mind, *hello, sweet*

Cindy. They'd planned on naming a girl Lucinda Robin, Pam had confided, but after what happened, *Robin* was too close to *Robert*. They'd dropped that middle name. Her new granddaughter's name was Lucinda Anne.

Eliza wished Ellen were coming so she could cuddle her new niece, this baby angel, but Ellen had decided to stay in her apartment for the holiday. Her roommates would be gone, and she wanted, she'd said, some alone time. Some rest, some peace. Eliza hoped for both for her daughter, but it was easier to close the door on roommates than on memories.

Everyone went back to bed, though Eliza's sleep was restless. Later that Thanksgiving morning, her daughter-in-law's mother, Mrs. Fortenberry, bustled in with a casserole dish of sweet potatoes and marshmallows that needed heating and directed Hugh to her car for the rest. Hugh brought in the French-cut green beans and mushrooms, and went back for the pies: coconut meringue and chocolate cream. Mona Fortenberry was a bottom-heavy woman with a taste for high heels and snug suits. Today her blond hair was tufted and sprayed and her burnt-orange suit featured a fount of sequins on the collar. Eliza, in the nicest of her shirtwaist dresses—a blue, sheened rayon, three-quarter sleeves that turned up in cuffs—felt plain but, noticing how the suit sleeves strained when Mona set her casserole dish down, a little relieved not to be upholstered. Mona took over in the kitchen, advising Pam that the turkey was ready and should be let to sit for ten minutes. Peering into Eliza's skillet, she said, "Just a tad, huh?" and sprinkled cornstarch into the gravy. Eliza relinquished the stirring spoon, got herself a shoulder towel, and picked up the baby, who had been fussing in her bassinet.

"Pam said you were bringing a holiday tablecloth, Eliza," said Mona once they were seated before plates and silverware set atop red-and-white-checked oilcloth. Pam and Hugh glanced at each other and then at Eliza.

"Well, there was an accident with it. If I'da thought when I got here, we could have called you. I bet you have some."

"You'd win that bet," Pam said with a secret glance at Eliza.

Hugh pronounced grace and the passing began.

"How was your trip?" Mona handed Eliza the mashed potatoes and Eliza spooned a scoop on Betsy's plate and on hers. "Eventful," she said. Back in the kitchen, she'd stuck a finger in the cranberry sauce, found it tart and crunchy rather than jelly-slick, and liked it.

"I bet it was, on a Greyhound bus. Did you run into any characters?"

"Some kids," Eliza said, "in the seat behind me—"

Mona launched into a story about her and her husband's trip to Hawaii some years back when something electrical on their plane had caught fire and everyone had had to slide down a rubber emergency slide in the dark.

People had piled up on one another, scared to death, although at least one fool was whooping and laughing. Mona smiled on the table. "Now, *that* was eventful!"

Eliza did not finish telling her own story right then; there would be time later. Instead she smiled back at Mona.

That night, after Mona Fortenberry had left with wrapped leftovers, after Betsy, John, and the baby were asleep, Pam asked what possible kind of accident could happen to a damask tablecloth on a Greyhound bus. "Oh, wait, but first, Eliza, tell us why that woman"—they all called Robert's other wife *that woman*—"hasn't been forced to let her claim go on your house."

Hugh's face became vague, breakable. "I'll never get over it," he said softly, "I know that. Never get over him doing it. Ellen, she can call him every name in the book, but me, it just...put ruin in me."

Pam, reddening, took his hand. She was brewing up a protective fury that Eliza knew well.

"I know it did," Eliza said.

Pam burst out, "You're the one the son of a bitch did it to! And you never did a thing to deserve it!"

In February, in March and April, Eliza had believed in this statement more firmly than in the sun's crossing the sky. But once you get caught in a momentum that drives you on, you don't always pick the sights you pass. One of them was the Eliza Kratke that did not exist anymore. Satisfied, placid, taking for granted, refusing to ask Robert what the matter was when she knew there was a perilous wrong. She was only now accusing that self, and she was obliged to behold her.

She touched her son's hair. "Can't everybody's story be pretty, Hugh. But I would give anything in this world if yours was."

Pam ran into the kitchen and came back twice, setting down glasses of bourbon for Eliza and Hugh and a bottle of beer for herself. "Good for my milk producers," she said, shimmying her breasts.

Eliza took a sip of bourbon and told them about her bus trip. How the pair in the bus's last seat had kept up a stream of murmurs and some grunts while Winnie, the woman in the seat next to Eliza, finished the story of her troublesome grandmother and moved on to other touchy relatives. Then, a half hour into their trip, when the view past the windows showed only black and blacker, the girl had thrown up and rolled back, moaning. Even over the bus noise, Eliza and her seatmate could not have missed the sound of retching or the soured smell that wafted to them a moment later. Or the groans and the whimpering that followed. Winnie produced a travel pack of Kleenex and passed it over the seat to the boy.

"Carsick, poor thing," she said, and Eliza felt the Fairlane again, an enclosure speeding down Pershing, Robert with vomit on his lips.

"Jesus, that feels better," the girl said thickly.

"Are you all right?" Eliza asked.

The boy answered for her. "Well, she was all right. I'm

thinking...she says she can make it but maybe...I don't know." His deep voice rose defensively on this admission.

Eliza got up from her seat and walked a step toward them. Studying the girl splayed out, her head in the boy's lap, Eliza thought, *Oh Lord.* "Do you have something in your pack to mop this up?" she asked the boy. He pointed to the packs on the floor. "My green one's got T-shirts." Eliza squatted, holding on to a seat, sopped the floor clean.

The girl groaned.

"How fast are they coming?" Eliza asked.

The girl yelped. Her knees jerked out widely, the left jamming against the seat back, the right narrowly missing Eliza's chin.

"Just a minute," Eliza said, trying to sound calm when she was not. Hurriedly, she made her way up the darkened aisle, clamping her hands on the seat backs for balance, past people whose cheeks were stuck to the windows and others with their heads thrown back or tucked in their necks so they would have terrific cricks once they got wherever they were going. She'd leaned toward the gray-haired driver and told him he would have to find a hospital. "Out here?" he said, but when she told him why, he got on his radio and upped the gas.

She went back, searching each pair of seats, not bothering with those where kids huddled or where folded-hands men sat with ball caps tilted over their faces. Finding a doctor on a Greyhound bus would be like finding a pearl in a hamburger. Eliza woke the grown women, asking for a nurse, keeping her *'Scuse me*s soft. Eyes flipped or cracked open; one woman startled up in her seat, a hand warding Eliza off. She'd gotten clear back to her own seat, hoping that maybe Winnie was a nurse, but Winnie negatived that. Eliza leaned across the aisle and roused the small woman hugging her pocketbook to her chest. The woman rubbed an eye and sat up, quickly checked her arms for her purse. Her shoulders relaxed then and she focused on Eliza. "Say again. What you want, now?"

"You wouldn't be a nurse, would you?"

"Nurse's aide. You sick? Listen, don't think I'm carrying any pills—"

"Please," Eliza said, her eyes wide, "just come here and look."

The woman blinked at her and then woke the child beside her, a girl of maybe twelve, said, "Patrice, you hold on to my purse, you hear?"

Eliza stepped back for the woman to pass. "Jesus Lord," the nurse said. She sat down at the girl's feet, spread a hand on the belly. She lifted the girl's skirt.

Eliza had gotten out of her way, was perching on the armrest of her own seat. Glancing back, she saw several sets of eyes watching—the women she'd waked.

The nurse poured water from a thermos onto her hands and dried them with a handkerchief Patrice handed her. "You got to get those underpants off, girl." She turned to Eliza. "What you told the driver?"

"Hospital," Eliza said, and though she tried to suppress it, her brain repeated: *Doctor, doctor, doctor.*

The nurse nodded. "Lift your butt, baby. I know it hurt. I know." Her hands disappeared under the long skirt, wrestled out the wet scrap of panties, and dropped them onto the floor. Her hands disappeared again. The girl's loud moan ended in grunting: *Uhn-uhn-uhn-uhn.*

"Boy, you got any clean clothes in your suitcase? I mean fresh-wash clothes, *clean,* cover up this old bus seat."

The boy stuttered and then shook his head no. "Lady," she said, turning to Eliza, "see what you can fin'."

Eliza squatted and retrieved the paper sack with her white damask tablecloth. She pulled out the heavy, folded rectangle. "Fresh-washed and ironed," she said.

"Hep me git it under her," the nurse said tersely. Eliza unfurled the cloth from its rectangle, careful to keep it from the floor. The nurse took its white scalloped edge and began to feed it under the girl's hips. "Lift up, baby," she said.

"I cain't," the girl moaned.

"Yeah, you can."

"Look, we're supposed to go to this one hospital. That's the deal," the boy said as though he might be about to interfere with the proceedings.

"Yeah, well, this baby want the bus," the nurse snapped.

They had hardly gotten the tablecloth stretched beneath her hips when the girl screamed, "Oh God, oh God,

I cain't hold it no more," and went on screaming a single syllable. The boy, his face contorting like hers, slanted away as if trying to counterbalance the immense momentum within her. He raked at a hank of his own hair like relief would be gained when it tore out. The nurse threw the skirt back, exposing the great mound, misshapen in its struggle, the girl's thin, pearlish flanks. The woman brought her hands together between the girl's legs. "Go on, baby. Better push." She spoke out of the side of her mouth to Eliza without taking her eyes from the girl: "Run and aks the driver to stop this bus. And git me a knife somewheres."

Eliza ran down the aisle. By now the passengers were awake, many turned toward the back. She ignored the questions that flew at her. "Somebody's having a baby!" a voice exclaimed. "Knife," Eliza told the driver, "and pull over. Smooth as you can."

The driver understood. Whispering, as if the reduction in volume could lessen the jolt of the bus's wheels onto the shoulder, he told her the state police were on the way. One-handed, he slid a Swiss Army knife from his pocket.

But it had been too late for that. Someone else passed the nurse a knife once the bus was still, on the shoulder, canted slightly to the right. By then all the riders, even children, were facing the bus's last seat.

The passengers jumped, exclaimed, cursed, averted their children's eyes by wrapping those small faces into themselves when the girl roared—like she was attacking, like the world was a tiny, modeled set of stop signs, streets, and houses and she would bring it down.

But once the thready cry of another voice rose up, the riders were unwilling to let out a sound that might obstruct its upward rising. Enchanted, they turned toward each other open-mouthed, comparing silent grins, Eliza included. After a while the word *boy* began to rustle back to front; *boy, boy,* whispered seat to seat.

The police had led an ambulance caterwauling behind them. The emergency workers lifted the girl and her wet, red, besmeared, mewling son onto a stretcher and hustled them into their domain. The boy, trailing, had to return for the backpacks. Midway on his trip down the aisle, the passengers, most of them standing so as to follow the action around the red-flashing ambulance, burst into applause and yelled out congratulations. Eliza added hers. He ducked his head and fled down the steps. An arm reached from the emergency vehicle's yellow interior, where the girl's bare, bloodied feet could be seen, and hauled the boy on. Then the ambulance whirled wailing away.

The passengers applauded the nurse as she returned to her seat. Eliza trailed behind the bus driver, who'd come back to thank the nurse, but the woman reached for her daughter and embraced her, holding the child's head to her chest. Then she patted her on the rear, and Patrice hopped back into the seat, her arm still laced through the short handles of her mother's purse, which was hugged in her armpit.

"God A'mighty, I couldn'ta done it," said the driver. "You people just got the know-how." He doffed his Greyhound hat to her before heading back up the aisle.

"You did a fine job," Eliza added, and all around riders chimed in to agree.

"Yeah, well," the nurse said, shaking her head. "All that and you know what that boy say? They gon' give that chile away."

Shocked, Eliza stared into the nurse's rueful eyes. The woman's voice had carried perhaps more than she meant it to. Conversations ceased. The people standing, so lately bathed in flashing red light, now slid down in the dark.

For a bit Eliza worked to turn it, this news, tried to make something better of it, as maybe the child would land with glad people who could greet him with more than a backpack and a bus ticket. But there was no way to unwreck that moment and many moments after. Winnie turned to Eliza with a wondering face and said sadly, "And they took your cloth with them, didn't they? Not that the blood would've scrubbed out or anything. But it was a damask, wasn't it?" Eliza nodded. She had forgotten the tablecloth.

Over on her side of the aisle, the nurse crossed her legs, crossed one arm in front of her, and set her other elbow on it in the way big or fat people never do, her little body barricaded behind all the crossing. She wore tennis shoes, and one lace was gone.

* * *

Pam leaned her forehead on her palm. "'Scuse me, Eliza, but that's a damn sad Thanksgiving story. Poor little muffin. That poor orphan baby."

Eliza nodded. "I know."

"If it wouldn't wake her up, I'd go grab my baby girl and hug her."

"Well, maybe, then…I guess maybe for you, Pam, it's not all sad. Or for Hugh. Or even for me."

They were a measure, weren't they, the ragtag couple in the back of the bus. She hoped they would have better days. She wondered how they would remember that one.

XVII

On Sunday, Eliza couldn't leave Hugh and Pam and the kids without tears on her cheeks. That phenomenon occurred beyond her will; she could not help it. She hugged Hugh extra-long and Pam did the same with her, and she kissed all the children. Consequently, she rode the bus dry-eyed and peaceful. A Sunday trip—she had all the time in the world to read *American Dog*. To her surprise she came across an article on page 45 by a Morton Winters, "Advances in the Treatment of Heartworms," that explained the typewriter and the neat stacks of paper on Morton's desk. A shiny, full-color picture of the white, blunt-faced dog accompanied the story. Caesar? Eliza

smiled. She would have pointed out the article to a seatmate, but she sat alone.

She lived next door to a writer. That was exciting. Of
course, one who rented at the Vidalia was probably not
a top-dollar bestseller writer. But top dollars were not
Eliza's target. A *living* was her target; that word had
begun to enlarge in a way she hardly understood. The sentence *She earned a living with her pen* floated into Eliza's
mind, then the image of a woman with long skirts sitting
at a table holding a quill, a steely look in her eyes. Har-
riet Beecher Stowe. Louisa May Alcott. Those were the
names that appeared for Eliza—to her, they were roman-
tic, daring, otherworldly. For all she knew, a great number
of women, if they were all added up, had earned a living
with their pens. Morton did it, though with a typewriter,
not a quill. But that sentence would never be applied to
Eliza Kratke.

An idea, strung with bunting, christened by champagne on some strange shore, emerged majestically in her
harbor. It did not dock but remained, for the rest of the bus
trip and several weeks after, close in on the clear water,
ready to sail in either direction—the idea that Eliza Kratke
might shed that name. She could wash her hands of *Kratke*.
She could become Eliza Brock again.

Louise had promised to pick her up at four p.m. At a
quarter to five, as Eliza continued to keep watch for the
churning Volkswagen, she felt her annoyance kindle into
anger. Travelers crowded the bus lobby with their suitcases

and bundles, more than one brown grocery bag set pro-
prietarily near its owner's ankle. The smeared floor was
scattered with candy wrappers and cigarette butts. Noises
of many kinds crashed into one another. For the fourth
time, Eliza got up and shaded her eyes to scan through the
broad window beneath GREYHOUND spelled backward. At
that moment, the sun and its red light slid away in silence.
Gone, irretrievable. For that moment the conversations
and competing transistor radios, the PA system, the chasing children, and her annoyance dimmed. She was waiting when she didn't want to be waiting. On her feet in a
grubby bus lobby when she could be at home with Percy
and the radio. Standing here, moreover, relying on the
word of Louise.

Eliza's mouth opened and a breath hopped past her
teeth, not a full laugh, just astonishment, as she entertained the image of Louise Molineaux in all the grandeur
of her protective coloring—the swinging shawl of hair,
the speeding Volkswagen, the self-absorbed chatter, the
combativeness, cleverness, flightiness, the sapphires of
self-interest that were her eyes. *You silly fool,* Eliza called
herself without rancor. Then she called a taxi. This was
one of those extra expenses that could not be avoided, even
if it brought on a round of tomato sandwiches. She savored
how safe and comfortable it felt to be tranquilly chauf-
feured back to the Vidalia.

* * *

When she picked up Percy at Morton's, she learned that there had been an event.

Morton had come back from a middle-of-the-night walk to find his door ajar and his apartment torn up: drawers emptied, dog beds and mattress disarranged, books and papers scattered, and his equipment—he indicated a microscope and some odd-shaped glassware—uncovered. Not broken, thank goodness. He'd called the cops and they had come but the lead one soon flipped his little notebook closed. He hadn't been interested in a robbery scene where nothing had been robbed.

Louise and now Morton. A bad coincidence. A very bad coincidence.

Uneasy herself, Eliza could not say that Morton looked more disturbed than usual, but she understood by his immediate recital of the story that the break-in had deeply upset him. Enough so that he had talked to Ike about it. This surprised Eliza. Ike was often up late at night studying, Morton explained. His light was on. By sticking his head out the window of his second-floor apartment, Ike could see Morton's door, so he could check on it occasionally. If the door was ajar, he would blow a whistle Morton had given him, and Morton and the dogs would run home.

"I don't think that's a good idea. Then what will you do? These are criminals, Morton. They might have guns or knives."

"I know who it is." For a second, Morton met her eye triumphantly, then turned away. "It's that professor over at the university, Dr. Bleckman. He wants to know what I'm finding out." Morton squatted to rub Caesar's ears. "*We'll* never tell him, will we? He'll just have to read it like *everybody else,* won't he, boy?"

"What do you mean, 'finding out'?"

Percy was straining from Eliza's arms, courting Morton's attention. Morton scratched the old dog's head. "Oh, just some work I've been doing. Professional jealousy. But you don't have to worry, Eliza. You're safe."

She didn't feel safe. For the first time since she'd begun renting at the Vidalia, she didn't feel safe. She told Morton about Louise's break-in, what all she'd lost. That drug addicts had done it.

"Won't happen, Eliza. No, it won't." He had it all worked out. He'd walk the dogs in shifts so that one dog was always on guard, there was Ike and the whistle, and he pointed to the two new locks—their brass was the only thing that shone in the room besides the dogs' eyes.

"And when I'm sleeping, the dogs are watching."

"Well, hurray, Morton," Eliza said, "maybe you've solved it. By the way, I enjoyed reading your story in that magazine. Thank you again. C'mon, Percy, we have to leave heaven now."

Beneath the caverns of his eyes, Morton's coffee-stained smile was brilliant.

Percy crooned longingly in his throat as he departed the Land of Arf.

Eliza set him down in her cold room and turned on the

heat and then the radio. They were playing Duke Ellington, one of the forties tunes she'd hummed for years under her breath. Robert and she had danced in their own living room to Duke Ellington's music when Robert had come home whole from the war. Robert, three and a half years younger than Eliza, had been a good dancer; she was not. Too self-conscious. But that night, with no one to see, they had twirled like Fred and Ginger. He'd loved her then, hadn't he? They were happy. At least, that was how she remembered it. Back when it was not deadening to remember things.

Stop.

XVIII

Louise was not at school on Monday; she did not come all week. The next Monday, she trailed into the Business Math classroom carrying a book. The girl was paler than usual, if that were possible. "I'm melting, mellll-ting," she croaked, writhing like the Wicked Witch of the West.

She went over to the desk in back of Eliza where Jeannie Ruffin sat and claimed it as her rightful one. "Go sit somewhere else. This one fits me," Louise said.

"They're all just exactly the same," Jeannie said, not getting up, hand clamped on the back rest.

"This one is better for my back," Louise said. "It slants ten degrees."

"Oh. Well, okay." Jeannie unfolded herself and gathered her books. Once in another chair, she looked back doubtfully.

Ensconced, Louise grinned.

"Shit-ass," Jeannie hissed.

"Giraffe." After Louise's face relaxed from its moue of malice, she shot a glance at Eliza.

Eliza was entertained by the girl's tricks, although she was still irate at Louise for stranding her at the bus station. She was genuinely fond of her, she realized, even if she couldn't count on her. Louise was part of the liveliness.

"Did you get yourself some extra locks?" Eliza asked.

Louise waved away *locks*. "Not yet." She reported she had spent a week of nights on friends' couches.

"What friends are those?" Eliza asked pointedly.

"Are you going to tell me to get some manners?" Louise said.

"Would you get some if I did?"

"I could have manners if I wanted," Louise protested.

"That'll be the day."

A dark cloud passed over Louise's face and blew on, leaving it in the sunshine. She stood from the desk, limped over to Jeannie, and tapped her on the shoulder. The tall girl turned and recoiled as if a cobra had risen up on its tail behind her.

"I beg your pardon," Louise said. "Thank you for so graciously giving me the desk."

Jeannie gawked. She looked to Eliza, who shrugged,

and then, suspiciously, back at Louise. "Okay," she said, and twisted away.

"See," Louise said, returning to her chair. Then she launched into the story of her week on the run, hiding from the people who'd robbed her apartment.

"But, Louise—if they already robbed you, why would they go looking for you? 'Specially if you don't have any more to rob."

"Junkies have junk for brains, Eliza. Cars followed us, I swear. We slept on a different friend's couch every night."

The math teacher stepped into the room, flipped on the lights, and dropped her satchel on the captain's desk.

"My boyfriend's friends," Louise said, shading her eyes from the cones' yellow light, "since you're so mean as to remind me I don't have any. Hey, will you eat with me today?"

At lunchtime, Sandra, the office lady, waved down Louise and Eliza walking by, asked for help with Christmas decorations. Louise drooped laterally into a classroom, citing cramps. Eliza rallied. She and Sandra wrestled the artificial tree, white with tarnished silver globes, out of the back of a closet to a position by the double doors, its flat side to the wall. MERRY was reduced to MERY when Sandra could locate only the single R. Eliza taped the letters high around the glass front that served as Sandra's window to the world and the channel through which all Carlton information flowed. When she stepped down from the chair, a man in a flashy business suit was obliged to veer around her.

The man leaned toward the window, asked Sandra if Louise Molineaux was here today. Sandra, never mind that she clutched a camel in one hand and a king of the Orient in the other, became the epitome of Carlton: "And who might I say is inquiring for Miss Molineaux?"

Eliza did not stay to hear the answer. The sleek man leaning into the window was not one she would forget: Ray Paley.

She found Louise in the classroom in which they'd met, her cheek on a desk, the long curtain of hair dangling, blowing lightly in the exhalation of a heater grate. She bent and touched the girl's shoulder. "Louise," she said.

Louise sprang awake. "What?"

"There's a bill collector asking Sandra for you. Do you owe somebody?"

"Bill collector." Tired blue eyes blinked. "No. Yeah. I mean, not exactly. What'd Sandra tell him?"

"I didn't stay to hear. Listen, this man came after me once, and he's like to find whoever he's looking for. If you're gonna get, you better get now."

"Ray Paley came after *you*? What for?"

So she did know him. The "robbers," the week of hiding, explained. Louise had done just as she, Eliza, had done. She liked Louise, but in the way a person might repeatedly visit a fuzzy tiger cub in a cage—her own sense of self-preservation did not allow her to discount the cub's essential nature. But genuine sympathy and an urge to help flooded Eliza. "Paley wanted my car. Are you going or do you have the wherewithal to settle up?"

Louise grabbed her purse. "It's him that doesn't have the wherewithal," she said, hiking her chin so high, she was nearly facing the pressed-tin ceiling. "I'll come by the Vidalia for my grandfather's box." She ran to the door in a lurching gallop that caused Eliza to wince. "My notebooks are yours forever, Eliza," she said as if renouncing all her earthly riches. She hesitated, lips pursed, pondering the next line of her speech.

"Go on, Louise!"

Louise peered out and, apparently finding the way clear, said, "I *did so* have a friend." She pointed to Eliza and was off down the corridor that led to a side door.

Eliza sat for a minute focused on the mess that was Louise, wondering how much the girl owed on the Volkswagen and where she would go. Then she left the classroom, intending to finish the decorations. Sandra was leading Ray Paley down the hall. Eliza had thought the secretary would discourage him at the office, but who knows what story the bill collector had told her.

Ray Paley's gaze flicked over her, returned, and stuck. He stopped walking. "Ahhh," he said. "Mrs. Kratke, isn't it?"

What do you know, Eliza thought, *exactly right.* She nodded.

His lips, beginning to curl, dropped back into a suspicious downturn. "What are you doing *here*?"

"Mrs. Kratke is one of our top students, Mr. Paley," Sandra put in.

"Students? A student? So you know Louise."

Almost but not quite unconsciously, Eliza had hunched her shoulders. Before she commanded it to be, her face had made itself as bland as butter. "So many girls here, I can't keep track. She the one with red hair?"

Sandra's bottom lip sagged, leaving her mouth ajar.

"Louise," he said, squinting, "is about yay high"—he raised his hand to Eliza's chin—"and she's got long black hair. Her spine's crooked with the scoliosis, so she limps a little. Blue eyes."

Eliza felt alarm that he should know so much about Louise. Nevertheless, she produced a soft *tsk* of bewilderment. "I swan, doesn't ring a bell. She must be in the advanced classes."

"She is." Ray Paley's brows ran together. "I think."

Shaking her head in a way that suggested palsy as much as ignorance, Eliza turned to leave. Too bad she could not say what the kids at the Vidalia did when they dismissed someone bothersome: "Well, it's been *real*." This statement was usually accompanied by a blasé expression even while its utterer was rejoicing in his or her cleverness.

Before being forced into retirement and having to take the job at Carlton, Sandra had been an executive secretary at Houston's Hughes Tool, a company with five thousand employees. She might not know what was up but she knew something was. "This way, Mr. Paley," she said, ushering him on.

"Wait a minute. Wait a damn minute here." His moment of confusion gone, he turned on Eliza. "This is important. Louise is in trouble. I mean, big trouble."

Eliza's concern deepened even as she maintained the blandness. "What are you after the poor girl for?"

Ray Paley clutched her elbow. As on the day he'd tried to take the Fairlane, he radiated authority; the smirk, however, was missing. "Stop playing me, goddamn it. I know who you are."

You know who I am, Eliza thought. His presumption flooded her with indignation, which receded as she silently realized: *Nobody now on earth, including my children, knows who I am. Not a wife, a mother whose kids are grown, with no neighborhood friend, no job to tell me what I am. Just a kind of in-between person who lives in a temporary place with people who live near her temporarily. Who doesn't know what'll happen tomorrow. One who's going day by day, best she can. You can't see that about me.*

Her facial muscles hardened. Her left eyelid tugged as that eyebrow arched. It was a look she had practiced in the mirror as a girl and that she had used on the children when, flustered over some misdeed, they lied to her.

Paley let her elbow go.

"Carlton Business College does not accept profanity on the premises." At her most frosty, Sandra acquired a

British intonation. "It would be best that you seek Miss Molineaux at her residence, sir."

"Think I hadn't tried there? She's my daughter."

Louise? Eliza, staring, shocked, took a step back. But a doubt crept in. Paley's daughter? Maybe. Maybe not.

In the office, she retrieved her coat, purse, and books next to the Virgin Mary, her face paled from years of adoration, and hurried down the front steps. The bus was just lumbering away from the stop. Shouting, Eliza ran to catch it.

Friday afternoon before the week of final exams, when she had had to relinquish her pencil and listen as the General Ledger teacher filled the chalkboard, Eliza knew she would have to give up her Saturday ironing. Whatever good the herbs were doing, if any, was not enough to counter the extra stress of pressing wrinkles from cotton. Her hands lay throbbing on the blond desk, the pains extending as if on wires, down her forearms, twinging in her elbows.

Eliza did not have to fire Malcolm. Malcolm fired her first. He appeared in her doorway as he had the day they met, behind him the stairs and beyond, the scratchy, bare-branched trees lining Sixth Street. The beautiful gold leaves were long gone.

"Manager business's not what it's cracked up to be, Miz Kratke," he told her. "They's wanting me to work night and day on salary. Last week I put in seventy-two hours. You go and figure it, you're better on hourly. I told them I'd take back the old job, but they said that set a bad example. Handed me my hat," he said sullenly, "so to speak."

Eliza sucked her teeth. "You'll find something," she said.

Malcolm looked distraught. "Think so?"

Eliza, head canted, brow furrowed with incredulity, was thinking of all the traps we hurled ourselves into. How we slammed the door after ourselves, rattled it from time to time, moped from one side of the cage to the other. She was thinking of herself in the days after the funeral, the long days of hibernation, rage, and festering shame. Maybe those days were needful, but how they'd hurt. This boy standing here with his white-sidewall haircut and agonized expression—he was maybe thirty, maybe even younger. He harbored ambition, and he was willing to work. He was not stupid enough to work himself to death or desperate enough. Fortune had smiled on him, for the times he was living in were not so cruel as to require he do that. Of course he would get on.

"Well, naturally, Malcolm," she said.

He stared a wishful smile into her face as if looking into his own pink crystal ball. "Thank you for saying that, Miz Kratke. I appreciate it." His shoulders, bunched toward his ears, relaxed, then bunched again. "My mama's pretty disgusted with me. I got to go room with her awhile." And *whisht,* like that, Malcolm Bettcher was subtracted from the Vidalia into other places, forging tracks that did not cross Eliza's.

XIX

Ellen insisted on visiting for Christmas, despite Eliza's misgivings. Her daughter, twenty-four, lived a hundred miles away, worked in one of those enormous warehouse stores that sold everything, and attended a state college three nights a week. That was not an easy load, Eliza knew. Ellen was serious, hardworking, and Eliza thought she looked tireder than she ought to. She was no Louise, delighting in being craftier than the world at large. A big spoonful of the self-confidence that Louise had, unproven though it might be, would do her daughter a world of good, Eliza believed. After throwing her arms around Eliza at the door, Ellen walked in and scanned the room in a military manner.

"God. Damn it."

"Nell," Eliza said.

Hands on hips, Ellen stalked to the kitchen, studied the three-quarter-size stove and refrigerator, then sat on the bed, grimacing as it sank. She scooped up Percy and cradled him to her chest like a baby. Percy's hind legs stuck up stiffly.

"Mother."

The eyes Eliza thought beautiful were narrowed; her daughter's voice grated. She spoke so deliberately, it was as if she had breath enough only for a few words at a time. "If you don't go. And make that woman get her filthy claws out of our house. I'm going to. I swear it."

"It's not bad here. I'm used to it."

"It's the pits! Has Hugh seen this place?"

Eliza dragged over the chair. "You're old enough to understand why I don't want to ever see that woman again."

But she was talking to the back of Ellen's head. Her rageful girl had released Percy and flipped over onto her stomach and was now sobbing into the pillow.

Anger rose in Eliza. *Wherever you are, Robert, I hope you can see what you've done to your children.*

She roused Ellen with a plan of Christmas sugar cookies—stirring, rolling, baking, and decorating. They used the half-moon table as a workspace. The little oven worked fine; Eliza's room filled up with a cinnamon smell. She made coffee too and they ate the cookies hot from the pan. Eliza hadn't permitted this when Ellen was growing up. Eliza kept a smile on her face as she proposed taking some cookies to her friends. Ellen followed her to the Land of Arf, to Ike's exotic lair, to Jeannie Ruffin's apartment. Jeannie wasn't home, was probably at her parents', but Morton and Ike welcomed the warm cookies wrapped in a paper napkin. She caught Ellen studying her later over their dinner of chicken, collards, and corn bread. She wished Mary were there in the parking lot so she could introduce her daughter to another friend.

"So you're okay?" Ellen said with narrowed eyes. "Those young guys—the guy with the dogs and the guy with the Aladdin room—they're really your friends? They're, like, half your age, Ma."

"Well," Eliza said, "I think I'd say they are."

"What happened to Gloria?"

"She's got her family. In the old neighborhood. I'm here now, Ellen."

"I see that, duh. But Gloria's still your friend?"

"Sure. Would you like to see the school? Probably all locked up, but we can take the trip tomorrow."

The next day, they went there on the bus. Ellen surveyed Carlton's medium-grand facade, and they sat in the small park underneath the bare trees. It was a pleasant day, chill at the edges but warm in the middle. Birds chirped, switching places up in the branches. Eliza coaxed Ellen to talk about school, her job, anything she would talk about. Eliza listened, her hands still.

Consequently, three days past Christmas, Eliza called Earl Fitzwalter. When he started his soft-shoe about the lien delay, she told him, "It's not that. I shouldn't ask this, you've done so much for me, but..." He hadn't done anything for her yet, but she thought it best to say he had. It was the way her mother would have put it.

An edgy silence met her ear.

"I was wondering if you could run through a name change for me. I know it has to be legal."

A snort. "Eliza, you getting married? Boy, aren't you the—"

"No, Earl. I want to take back my maiden name."

A ruminative silence. "Under the circumstances, I don't blame you. You know you'll have to sign the application."

Eliza hadn't thought of this. But the solution was on her tongue immediately. "I can come to your office."

"They've got lawyers over there where you—" Earl said.

Eliza broke in. "I trust you."

"Well, all right, if you want to come all the way back here, that'll work. Can Hugh drive you?"

"I'll take the bus," Eliza said.

Why she felt she had to do this first, put in for the name change, Eliza wasn't entirely sure. It was a little like getting dressed while Paley's men waited in her living room. It felt like a prop. Like a theatrical item—but not hollow. Something tough and sturdy that literally propped her up, that strengthened her. She decided not to question that feeling.

When Eliza arrived at Earl's office that afternoon, he told her he had something for her—the other wife's phone number. He'd called the woman, he claimed, but nobody answered. Eliza was learning about Earl Fitzwalter. He'd always been just her neighbor Velma's husband, a shadowy fixture. Now she noticed how he'd stare away from her as he spoke. She didn't believe him, but she needed him. She'd visited the records bureau and gotten copies of her birth certificate and marriage certificate to be submitted to a court. Eliza handed these over, saying she would pick them up once Earl was done with them. She added her driver's license, since she wasn't using it anyway. She bent to his desk and signed the papers.

The name change would take a little while, Earl said, but it was no problem for him. He snapped his fingers. Routine. And he'd call that woman again, he told Eliza, soon as he got the chance. Unless of course *she* wanted to. Maybe they'd get further, you know, woman to woman. He glanced at his watch.

Of course she didn't want to call Robert's other wife. But Ellen's collapse had steeled her nerve. Eliza felt prodded by the picture of her daughter sobbing into a pillow. As though her mother were hopeless, helpless, a pitiable, aged woman in a hovel. She was not. One evening, Eliza just snatched up the paper that Earl Fitzwalter had given her with the woman's number scrawled on it. She'd stared at it before, but this time, she strode out to the pay phone and dropped in some dimes. Christmas lights were still entwined with the plastic onions around the office door. It was not that cold for a January evening, but it was breezy, and she was trembling.

A high voice answered. "Hello."

"This is Eliza Kratke." Was there a tremor in her voice? "You know who I am. I'm calling to talk about the lien you put on my house."

The high voice immediately rose to piercing: "I don't want to talk to you. I didn't know anything about you!"

Eliza was gripping the phone cord with her right hand. If she got into an argument with this woman, it would never end. She plowed on. "I need to sell my house that I lived in for thirty years. I can't sell it with that lien. I'm asking you to take it off."

"I didn't know about you! It was terrible, terrible to find out! And there was nothing I could say to...my husband because he was...he was..."

My husband. Those words like a slap to her face.

The other woman hadn't known Robert was married. "Terrible," Eliza managed to get out. That made Robert's betrayals even worse, didn't it?

The impetus to call June Rummidge, spur of the moment as it was, before she lost her nerve, now flattened out. She became...not calm, really, but deliberate. She wanted her words to push this woman, push her. "Were you mad at Robert? Is that why you did this? You couldn't

get to him but you could get to me? You don't have any
right to my house."

"I have my marriage papers!"

"And I have mine."

The woman broke into wild sobs.

"You know whose came first. Don't you?" Eliza said.

A crash in her ear, and she heard the dial tone.

So much for woman to woman. She hung up the phone
and sagged against the Vidalia's wall. The breeze lofted,
and Eliza brushed hair off her forehead. The moon was
young, just the barest crescent. Earl Fitzwalter seemed
much more confident about the name change than about
the lien. She would have to keep on him. She passed the
rat-a-tat typing in number 1, entered number 2, locked the
door. She picked up Percy. The trembling returned now
despite Eliza being in her own domain. She fixed herself
on her bed, back against the headboard and knees raised,
sheltering the dog on the shelf of her lap. Eliza closed her
eyes and pretended she and Percy were on a boat, sailing
on a waveless sea, with that pinch of a moon overhead.
Until calm filled her.

XX

Louise did not attend Carlton's meager but pompous graduation ceremony held on a Sunday afternoon in January. Why should she? Carlton would mail you your certificate.

Eliza, having completed only the first semester, watched the doings from a folding chair. Terry and Jeannie Ruffin, dressed up, marched across the stage, beaming as they collected their certificates. Eliza felt a pang for Louise but supposed she'd moved on, much as Malcolm Bettcher had. As Terry and Jeannie Ruffin would. That was to be expected. But she missed the girl's vivid little self, her fresh air. By now she'd connected Louise with her walk down the stairs from Ike's room as the leaves flew, when she'd felt a kind of exhilaration in her difference from the old Eliza.

It was time for her own next trial.

Once a student graduated in good standing from Carlton, the business college guaranteed him or her six interviews. That was one of Carlton's attractions. Of course, Eliza was not a Carlton graduate. What she was, was the contemporary of Sandra, a professional woman edged out of a good job when she wasn't as picturesque as she'd previously been. After the graduation ceremony, as Eliza was leaving, Sandra approached her with a folded sheet of paper. "For you," she said, holding a finger to her lips. "Shhh. And I mean, shhh!"

On the paper were names and addresses of six employers in Sandra's flawless typescript.

Eliza had prepared herself for performing a job; she felt much less prepared for landing one. In January, dressed nicely, she took the bus to four places listed on her paper. The way potential employers probed, their manner light, a little confidential, talking about "How we'd want you to do things here" and "If you go to work for us," confused her.

The first interviewers pretended to take her into their club for the duration of the interview, and Eliza's hopes rose. She looked around with interest at the business—auto parts or insurance or a small restaurant. She noted

the messy or neat desks, how formally or not the inter-
viewer was dressed, the smell of the place—oil or paper
or air freshener or cooking—some banter she might hear
exchanged, and she inserted herself into that place, hanging up her coat, starting coffee, answering the telephone,
gathering receipts. The potential employers spent time
talking about their "crew" and how they were like a family or how you had to be crazy to work here, *ha-ha*. In her
twenty minutes at each location, Eliza identified no fam-
ilies or craziness. She wondered why the employers liked
to feature themselves this way. After the interviews, she
understood that they had judged her every word, her dress,
her appreciation of their jokey conversation, the business
courses she had taken, her lack of experience. Mild faces
x-rayed her answers and her person. They spoke of a pro-
bationary period when she could be taken on approval,
like an orphan who has a week to be judged lovable or
returned to the county.

When she left, they all shook her hand in a cheerful
way, as though she would see them shortly. She did not see
them shortly. Sandra would call with the news.

"Oh, Eliza, this one's not to be," she'd say. "Phoo on
them. On to the next."

Carlton had a seemingly endless list; many employers called the school first. So diligently had she done her
homework and studied for the tests that Eliza might have
graduated with the honor group if she had stayed on. Terry
headed that group, her coffee visitor, the young man with

the floaty style. A former dancer, originally with the Joffrey Ballet and then with a company in far-off New York City, Terry aced the tests, the accounting, and the role-playing problems. His business letters were succinct wonders of tact, even when he was dunning customers for money or denying credit or placating a disgruntled ex-employee. Terry was organized, shrewd, able to fade into the background or produce a merry atmosphere on demand and dead-on at intuiting what that demand was. Beside him, Eliza felt blocky and one-dimensional, depressingly earnest, and—though she wasn't yet a genuine antique—elderly. There was a slogan going around: *What you see is what you get.* That was Eliza. Terry was *Whatever you need is what I'll give you.* Terry had not landed a job yet either.

"Discrimination, pure and simple," he said to Eliza after proposing they ride together for the rest of their interviews. Terry had arrived at her room in the Vidalia with coffee—ground beans in a small sack—and a half-pint of table cream.

"No offense," he said, "but that stuff we had the first visit..." His lips formed an upside-down U while his eyes rolled. Eliza took no offense. He made her feel included—why he did, she couldn't say.

"I'm queer and you're old. End of story. As far as *they're* concerned." Terry announced that and swept on so Eliza did not have time to be embarrassed by *queer* or wounded by *old*. Once he said it, it was established, just like that.

"We're dealing with closed minds. That's our obstacle. Black people are out there clamoring for equality. As they should be. But what about us? Where's our march? Who even cares? Oh, I could get a job dressing windows. But my mind reels off numbers, not scarves and pumps. Employers don't see me as their secretary. Or you either. They see Jeannie Ruffin. Twenty, cute, yam and tiny marshmallows for a brain. Look, in their heart of hearts, they really want somebody who can run everything perfectly but without taking credit. Somebody who's a lot smarter than they are but acts like the boss is Einstein. That's the unspoken deal, Eliza. The pact."

"Discrimination," Eliza repeated. She had diagnosed her problem correctly without giving it its proper name.

"Oh, catch up!" Half a step with his long legs and he slouched at the counter. "Listen, I haven't clarified my point." He measured out the coffee with his special spoon, filled the percolator's basket, tamped it down, and set the percolator on the burner. He whirled around. His shirt was a Hawaiian print in turquoise and dusty pink. Rayon; Eliza admired how it swirled.

"The crucial point is that, if they're looking for brainy and efficient, they'll choose us. But given that we're brainy, efficient, and assertive—as in, *I want full credit for my work*—they'll choose marshmallows. Get it?"

"Well, but, Terry, Mrs. Cartwright taught us that in Personal Relations. I don't understand what you think is new about it."

"What's new about it is we have to apply it to the interview. Right away. That's all the time we've got to get our...*value* across." Terry's palms flipped outward.

Eliza was shaking her head. "I wouldn't know where to start."

Terry sat down and popped a breath mint in his mouth from the roll he always carried. He crossed his legs, top foot vibrating. "I just told you. The interview."

She appreciated his effort but he was making her feel worse. "No, I mean I wouldn't know how to...to do what you just said."

His foot lost vibration. "Me neither." He hung his head. "Oh, to be an *aide* in France." This was his ongoing joke, but it was not funny because Eliza sensed the thread of hope in it.

Eliza sat too. Every so often, Terry's foot would give a whap, like an annoyed cat's tail.

Eliza sighed. "You know, you don't have to dry-clean that shirt. Wash it by hand in Woolite and cold water and hang it on the showerhead to drip dry. When it's still the least bit damp—don't let it get all the way dry—iron it. It'll come out just as good and save you a dollar..." She trailed off.

Terry stared at her, frowning.

Her attempt at a smile was bent. Such advice was

paltry and far off the subject and, what's more, deflating. It displayed her for just what she'd been: an old housewife. Only now she didn't have a house and she wasn't a wife, and in Eliza's position, old didn't factor; she still had to work. Avoiding his eyes, she got up to attend to the percolator that was shimmying and spitting on the stove and filled their cups. Terry would give up on her. He should. She'd miss his including her, that attitude he had that treated their differences as the very qualities that yoked them together. She took her seat again, searching for an excuse that would allow him to leave guiltlessly.

He was still staring at her, his eyes wider. She knew he didn't wear that black eyeliner on his interviews, which was almost too bad; it was attractive, she thought. Maybe she should try some.

Terry's palms came toward her and cupped her face. He pulled her forward and gave her a noisy kiss. Eliza choked on her swallow of coffee.

He rose as slowly and smoothly as if an invisible wire hooked through the Hawaiian collar were lifting him from the chair. Terry positioned his arms by his sides, curved out and showing space. He jumped straight up, fluttering, somehow, his large feet. He thumped down again, knees deeply bent, rattling the cups and spoons on the table, the percolator on its burner.

Part of Eliza followed this performance; another part was riffling through her memory like the Rolodex Mrs. Jennings had demonstrated in Business Communications.

When was the last time Robert had kissed her? Wrong question: When was the last time he had liked kissing her?

Terry slid into the chair across from her, the chair Eliza borrowed from the Vidalia management each time she expected a guest. He took her hands in his, careful not to squeeze. He leaned close, and a puff of his mint and coffee breath reached her when he whispered tenderly, *"Eureka."*

Eliza whispered back. *"Eureka* what?"

He'd begun to explain a plan when someone banged on Eliza's door. It flew open, rebounded hollowly against the wall. Louise—whom she hadn't seen in weeks—caught it on its way back, lurched farther inside, and shoved it behind her. It bounced, failing to latch. Louise pivoted, took hold of the knob, slammed the door once to punish it and then again securely. Purplish smudges marred the perfect skin beneath her blue eyes, whose glare enlarged and surged at them in the way Eliza remembered the sudden giganticizing of a shark from the one 3D movie she had ever seen. She'd recoiled back then. She did the same now.

"What are *you* doing here?" Louise cried at Terry.

His mouth remained open.

She gazed bitterly at Eliza. "You're *my* friend, Eliza. Not his."

"Louise, honey, it's okay to have more than one friend."

"That's what *you* say. Remember, I was your friend *first*. I came for my property."

Eliza fetched the notebooks on her dresser.

"No, not them! Don't you remember I gave those to

you forever? My important property that I gave you for safekeeping."

Eliza remembered and retrieved Louise's grandfather's enameled box from beneath two icetrays in her freezer compartment. This is where Eliza's mother had safe-guarded larger bills like twenties until she needed them. Instead of in her purse, which might be grabbed or lost.

Eliza had been curious about the box's rattly contents, but she hadn't disturbed its duct tape. She held it out.

"Ow, cold." The girl glanced over each shoulder, then stuffed the box in her bag. She treated Eliza to another aggrieved stare. "I doubt we'll ever see each other again. Not for the rest of our lives. So goodbye."

Eliza crossed the distance between them, noting Louise's drama yet feeling a pang for her. "Well, my good-ness, goodbye, Louise. I hope they see how good your drawing is over there in London, how perfect it is. I'll miss you."

The girl looked gratified. "Thank you, Eliza." She leaned forward, touched Eliza's hand. Hesitantly, as though it might be dangerous or valuable or forbidden. Then she pulled her own hand back and was gone.

XXI

Eliza wore her navy suit, Terry his, which included a vest over a shirt the pale blue of a boy baby's layette. They had a paper from Sandra with the names of employers and interviews spaced so that one of them could wait for the other in Terry's Corvair.

"Your haircut looks nice," Eliza told Terry.

"Are you sure?" Terry patted the bare skin around his ear, his forehead wrinkled. "Is it awful enough?"

The plan was improv he had said after his soft *Eureka*, and he defined it for Eliza this way: During the interview, Terry and Eliza had to show the employers something they knew how to do well; they had to impress them, not just sit back like a knot on a tree and answer questions. Give a little demonstration. On the spot. This was what Terry had thought of when Eliza gave her rayon advice. It was something she knew that was practical and useful. They both knew about business now, and they could show that. Find out what the bosses needed most and then give it to them.

The plan had dazzled his face but not Eliza's. "How do we find out?"

"Two ways. Sandra gives us these names of the places and we learn what we can about them in advance. Use the manuals at Carlton and read up on that kind of business. Call the Better Business Bureau. See who their competitors are. In the case of huge businesses, see how their stock's doing."

"What's the other way?"

Terry lifted a shoulder and let it fall jauntily. "Ask them."

So they did their homework, dug up some facts about each place—products, processes of the trade or the business itself. When they drove up to Andover Tool, a sprawling plant with an acre of parked cars, a middle-aged man in overalls carrying a lunch box threw a sour glance their way as he trudged by. This man and others like him, slamming the doors to their pickups, were familiar to Eliza. They looked like Robert and the railroad men he'd worked with, their faces reddened and deeply creased, their hair slicked down with water, some shot with gray, or covered with baseball caps.

"Shift change," she said.

This was supposed to be Terry's fourth interview. His head tipped worriedly toward the workers filing by. "No offense in a thousand years, Eliza, but I think you should take this one."

"No, Terry, it belongs to you. Number four. I've already done four interviews."

"Nope, nope, not my milieu. I surrender it to you. I still have two more."

Eliza wandered through the tan-painted halls until she found a frosted glass door marked PERSONNEL. It was her fifth time standing before such a door. Her second-to-last time, possibly, since Carlton promised only six interviews. She took a breath and arranged her mouth in a neutral smile.

The woman at the desk had hair as uniformly black as the parking lot's tarmac. "Can I help you?" she said after she'd set her cigarette in the ashtray on her desk.

"I'm here about the secretary job."

The woman blinked at her. She had very thick false eyelashes, and on one eye, the end of the lashes had peeled loose from the lid. "You're from Carlton?"

"Yes…I am." She had narrowly avoided saying "ma'am," which she judged would be a mistake. "Eliza Kratke."

The woman seemed glad to consult a pad on her desk. "Not Terry Vandiver?"

"Mr. Vandiver has already found employment," Eliza said without thinking.

"*Mr.?*" The eyelashes blinked again. "Carlton's full of surprises these days. Well, follow me. The first thing's a typing test."

Eliza typed and worked a ten-key and took dictation in shorthand. The woman's eyes met hers once or twice, and Eliza read there, in the deadness, the beat of unease, a tinge of indignation that her time was being wasted with this charade, and Eliza knew that this was her last visit to Andover Tool. What were the instructions that Eliza would never hear? *Get me a pretty one,* said in a joking voice?

Walking back through the parking lot, Eliza nodded at a worker hurrying toward the entrance. He nodded back politely, matter-of-factly, as though she were a normal human being in the world and not a supplicant.

"Well?" Terry said, eyes stretched wide. He'd been running the engine for the heater. "Did you use the plan?"

The plan. She'd known Andover's products, the number of employees; a lot of good that had done her. The Corvair was low to the ground; Eliza ducked, swung her purse into the footwell, then folded over and plunked herself heavily into its bucket seat. She washed her cold hands in the blast from the heater. "I might as well have been a pregnant cat begging at her door."

Not for the first time, she thought that the past several months, the expense and the effort of business school, might have been for naught. Money wasted. She'd entertained that idea all along but at a distance, safely, not with the frank fear that approached her now. In her mind's eye, she saw a black oblong pressing toward her, as though the emptiness framed by a terrible doorway had detached and was approaching on its own.

At Kramer's Karpet Outlet, Terry's fifth interview, Eliza watched through the store's expanse of plate glass as Terry spoke to a man in droopy, dark pants and a long-sleeved white shirt with a name tag. The man stepped back, made hand signals. Terry returned to the car immediately. He looked so nice, his elegant topcoat flying open in the wind to reveal the pressed suit and striped tie, the vest over the blue shirt. How could they not even give him a chance?

Terry turned the Corvair around and grabbed the note with Sandra's list. He reversed again and pointed the car the other way. "Okay, okay, so I just asked for directions." They waited for traffic to pass.

"Terry, you're wasting your interviews."

He waved a hand. "I can read them," he said. "I've done it all my life."

Stinson Brothers Fine Cabinetry was the sixth employer on Terry's list. "You understand," he said, gesturing toward the beige metal building, the trampled sawdust by the front door, the pickups in the parking area, "this is Carlton's fine print. Six interviews, period. Could be with the circus, the city morgue—no, *those* would be *good* interviews..." He went in, leaving the engine running. Several minutes later, as he walked back to the car, two faces appeared in the shop window. He slammed the car door and looked back at the faces, muttering, "Life-threatening." Eliza felt awful for him, his interviews spent. She said nothing about the plan.

Terry pulled in at a Chinese restaurant. They went inside and sat down, and he ordered them jasmine tea and a plate of fortune cookies. "Start opening," he commanded.

"But what will—" She gazed down on the plate of puffy half-moons.

Terry's finger jabbed at her. "Open," he said. He peered at the white strip he'd extracted. "'You will be joined with an old forgotten friend.' God, I hope not. What does yours say?"

Eliza had pulled out a strip without breaking the cookie. "'You long to see the Great Pyramids in Egypt.'"

They broke and crunched and read, letting the pieces of paper fall to the table between them. "'Executive ability is prominent in your makeup.' Maybe the eyeliner?" Terry's smile was sickly.

"'Confucius say,'" Eliza read, "'top of ladder nice place but very lonesome.'"

"How would we know? 'If you are waiting for something to turn up, start on your own shirtsleeves.'" His brow wrinkled. "What?"

"Means roll up your sleeves. Here," Eliza said, "you take this one."

"'You stand in your own light. Make it shine.'" He sighed. "'Make it dim' is more like it." But he folded the fortune and tucked it in his jacket pocket. "This usually works," he said. "If you open enough, you have to get a 'Good news will come to you from far away.' That's why you eat those water chestnut buttons." Terry gathered the fortunes and crumpled them together. He propped his head in his hand, dragging the skin of his cheek down.

Eliza studied the hanging red lanterns, the picture on the wall by their booth; painted on some kind of slatted mat, it showed black ships sailing on a white sea. Either the ships, made with clever brushstrokes, were small or they were far away. At a table by the kitchen door sat three Chinese teenagers, their chopsticks inserting noodles efficiently into their mouths. *Now, there's your family,* she thought, *not like the family the prospective employers liked to imagine they had.* Maybe the kids griped about working at the restaurant, maybe they didn't even think about it. Work, noodles. Work, corn bread. It was all so simple if you had it. Then you picked out other problems to have.

"You know, Terry," Eliza said, "if worse comes to worst, President Johnson has his war on poverty going."

"Please. The draft board doesn't want me."

Eliza smiled with him, but then she saw his eyes were welling. She got up, slid in the booth beside him, and put her arm around him. Terry laid his head on her shoulder. "You should see how they look at me," he murmured.

Eliza tightened her arm.

The black ships floated becalmed on their white sea.

Two of the teenagers were rolling silver into red cloth napkins. The third turned the pages of a thick book. Outside the plate-glass window, beyond the painted red and gold arc spelling out CHINA GATE backward, the light deepened.

"I should've used our plan on that woman at Andover," she said with a small, ironic smile. "I coulda recommended Elmer's Glue for her eyelashes. One side like to've dropped off in her ashtray."

"You don't really mean that." Sitting up, Terry ripped a paper napkin from the dispenser and tamped beneath each eye. "The fabulous thing about you is that the lies you tell are so moral. That's not true. You said it just for me."

"Maybe so," Eliza said, sliding out of the booth. "But it's true enough."

XXII

Caesar lay in front of Eliza's door, one paw crossed over the other. That was strange, but then, Caesar's owner was strange. She would have given the stolid white dog more than one pat on his head, but the weight of the day urged her past him to lie on her bed. Sure, she had one interview left, but Terry had none.

The radio stayed off. A tear leaked out and dried on her cheek; she could put no energy into weeping. Instead, lying there, she cast around for some action to hold devastation at bay. At one time she had taken comfort in making lists. *I could,* she thought, *(1) bother Earl Fitzwalter again to hurry up with that lien; (2) go to that woman's house and demand she sign the quitclaim on the spot; (3) secretly petition Sandra to give me more interviews; (4) check the few newspaper ads for clerical jobs; (5) see about... caretaker jobs.* Though these were options—she did have options—the list offered no real comfort.

Someone knocked loudly on her door. Sighing, she pulled herself up and opened it to Morton, who commanded Caesar to stay by the threshold, scanned the parking lot, then closed the door. His deep-set eyes were wide open. "There were two men here asking about you, Eliza. Like, serious men. You know who they are?"

Eliza blinked to clear her vision. "What'd they want?"

"To know when you got home. What your routine was, if a lot of people came to see you, nosy stuff like that." Morton picked up Percy and scratched the dog's head as he sat on Eliza's chair. He relaxed then. "You're not...on the run, are you?"

"I don't think so." She told him about Ray Paley, but that was over now.

Morton's eyes stayed wide open. "So you outfoxed that guy?"

"More like he let me get away with it."

"Well, I've started thinking. What if I was wrong about Dr. Bleckman from the university searching my room? What if whoever did it was after you and got the wrong room?"

"But...what for? Did they tell you what they were looking for?"

"You."

"No, I mean why."

"They didn't say. Shifty guys, black suits and all. Here." Morton set Percy down and dug in his pocket. He handed Eliza a red whistle on a cord. "You can wear that around your neck. It's loud. You need help, we'll come."

Alarmed, she accepted the whistle. She snapped it into her purse and laid the purse down on the floor by the bed, where it was an arm's length away. She said thanks and goodbye to Morton and scavenged through her mind for some reason unknown men would have come looking for her.

Nothing.

Wait.

Oh no, no—a stab and a lurching in her stomach. Could there be something else underhanded that Robert had done? At the railroad, maybe? Something Eliza would be required to take responsibility for? The word rose up before her: *embezzlement.* Before Robert's death, she would never have considered accusing him of such a thing. Not Robert. But now...She stopped there, did not want to take one more step down that frightful road. She flipped on the radio, put on her nightgown, and clutched the covers with both hands.

Please not more, she said as a prayer, her chest heavy. Then, in order not to imagine what else Robert could have done or what his other wife could have done, she branched out, saying prayers aloud for her kids and grandkids, each of them, for Louise, for Terry, for Sandra, for the poor people out on the West Coast who were washing away in floods, for the people up in frozen Alaska who'd had a spring earthquake so violent, their streets had cracked wide open. She was also grateful that Lyndon Johnson was the president and not Barry Goldwater, who would not care about fighting any war on poverty. Eliza knew in her heart these were not true prayers, as she was using them to help herself. But the whispering, the repetition, the picturing of each person or persons, eased her.

The radio was softly playing a song by the Beatles. Eliza didn't know its name. It was jolty. She rolled over and turned it off, closed her eyes. Then she leaned down and blindly felt her purse beside the bed. The whistle was there.

Terry surprised her by appearing at her door the next morning in yesterday's suit, announcing that he was Eliza's chauffeur today. She was touched, though she noted the strain behind the valor. This last appointment dealt out by Carlton was Cassen and Associates, Attorneys-at-Law. It was Eliza's. Her sixth.

"Sixth time is the charm," Terry said solemnly. "They're going to love you."

As Eliza walked toward a set of mahogany double doors, a youngish woman in a short skirt and white stockings burst out, clutching some items to her chest. Her eyes were hugely and blackly enlarged while her mouth was erased by lipstick the flesh color of a Band-Aid. She ran to a car parked nearby, threw the armload inside it, climbed in, slammed the door, and revved the engine. The car lunged backward, then braked with a screech. The driver leaned out her window; her eyes, blazing from their black enclosures, seemed to vacuum up Eliza's person. "I'll just bet you're the interview. Aren't you."

Eliza had completed half of a cautious nod when the woman pinched her thumb and index finger into a circle. "Cinch," she snarled. The car peeled away.

Eliza's shoes sank into a pale blue carpet. She approached the waiting area in which three velvet wing chairs, two striped taupe and blue and one plain taupe, were arranged conversationally, fronted by a glass coffee table fanned with *Time* magazines. A broad receptionist's desk, mahogany like the entrance doors and bare of papers, sat beneath a sunburst wall design that proved to be a clock. The teal-blue receiver of a phone dangled from its spiraled cord and a teal-blue vase spilling dried cattails lay across the desk. Beneath the desk, a heavy young woman was gathering scattered papers. Some were wadded, like rejected letters; those she tossed into a wastebasket. One sheet was scuffed and bore a small, round hole as if from a bullet or the point of a high heel; that one, she wadded up herself. She stood and adjusted her teased brown hair, the pouf of which had canted to the left.

"Oh," she said when she saw Eliza. She hesitated, as if translating what she was about to say into another language. "Good afternoon. Welcome to Cassen and

Associates. May I help you?" Quickly she righted the teal-blue vase and brushed cattail debris off the desk.

"I'm here about the job."

The young woman put a hand, fingers stiffly spread, to her collarbone, over her plain white blouse. "Not the reception one? I just got it. I'm going to wear better clothes tomorrow."

"The information I have says it's executive secretary."

The girl broke into a smile that reminded Eliza of the sunburst clock on the wall. "Oh, right," she said, almost to herself. "She's gone too." She formalized her voice: "If you'll be so kind as to wait, I'll see if Mr. Cassen is available now." She left, returned in a minute, and arabesqued her palm in the air, inviting Eliza to follow.

Eliza passed through a compact office with a desk, a Selectric, a Rolodex, file cabinets—the executive secretary's—into the boss's domain. It was a far cry from Earl Fitzwalter's modest suite; this room was spacious, the glass-cased bookshelves polished and the plush wall-to-wall overlaid by a Turkish carpet of many colors. Brass-framed prints hung above the bookshelves. A luxurious room; it smelled good to her, homey. Like, in fact, barbecue sauce.

The lawyer wiped his fingers with a paper napkin and came out from behind a much larger desk, strewn with folders, accordion files, and a paper plate with potato chip remnants and half a pickle. Eliza gauged his age to be forty-eight or thereabouts. He held out his hand. His face was acne-scarred and handsome, marred at the cheekbone by a wedge-shaped abrasion atop a robin's-egg-size lump.

"Eliza Kratke," she said and gave him her hand.

"Harold Cassen. Sit down." He flipped his tie back over his shirt. "Tell me about your experience, young lady."

Young lady. Eliza smiled weakly. Anyone using that term ostensibly meant to flatter, but it was two-faced flattery, a kind of inside joke enjoyed only by the joker. She detailed the courses she had taken and the skills she had learned at Carlton.

"Can you work under pressure? Pretty crazy around here sometimes."

Eliza allowed that she could work under pressure.

"Know how to run interference for the boss? Field phone calls from undesirables such as, say, my wife?" He laughed slyly. "Just kidding."

Eliza bent her lips.

"Sometimes our clients calling from jail can be awfully persuasive. Weeping and wailing. That would be exclusively the secretary's domain." Cassen shook his head in distaste. "And any irate husbands. We also do high-end divorces here. Last year a rancher sent us his check written on a piece of cowhide. We couldn't believe it, big old messy piece of..." The lawyer grinned. "Glad he didn't deliver it himself."

Looking away from his face, in sympathy with the rancher, she glanced down and saw a speck of barbecue sauce on his shirt.

"Of course, the depositions and such require first-rate typing. Sometimes we work killer hours when a case gets close to court and naturally during a trial. Seventy, eighty hours a week. We're a fightin' machine. But you wouldn't have any rugrats at home, and I don't guess you'd be getting knocked up. That's a plus."

Seventy, eighty hours. She imagined the solid pain in her hands from seventy hours of typing, the stiffness. She glanced around the attractive office, a different world from Andover Tool. Her last interview. This was the last one. She could use the plan, clean that spot of sauce from his shirt with the tiny jar of spot cleaner in her purse. But. Seventy or eighty hours typing. She was a practical woman. Sensible. She knew what to do, and that was not the moral or the correct or the proper thing. It was just the right thing to do.

Eliza tried for her most warming smile. "Mr. Cassen, it's not that I wouldn't like to work here—it sounds so interesting—but a fellow graduate of Carlton is outside, and I just have this feeling he might do better for your job. Would you let me run get him for you?" She kept her seat so he wouldn't have to look up at her, and she beamed as best she could. "He won't get pregnant either."

"A man for a secretary?"

"Oh, yes, sir, just like the government in France and so on, they're all men. I think they call them *aides*."

But the lawyer had drawn back, grimacing, waving

away her suggestion. His tie slipped forward into his barbecue plate.

"He types like the wind, Mr. Cassen. He knows how to handle upset people, and he can keep secrets. Don't you think men do that better than women?"

"Hell yes. But I still don't want—"

"Mr. Cassen." She dived into the plan as if into clean water. "Has your life ever changed for the better?"

"Well, sure, but—"

"You know beforehand it was going to?"

"Pretty close. I won a case last year—"

"The Memorial Hospital case, wasn't it?"

Harold Cassen's mouth closed; she had his attention.

"All those nurses breathing in some chemical until they were too sick to work. The young man sitting right outside, the one I think might change your business for the better? He told me all about it. Please, sir. Just one minute."

Back at the car, she opened Terry's door and filled him in quickly. He started toward the building but she called him back to give him the jar of spot remover.

"That's *your* thing." Terry was still protesting, straightening his tie and patting his hair back at the same time.

Apropos of nothing, a favorite saying of Robert's issued from her; this was how easily and unfairly Robert could break in. "Smoke 'em if you got 'em," Eliza said.

Terry's brow furrowed. "What?"

She pointed her finger like Fate; Terry scurried. At the door, he paused, gazing back at her momentarily, his face contorted into a mask of tragedy. Then he pulled his body up and into itself, utterly straight, gracefully aligned, two inches taller than he'd been half an hour ago, and sallied in.

She waited, telling herself that she would never have felt right in Harold Cassen's plush lair. A seventy-hour typing week would have crippled her. Trying not to host the image of dirty bathwater—her six chances—gurgling down a drain. Coughing out into a Kleenex the taste of Robert's voice in her mouth.

Eliza got chilly enough to change to the driver's seat so she could start the engine and run the heater. It was forty minutes before Terry loped back to the car, overcoat flapping, and said, "Drive!" Eliza nudged into the stream of traffic on the feeder road to the freeway. Terry was sitting bolt upright by the window, his head close to touching the Corvair's low roof, sweat on his upper lip. Eliza drove back to the Chinese restaurant and parked in a space near its bright window, the arc spelling out CHINA GATE in gilt and lucky red. They did not get out.

"After I went to New York," Terry said, looking away, "I got a note from my sister saying they were moving. A few weeks later she sent me a letter saying she missed me but Dad said to tell me not to bother coming home. Got a couple letters from Mom." Terry wasn't talking like himself. His speech was excruciatingly precise and quiet, as if he were building a card house with his voice.

"I showed him I knew the details of the Memorial Hospital case. Sacrificed a handkerchief by dousing it with spot cleaner and handing it to him while I was talking about how to get receivables moving. Color-coding files, fine points of call screening—I just threw out darts to see if any stuck. The one that did was about difficult people. I said I could deal with the psychology of difficult people. Chapter nineteen of *Human Relations*. That was a heading, can you see it, about halfway down the page? 'The Psychology of Difficult People.'"

"So you got the job."

Harold Cassen had sat back, apparently running an internal balance sheet. Terry was flooded with delicious understanding, pleasanter than Warren Beatty or chocolate sprinkles for life. He said in that distant, careful voice that his interview had gone more than well. It was ace. He'd done his best, and he had aced it.

Except an ace wasn't enough to win.

Terry told Eliza that the lawyer had phoned his brother in Boston. "Hey, Arlie," he'd said, "got the answer to your headaches." The brother ran an art gallery, managing neurotic, haughty, idiosyncratic, superstitious art types, which, Terry told him, would be very much like managing the neurotic, haughty, idiosyncratic, superstitious dancers he had worked with for years. This was Cassen's queer brother, though he didn't say that, and the brother, Arlen, when Terry answered his questions, didn't have to.

"I've had a bottle of champagne in the fridge for two years, Eliza. Now I don't know whether to drink it or pour it down the crapper."

Eliza started the car and drove from the China Gate to the Vidalia, where she pulled the parking brake and got out.

"Are you going to Boston, Terry?"

"On wild horses."

"Then don't make champagne into a problem." Eliza smiled and turned toward her door.

"Wait." Terry called her back. "I know we didn't do great. But I want to tell you that it's been nice not to do great *together*. I mean, I feel that way. I'm not speaking for you. But not getting into an empty car *after* was heaven."

Eliza kissed the tips of two unpolished fingers and set the kiss on Terry's head.

XXIII

In the morning first thing, she peered out her curtains at the parking lot and froze. Morton and his dogs were outside in the daylight, facing a black car with a man…no, looked like two men in it. He held the leashes; the dogs sat obediently. But alertly—it was easy to see they'd lunge the second Morton commanded.

Criminals did not come in the daytime in a late-model black car. They did not wait for you to get out of bed.

Eliza dressed as if for school, made herself coffee, and sat at her table. Her purse with the red whistle sat beside her cup. After a while, a door slammed and voices rose. Finally, a sharp knock at the door.

She felt like blowing the whistle in their faces, the two

men standing there in black suits and dark ties. She hadn't done anything against the law. And if Robert had, it wasn't her doing. Wasn't her fault or responsibility, and she would tell them that! They didn't have any cause to scare her like this. If they *were* the law. Morton and the dogs stood off to the side now, a few yards in back of the men but still alert. She could not catch Morton's eye beneath the ball cap.

"Eliza Kratke?" the taller man said.

"Brock."

"You're not Eliza Kratke?"

"Well, I am, but I'm expecting a name change to come through any day now."

"A name change."

Eliza nodded and continued to look at him.

"Do you have some ID?" he asked.

Eliza gave the man her driver's license—she had picked it up from Earl Fitzwalter's. The man read off "'Kratke, Eliza'" and the address. "That's a former address?"

She nodded again.

The taller man showed her a leather holder with a gold badge in the middle; she made out an eagle on top. "I'm Agent Gatlin and that's Agent Keller, and we need you to come with us, Mrs. Kratke."

"What for?"

"We'll have a discussion about that soon. Please follow us, ma'am."

What else could she do? They escorted her to the car, where the shorter agent helped her into the back seat.

His head jerked around at the sound of a piercing whistle. Eliza angled back toward the motel. Ike had burst from his door and was galloping down the stairs, his long hair flying.

Morton and the dogs drew nearer to the black car. "You all right, Eliza?" he called.

"I reckon so. They're the law, Morton, so I got to go with them."

"You call us if you need us! We'll be right here waiting."

Eliza raised her hand to her two neighbors, witnesses if it came to that. Morton was speaking into Ike's ear, but his gaze was on the car. Its door closed.

They took her to a police station, to a room behind a glass window much like the one Sandra at the business school worked behind. A man sitting at a long desk guided her fingers to a black ink pad and, grasping each one in turn, rolled them across white paper. The sight of the black ink on her fingers nauseated her.

"But what are you arresting me for?"

"You're not under arrest, Mrs. Kratke." The taller one, Gatlin, said this. "We just need to ask you some questions. We're taking your prints for comparison."

"To what?" Eliza hated that her voice sounded screechy. No one answered.

The two men led her to a room with a smooth metal table and metal chairs. They asked her meaningless questions

Lisa Sandlin

about her life: Where her family was from, when she'd moved from the address on her driver's license, how long she'd lived at the Vidalia. Her marital status, number of children, occupation. She still clutched the tissue they'd given her to clean the ink from her fingers. It had not done the job. The taller agent, Gatlin—though now that he was sitting down, she couldn't tell he was the taller—asked her how long she had been working with Louise Molineaux. He set his pencil to a yellow pad.

Louise?

Confused, she told them since school had started. "Back in September." It was now late January. Headed up for February, when it would be one year since Robert had died. Scot-free, no reckoning for him, wreckage all around. Five months since she'd met Louise—it seemed many more. The greater news: The agents hadn't come because of something Robert had done. That was a huge relief.

The man was jotting notes. What was Eliza's role in their operation?

Operation? What role? She didn't have a role. She and Louise would do homework together or work on a problem over lunch as they ate.

"What kind of problem?"

"Louise isn't so good with figuring markups or percentages."

"Mrs. Kratke. How else did you work with her?"

"That's it. Otherwise, she does all right. Been at it two years. She started way before I did."

"Started?"

"Carlton."

"Carlton. First name?"

She canted her head at them.

The shorter one leaned over and said something to Gatlin. "Oh, okay," he murmured.

A uniformed police officer entered the room, set a box on the table, nodded to the other men.

"All right, Mrs. Kratke, what can you tell me about these?" Gatlin reached into the box and pulled out two of Louise's notebooks, both of which had formerly been stacked on Eliza's dresser. "Is there a key to decipher them?"

"You took those out of my room." Eliza felt surprised and angered.

"We're authorized to remove evidence."

"Of what?"

Agent Gatlin opened a notebook so she could see two pages at once and tapped Louise's thick, back-slanted handwriting. "Can you read this?"

"I could if I had my purse. Which that man up front took away."

"You have a code sheet in there?"

"I have a compact. Hold that up to a mirror and you can read it."

She expected surprise, but the man showed none. His bland face seemed to drag down a little. "Right," he said. "All right." He flipped to a page with drawings: Jeannie Ruffin and one of the Abraham Lincolns. "And this?"

"This what? Louise draws faces in her notes. Historical ones. And other ones, students in our class."

His eyes narrowed. He reached into the box again. "Okay. Tell us about this." He set an enameled box, one Eliza recognized, in front of her. It no longer had the duct tape around it.

"That's Louise's. Belonged to her grandfather."

"Did you ever use it?"

"Use it? I kept it for her after her apartment got robbed. Louise was worried the robbers would come back. Returned it to her the last time I saw her."

"When would that have been?" When Eliza answered, Gatlin made a note on his pad. "Were you aware that Miss Molineaux's grandfather was known to certain circles back in his time? Criminal circles."

"No."

"But you were aware Miss Molineaux's apartment had been burglarized?"

"Yeah, I told you. She was real upset about it."

"Did you know the burglars had been arrested?"

Eliza shook her head.

The other officer—Eliza had forgotten his name—withdrew an envelope from his jacket and laid two bills on the table. A twenty-dollar bill and a hundred. Old ones, not very clean.

"Seen these before?"

"In better days, mister."

The man tapped Andrew Jackson. "The burglars had

232

sixteen of these on them when they were arrested. Five of the C-notes. They told the police where they got them. At the apartment of Louise Molineaux."

Eliza looked at the bills on the table, relieved again. These lawmen must be investigating the burglary—which she had nothing to do with. She felt powerfully sorry for Louise, though. This would be the money she'd saved. Her travel money. The money to start her new life—and thieves had taken it. No wonder she'd looked upset when Eliza had last seen her at the Vidalia. The burglars had stolen her future.

"That's Louise's money she saved, poor girl."

The two men looked at each other.

"What do you mean, Mrs. Kratke?"

"She was saving to go to England. Live there and study art. But I still don't understand what this has to do with me."

The forgotten-name agent sat back and lowered his eyelids. "Come on, Mrs. Kratke, we know Louise had plates. Did you run the press? Cut the sheets apart? What? Why don't you tell us what your role was in Louise Molineaux's operation."

"What sheets? Operation—mister, Louise can barely keep Louise going. Look, that heavy thing is Louise's granddaddy's box. It's a keepsake. She gave it to me so if her place got broken into again, they wouldn't get it. Then she came to see me, and I gave it back to her. That's all I know. That's it. That's the end."

Lisa Sandlin

"Who's 'they'?"

"The people that robbed her apartment."

"Who were they?"

"How would I know? I'm not a robber."

The man shook the box; it rattled like it had when Eliza shook it. He opened it and, as if he already knew the contents, pushed it across the table to her. Inside was an oblong metal plate, heavily engraved. Another beneath that one. The top one was the head of Benjamin Franklin. Just as finely drawn, but he did not have the same sly look as the one on Louise's tablet. He looked like regular old Benjamin Franklin.

Except he was facing the wrong way.

A light shock descended on Eliza. The picture cleared. Louise's sketches. Louise had not been drawing our Founding Fathers. Louise had been drawing money.

"Your prints will be compared to the prints on this plate," the forgotten-name agent said. "If we find yours, we'll have more to talk about."

Gatlin took over. "Meanwhile, Mrs. Kratke, please be patient. We'll need to hold you a while longer."

XXIV

The cell was not empty. A girl in jeans and a red T-shirt sat on a bunk, her knees up to her chest. She opened her eyes when Eliza entered, and her gaze followed the men who locked the cell and walked away. There was another bed, folded sheet and blanket at the end of it, but the mattress was splotchy. Eliza sniffed it, then sat herself on it and leaned back against the wall.

"Hey," the girl said.

"Hello."

"What are you here for?"

"A mistake." A flood of words waited to condemn the magnitude of these lawmen's mistake, but Eliza bit them back.

"Yeah. Me too. Mine was a man. What's yours?"

Eliza thought as she spoke so as to make more sense of this thing. Haltingly, she told the girl about Louise, whom she'd met at the business school they'd both attended, and gave a few details about the school. Then about the box Louise had asked her to keep, the men at the door, the black car.

"Bitch. She left you holding."

"Holding?"

"Dope, probably, that was in the box. So it'd be on you and not her."

"Oh. No, that wasn't it."

Eliza had not untaped the box to look into it. She'd trusted Louise without realizing she was trusting Louise. Had there ever been one good reason to trust Louise? Eliza had just become used to her. And, in spite of her exasperation, fond of her.

Look what that had gotten her. A jail cell.

She dropped her face into her hands and cried. She cried out of disgust at herself for her lack of self-preservation. Out of pure fear. Out of shame for the ink on her fingers, for the jeer of the flash on her face; she cried for the agents' casual power over her, the power men always had over women, and in hopeless anger at Louise, whose teeth she would have shaken loose if she were here in this cell. She cried for her mother sewing in thin dawn light, for the grooves worn in the downturned corners of her father's mouth, for his mind emptied in the last, bespattered-shirt years; she cried for her brother's numbed stumbling into a bullet-skimmed ocean; for Robert's cruel betrayal, silences, absences; for his other wife's callous efforts to steal her house. For the embitterment of her children and for her own littleness.

It took a long while for her to realize that the girl in the red T-shirt was standing in front of her, a wad of toilet paper waiting in her fist. Eliza took it to mop her eyes and nose, sat back against the concrete-block wall, gasping.

"Hey, listen, it's just an arrest," the girl said, cocking her hip, "not your immortal soul. They'll figure it out. There's bail. I've got out of jail before."

Eliza breathed for a while. "You're real kind," she said.

"C'mon. All I did was give you some toilet paper."

"You could've stayed over there" — Eliza indicated the other bed — "and not said a word to me."

"I would've been bored."

"Honey, you — what's your name?"

"Faye. Faye McKnight."

"What'd you do, Faye?"

"Rode along with my boyfriend while he ripped off a couple places. The dumbass came out with a fistful of money that wasn't money. That's why I'm here."

Eliza stared at the girl. Tangled strands of brown hair, one knee of her jeans worn through, bare feet. Matter-of-fact expression. This was Louise's robber. Or maybe assistant robber. Right in front of her. And Eliza liked her.

"I'm Eliza Brock. You're in jail not knowing how you're getting out and you're bored?"

Faye shrugged. "Something'll happen. I'll get out."

"Did you call somebody?"

"Not yet."

"Do you know a lawyer?"

"No."

"Then how do you think you're getting out without you do something?"

"You wait long enough, something happens." Faye snapped her fingers and flipped over a palm as though a big metal key would appear on it.

"Wait long enough and you're liable to have your chair jerked out from under you."

Faye sat down on Eliza's bed. "Why don't you tell me about this school you were going to. What's it good for?"

"Why?"

"Because... I don't know. It's boring in here. Just talk."

Eliza blew her nose. She told the girl about Carlton, about the accounting class, the business English, the stenography, the typing, the homework. Talking about these ordinary things lightened her chest some. She told about how her day went, how her time was spent and her money was stretched. When she stopped, Faye motioned at her to go on. So Eliza told her how she felt when she understood the profit-and-loss statement, the accounts payable and receivable, how each understanding was a bit of victory that allowed her to continue to believe she could make a new life out of nothing, out of a ruin. Faye did not ask her what the ruin was; she seemed to understand ruin.

Eliza said every day forward seemed to fix her a little further on her way somewhere. Or that's what she had told herself before now. At least once a day, she told herself. She practiced picturing herself at a job, in an office with a carpeted floor and a desk, where she performed her work satisfactorily. Where people were friendly to her or at least polite. She could even see herself out of the Sweet Vidalia Residence Inn and in a modest place where her children would visit. Maybe even a friend or two. Then she would put the image away, like hanging up a rayon dress, and start on her homework.

The girl looked at her wonderingly.

Eliza interpreted the look as judgment. "I'm sorry—I know there are setbacks. Ever'body has them. But this is just the only way I know how. One thing at a time. Payroll questions and then the test, then more problems and another test, and so forth."

Faye waved at Eliza to go on.

"Nothing left to say, honey. Days turn into a week and weeks turn into months. Then you're finished with what you started. You look back and the long time seems short. Anybody'd tell you that. Thank you for the tissue."

"No problem," the girl muttered. She appeared to be considering what Eliza had said. She returned to sit on her own bed, darted another look at Eliza.

Eliza made up her bed, took off her shoes. Tomorrow—
she gritted her teeth—she would have to call Earl Fitzwalter.

But she didn't. Eliza was bailed...or not bailed, exactly,
because she hadn't been arrested. She was escorted from
the cell back to the fingerprinting room, where a man sat
smoking. A plump, sleek Ray Paley in a sheened suit. She
was too surprised to make any kind of greeting.

"Louise told me you were here."

"How'd she know? Where is she?"

Paley, frowning, lifted the hand with the cigarette.
"Somewhere in this stockade. Listen, Mrs. Kratke—"

"Brock. The name's Brock now."

"Okay, Brock. I'm gonna do what I can for Louise. Got
her a lawyer, and he's talking to her now." He pinched out
his cigarette and flicked it away. "Those goddamn plates.
The old bastard died when she was seven or eight, but
Louise thought he hung the moon. I let her have 'em
because it was like giving her a...a family ring or a pocket
watch or something. It never dawned on me she'd use 'em."

"She's guilty, then, isn't she."

"What do you think? She and that boyfriend—they
had the paper, ink, the plates. Louise..." Paley pinched the
bridge of his nose. "Louise was born guilty. Fast mouth,
fights, schemes. A little actress. She gets mad at you, you
bring up her limp, but then she'll use it to get out of trouble. And stubborn...whoo. Know what I mean?" He lit

240

another cigarette and, looking down, drew on it. "But here's the thing I wanted to…she told me you believed in her. You." His eyes were incredulous.

They darkened as smoke issued from his nostrils. "You. Not me, that's what she means. That I didn't believe in her. She's right."

"Louise has a talent, Mr. Paley. Anybody could see that. I could see that."

"Well, I didn't."

"But you're gonna help her now."

"If she lets me." He shook his head. "By the way, she said you need a job. Call me next week and we'll talk about it. I saw that day at your house that somebody like you could do—"

"Somebody like me?"

He waved his hand at Eliza's whole form and turned as a man approached. It was the tall one, Gatlin; he called for Mr. Paley to follow him. Hope lifted Ray Paley's plump face. He jumped up, seemingly forgetting Eliza, and hurried after the agent.

Eliza could only guess what Paley had meant. Somebody like Eliza—a former housewife who could sell a secondhand car?

They were going to take her home to the Vidalia, though. At some point during her questioning, the agents had lost interest in her.

XXV

On a March morning when bluebonnets filled the courthouse beds, Eliza walked down a marble hall and sat on a bench beside Louise Molineaux. Ray and the lawyer were huddled on a bench directly across from them.

Louise startled. "Eliza. I didn't think I'd see you again. Why are you here?"

The girl wore a plain gray dress with a white collar, and her wealth of black hair had been cut to her ears, with a row of bangs on her forehead. She reminded Eliza of a cartoon boy from her childhood, Buster Brown, who wore his yellow hair in that style. Buster, a tricky sort of boy, had round white circles for eyes. Louise's blue eyes looked tired, heavy.

Eliza patted the knot of Louise's hands. "Just to sit here with you, I guess."

"I already pleaded. Been out on bail. You know that?"

"I heard."

"This is sentencing. You know max is twenty years? I don't get probation, I go to jail today. I mean this day." The blue eyes clutched at Eliza.

"Your daddy said."

Louise did not contradict *daddy* but she didn't react to it either. "If you plead guilty, the judge is s'posed to give you a bunch of time off your sentence. Maybe even probation. I don't have a record, Eliza. Except for shoplifting in high school. Everybody does that."

"What did the lawyer say?"

The girl faced downward. "He said blame Solly. Put it all on him. Say I'm just a silly girl that went along with her boyfriend. So silly I couldn't have figured out in a million years how to find just the right kind of paper for money, how to end up with ink the exact right color. Such an idiot I thought it was like a Monopoly game. You know, it was Solly's dad's print shop we used. Boy, is *he* mad."

"'Magine he is."

"I can do a lotta things, but I couldn't do that."

"Do what, Louise? Dump it all off on your boyfriend?"

"No. Act like I'm stupid. Swear on a Bible I'm stupid. Swear on a Bible that it wasn't my idea. That I hardly knew anything about it. 'Cause it was my idea. My grandfather's plates gave it to me. I knew. They mighta all had the same serial number, but those bills were *good*. And I am *not* stupid."

"No," Eliza said, "you're not." Louise sat up a notch straighter.

Here was pride, Eliza saw. It was holding Louise together; it was giving herself her own due. Eliza pictured the cell she had so lately been in and wondered if Louise's would be the same.

"When I didn't go along with the lawyer, Ray went nuts. So the lawyer called in the prosecutor to make a deal. Me and Solly hadn't spent any of the money yet." Louise turned her head to the right, then left. She whispered, " 'Cept for a couple tryouts. On the Jacksons. They passed like butter." A small, satisfied smile flitted across her face.

"Man, is it a lotta work. First thing, we tried bleaching some singles and made those into twenties. It was tough, getting the balance right, cutting even. I could smell the bleach. But I wanted to use the plate, I just wanted to, so Solly went along. After we cut 'em, we had to wrinkle the bills all up, walk on 'em, spill coffee on 'em, make 'em look old, since the date on the plates is 1921. Doing it all at night."

"Then those robbers came."

"Those assholes, you mean. And got caught. We wouldn't've got caught 'cept for *them*—and I know damn well that if they get off, it'll be because *my money* got 'em off. Coughed up the bills to the cops, told them where we lived. Home free for the assholes, 'cause counterfeiting is a big crime. Did you know it's a crime just to *have* my granddaddy's old plates?"

"No, I didn't know that." Eliza thought of the enamel box resting in her freezer compartment under the ice cubes. If those two agents had not mistaken Morton's place for hers, they'd have found the box. They could have charged her with a federal crime, and she would have been guilty.

That thought had apparently bypassed Louise's brain. "Well, that's what the lawyer got the prosecutor to agree to. Possession of counterfeiting materials. Not that I was passing or selling. Just making. The lawyer told the prosecutor I was an art student. That's true, by the way. I was seventeen, I took an art class at the community college. Drew apples and baskets. But..." Louise's small face became grim. "Ray said business school was where I belonged. That's what he'd pay for. That art school wouldn't get you a job as dogcatcher, and...and me being how I am, I was gonna need a job. Art school was a stupid idea. I was stupid to want it."

Eliza measured the woundedness, the resentment burning like a pyre in Louise's eyes.

"You're the only one believed different." Louise threw a glance at Eliza, then faced away.

She had believed different. That Abraham Lincoln face wasn't money—it was history on the page. Eliza realized that her admiration for the drawing, her appreciation of Louise's vitality, had softened her feelings toward the girl.

She reminded herself that Louise was a criminal, surely as Faye from the cell and her boyfriend were criminals. A year ago, there would not have been a question in her mind about a criminal like Louise.

"It's time."

They looked up. Ray and the lawyer stood in front of them.

Eliza took a seat in the courtroom directly behind the defense table as Louise was still hobbling painfully to her chair. She listened as Louise, standing but hunched in such a way that her crooked back looked crookeder, told her story. That was required for a plea of guilty, that you tell all your sins out loud and take full responsibility. Louise did it. Said she was sorry. Threw her young, almost-no-priors self on the mercy of the court.

Eliza's breath caught when the judge said, "Eighteen months." On one hand, a year and a half was far, far less than twenty. It was a light enough punishment, and Louise was definitely guilty. On the other hand, that was frail Louise Molineaux in an airless prison cell for all those months.

Ray Paley groaned and slapped a hand over his eyes when the bailiff began to lock on the cuffs. Louise looked back over her shoulder at him. Her eyes filled. Eliza stood up and caught her gaze. As long as Louise kept looking back, Eliza held eye contact, not stopping until Louise was led through the courtroom doors.

XXVI

During their telephone conversation a few days after Louise's sentencing, Ray Paley filled in Eliza on the job he had in mind. "Majority's office work, you know the deal, phones, bill paying, invoices, payroll. Oh, and monthly taxes. You learned all that at Carlton, right?"

"Right." Yes, she had learned that. Eliza felt pleased, buoyed—for knowing how each of those business tasks worked, for learning them. For Carlton. Not a waste of money after all. Maybe.

"Just hadn't worked out for Red to do it; numb-nuts can't balance the checking account. But listen, there'd also be some out-of-office work you might be good for. Repo-ing different stuff."

"What kind of stuff?" Eliza leaned back against the Vidalia's wall, her right hand covering her ear. Sixth Street was noisy today.

"Not heavy-duty stuff, like hooking up cars to tow. More personnel-facing."

"What does that mean?"

"People. The people we deal with get mad, Mrs.—can I call you Eliza? They get pissed, they yell; it's part of the job. You'd maybe be good for that. They wouldn't want to fight you."

It was a positive sign that he wanted to use her first name. But fight people?

"So whaddya think?"

What did Eliza think? "Yes," she said. "When would I start?"

"Next week. Payroll, workers' comp. Workers' comp's important in this biz."

"All right. Thank you, Mr. Paley."

"Ray. I'm the boss, but no *misters* around my shop."

Eliza hung up. It was quiet suddenly; the manic honkers on Sixth had let their war go and raced on down the street. She'd just had a job interview. And she had gotten the job. She walked blindly back to her room and hugged Percy.

Eliza entered Paley and Associates Collection Services wearing a cardigan sweater over a shirtwaist dress and her school shoes with the thick heels. Red and two other men, introduced to her as Freddie and Byron, exchanged deadly glances.

"This is Eliza," Ray said with an edge. "You'll remember her, Red. She kicked your butt." The heads of the other two men swiveled to Red.

"She's gonna get the shop working right. Help y'all out. So be polite, knuckleheads." He showed her to a desk in a corner with a crippled but serviceable chair — "Have to get a new one, one of these days." She noted how he called the office "the shop." He showed her the files where info was kept and the drawer where the checkbook and deposit slips lived; he pointed out folders for invoices that needed to be made up and sent out and gave her a list of his properties' tenants. "Today's payroll. But fix the bank account first, okay? We could have negative a million dollars in there for all I know."

Eliza noticed the cloud that passed over Red's face and the beetling look he shot her.

She began straightaway. Starting with a checkbook balance Ray assured her was correct — "Because I verified the damn number myself" — she combed through three months of statements. Put all the canceled checks in order and compared them to the numbers recorded in the checkbook, looking for discrepancies. Corrected as needed. Added in the deposits. Eliza silently exhaled with relief when the checkbook balanced to the penny. Then she took the five time cards lying on the desk, along with a rate and W-4 deduction posted on each one, and figured out payroll; she wrote the checks and handed them to Ray to sign. After that, she split out labor costs from the time cards—three hours for a First National Bank repo, two hours for an appliance store, four for a car dealership, et cetera, et cetera. Then she drew up a monthly sheet and entered these numbers there so that at month's end, Ray would be able to tell exactly how much time and money had been spent on each client. She explained the sheet to him as he peered over her shoulder. Clients could be put into categories if he liked, she told him, so that he could see what types of businesses were his strongest customers.

"If you want," Eliza said.

"Yeah, okay," Ray said, squinting at her. "I don't mind knowing that."

She compiled invoices, let Ray eyeball them, and typed them up. Found envelopes, found stamps. Tolerated side-eye from Red. Then the day was over.

Eliza worked the next day and the next, saying "Good morning" to everyone when she arrived. Studiously not minding if the men did not respond. She made coffee. Opened the mail. Concentrated on each task. Double-checked her work. Answered the phone courteously, wrote messages legibly. In a week, she began to get a "Morning" or two back.

When she got her first paycheck, Eliza walked down to the Safeway on a fine green evening and bought groceries.

Necessities. But also bacon. Strawberries. A small jar of apple butter. Better coffee and a carton of table cream like the one Terry had brought. She did not figure prices in her head. She put what she wanted into the basket and carried the wonderful sack home.

XXVII

Her first out-of-the-shop job. Red waited in the car and Eliza stood on a porch before a closed door. There was no bell. She knocked on the rattling screen door. The porch slanted so that she had to put one foot behind the other to keep her balance. She was so unsure of herself that her hair, knotted in a bun and fastened with bobby pins, seemed to crawl at the roots.

A curtain over the window rippled.

Eliza knocked again. Steps sounded from inside the house and voices. The curtain jerked.

The door opened slowly and a middle-aged Black man in a white undershirt peered out. He did not unlatch the screen door.

"Mr. Ford Johnson?"

He nodded.

Eliza tried to keep her voice normal, tremorless, though she felt herself almost buzzing. Her name change was coming, but she wasn't waiting on it. "Mr. Johnson, my name is Eliza Brock and I've come to collect payment for a color television you bought from McGinnis Appliance. Payments are three months behind."

The man's lips hardly moved when he said, "Got laid off."

"Oh," Eliza said. "I'm sorry to hear that." She was, though she had expected to hear some such variation. "That's hard."

"Yes'm, it hard." Creeping to the man's waist was a little boy, maybe five, who held on to the man by his trouser pocket.

Eliza unsnapped her purse and took out the papers from McGinnis. "This paperwork says forty-two dollars is due."

Mr. Johnson's gaze did not lower to the paper. "Might's well be five hundred. Don't got that neither."

They looked at each other through the shadowy screen door, though Eliza felt that the man was not really seeing her but the wolf, pure and simple. He would know, as she did, that the wolf came in different forms. What was she supposed to do now? The only resource she could think of—Carlton Business College—came to her: accounts payable, the ledger, the columns.

"Well, let's see could we work this." Eliza studied the

paper. Sweat was sinking into her hairline. "I don't suppose you could make a one-month payment? That would only be fourteen."

The man's squint relaxed infinitesimally. But then he looked beyond her, out to the street. "That your driver out there, huh. Brought some weaponry with him, I bet."

Eliza turned to glance at Red in the awful car. He was sitting up straight, glaring out the side window. The faded ginger hair joined his forehead invisibly; he appeared to be pink-flesh-colored, hair and all.

"Him?" She considered. "I guess I'd have to say he's more like my boss. Where I work, everybody's my boss." She smiled apologetically, as though this aspect of her job were her fault.

Mr. Johnson's head angled. "Why they sent you out to do this stuff?"

Well. He had good manners. He hadn't said *an old lady;* he'd said *you.* But he hadn't budged an inch from the door. So this wasn't going to work after all. She would fail, and she would go back to the Vidalia and to Percy and the pennies and the dimes.

"Mr. Johnson." Eliza tried to swallow the tremor but it won through. "I'm working. It may be a job nobody wants, taking things away from people, but it's mine. For today, anyway."

His head canted further, and it was as if Eliza were coming into focus. "So what you say about the fourteen dollars?"

A truck went by on the street. Nearby in a tree, a crow guffawed. There was music playing somewhere in the house; Eliza could hear those things now. "Well, see here, Mr. Johnson"—she held up the paper—"see, payments are missing from December, January, and February. Now, they send us out at three months. If you could just pay December, it would set you back to two. Then, if that's how you want it, I could come and get another payment around the end of the month. Just another fourteen, but that's goodwill. Shows you want to pay. Soon as you get a job, you can catch it up. Could you do that?"

The door was opened wider. Another boy, taller, appeared on the man's right.

"Sally," Mr. Johnson said.

A woman came up behind the man, her face stony. "Jus' let it go, Ford."

"Aw, Daddy," the smaller boy cried. "I like Mighty Mouse." His brother commanded him to shut up.

"She say we c'n pay fourteen, get caught up little at a time," he told his wife.

"If that's how you want to do, Mrs. Johnson," Eliza said, turning her focus to the woman, "I'll come back." This was not the procedure she was supposed to use. But it was a procedure, she recognized that. She had learned that. Down at Paley's, they might swagger in the door fanning greenbacks like a royal flush, but that was them. This was her. Ain't ever'body got to be the same, her mother used to say. With the back of the damp hand clutching the papers, Eliza swiped at the sweat puddled at her neck.

Sally Johnson disappeared from the door and returned with her purse. She swatted the butt of the little boy, who was squirming beneath his daddy's arm, and paid no attention to his yelp. She counted out a ten, three ones, and change. She had to unlatch the screen door to hand it over. Eliza put it into an envelope, thanked her, then held out her hand toward the woman. Reluctantly, the woman shook it, and when she had, Eliza held it out toward the man. "Thank you, Mr. Johnson. Be seeing you. Good luck getting that job, you hear?"

She walked down the tilty porch, steadied herself on a post by the steps. She had not succeeded. But she had not exactly failed either.

Red grinned wickedly, expectantly, when he reported her ridiculous hand-shaking to Ray, who took the fourteen like it was dirty Kleenex. Eliza listened to his withering lecture, Red smirking along: She was here to work the office part of the shop and do the occasional house call; she would have to do her job like everyone else. He was not in the charity business, and he didn't provide layaway service. Not hearing *Fired*, she waited it out. Then she dared to say, extremely politely, that while she understood Ray's point, her method might work; the jury was still out on that. Mr. Johnson might pay another fourteen when she returned to his porch, and if not, the television could be picked up then. They would just have to see. Ray's jaw tightened, but he said nothing. Eliza took the busted-spring desk chair to figure and write out the week's payroll.

Now she better understood the estrangement between Louise and her father. Ray Paley was so used to being boss that he hefted that title everywhere with him. Did not know how to set it down. Did not know that there were times he could or should set it down. Eliza knew what he did not—withering people up might also spite the nose on your own face. She'd known that even before she went to Carlton Business College and knew it more firmly afterward.

She wrote out the checks. The Palmer Method cursive she had learned as a child, the flourishes, the evenness—though less even than when she was younger—endowed each green check with an antique quality. She handed the checks to Ray at his desk so he could scratch his signature across them.

Before he'd finished signing the last one, Freddie Haines and Byron Barker drove up in an Airstream travel trailer. After flinging wide the office door so all could see the gleaming silver lozenge outside, Freddie performed an end-zone dance, high-stepping in place. Byron, entering with the keys, ruined it by whapping the back of his head. As *sons of bitches* and *broke-dick bastards* flew through the shop, Eliza slipped away to her desk, glad that her chair faced the wall even if the wall was decorated with a rouge-nippled blonde on a motorcycle. She snapped her paycheck into her purse and typed up a batch of threat letters, the kind that used to fill the little drawer of her end table.

Quitting time. Wait, no, it wasn't. Not quite. She needed to fix something.

Eliza stopped by the door where Red was sliding on a windbreaker. "Red," she said. His posture stiffened.

"If we're going to work together" — a hostile look from him — "I mean, if this job works out for me, I wanted to say I'm sorry for making your job hard when I did. I know you were being nice when you let me keep the car awhile. I want you to know I was grateful for that, I was. So...thanks."

Red's shoulders lowered. His lips curved so slightly no one would have called it a smile. Eliza caught the movement, though, before he resumed his tough attitude. Red stuck out his bottom lip and nodded to her. "'Kay," he said, turning away.

He angled back to her. "I *did* cut you a break. Cut you a big break."

"You did," she agreed.

"'Cause you reminded me of my ma."

Eliza recalled his manner when she'd reentered her living room dressed properly in her suit. Daydreaming was what she'd thought, but maybe he'd been lost in memories.

"I'm sorry, Red."

"'Kay," he said again. He sniffed and went out the door.

XXVIII

Eliza's next two out-of-the-shop jobs, done between the daily typing, figuring, and phone answering — "Good morning, Paley and Associates. May I help you?" — were a washer and dryer from Sears and a Mercury Marauder from Walt Walker Ford. For the first, she spoke to the woman at the house, then held the door open for Red, who rolled in the dolly and, with Byron's help, wrangled the appliances into the back of a truck. While the washer and dryer fled, Eliza consoled the weeping woman. It was nothing she hadn't done all her life. This particular job did not require acting.

"I hate the sobbers," Red offered on the way back, an actual foray into conversation. At the office, she let Red turn in the papers while, phone receiver balanced between ear and shoulder, she copied down a message from a bank manager.

As for the Marauder, it sat parked in a driveway with two concrete runners and weeds between them. A tall young man banged out of the door and sat on his steps, arms tightly folded. Red took one look and got out with her. He leaped the ditch while Eliza walked up the driveway, hurrying to get there first.

"Mr. Flowers?" The young man's navy-blue work shirt bore an oval patch with *Donnie* written on it in black. Eliza knew what the papers said but she glanced at them anyway. "Mr. Donald Flowers?"

"That's me. And I don't know who you are, lady, but your sonny boy there ain't taking my car."

"Eliza Brock with Paley and Associates," she said to the young man. "That's good news, Mr. Flowers. We'll be happy to collect the back payments and be on our way. It comes to two hundred and twelve dollars."

"Don't have it, lady. But you take my car and I ain't never gonna have it."

Red stepped forward. The car tool, the one that could pop a lock, he held pressed to his side, his straight arm over it. "Not our problem, Jack."

The young man unfolded to maybe six foot three and anted up to Red's face, stared down at him. "Name ain't Jack."

"I'on' care if it's Daffy Duck," Red said. "Pay the two twelve or she's outta here."

Two female voices said "Donnie" at the same time. The young man sharp-eyed Eliza and then said over his shoulder, "Shut up, Mama. I'ma handle this."

"Donnie." A broad forehead peeped out a slit in the door, blond strips curled around pink foam rollers. "Told you Ed'd give you that old Chevy, you ask him nice."

"How many times I have to say I don't want that pile of shit?"

The door cracked open farther, bringing into view a tall, wide-necked, wide-shouldered woman yanking the sash of a pink velour robe. "Don't talk that way front of an old lady." Her head hooked toward Eliza, whom she then spoke to directly. "Shame how children act these days, idn't it?"

"Yes, ma'am. Same with mine." Eliza shook her head and set her hand on Red's back. Red turned to her open-mouthed, top lip unattractively drawn back from his stained teeth. "Where'd all those manners we taught 'em go?" Eliza asked.

Her hand insinuated itself along his side and closed on the car tool.

"In one ear and out the other," the woman said, hands on hips.

"Look, Mama, this is my business! Go on back in the house now!"

"See what I mean."

Donnie Flowers formed a fist and slugged his palm with it. The big woman raised both hands, shook them in mock fear, and closed the door.

Immediately Red backed him into the yard and said in his bored voice, "Okay, big guy. This is a legal deal. It ain't personal."

Furious explanations and justifications spewed from Donnie Flowers. Eliza headed quietly for the Marauder. Red was droning on about rich sons of bitches at the bank, shrugging, holding up empty palms, edging backward across the dandelion yard.

The lock popped easily. The young man broke for the Marauder, hollering, but not until the engine turned over. Now she understood the crucial skill of speeding in reverse. She curved wide into the street, stomped the brake, knocked the automatic gear into drive, and stepped on the gas for a few blocks.

Smiling.

Driving recklessly, though, brought back the flight to the hospital with Robert. *Doctor, doctor, doctor, doctor.* The smile faded away. Eliza cut her speed and wound a circuitous route back to Paley's shop with the radio on high to ward off the memory of that reckless drive. Red was there when she pulled up; she parked the Marauder in a slot and walked in past him and Ray Paley and Byron Barker to answer the ringing phone. It was one of Ray's renters from a sad block Red called Desolation Row asking if she brought the rent money by, would Mr. Paley call off the sheriff.

"Honey, you bring it by, I'll call him myself."

A long sigh breathed from the receiver.

Eliza, feeling herself observed by the men, let it stand in for the sigh she was holding back.

That night at the Vidalia, Percy made an awkward lump in her lap, trying to curl a body that didn't want to curl anymore. Eliza, her hands in the herb concoction Ike had sold her, gave herself a pep talk. Hers wasn't a job with prestige, wasn't a job people would envy or show respect for. But the work wasn't a mystery either. She didn't have to type her sore fingers off, change leaking diapers, or feed an old person bites of cottage cheese. Her job just called for quick thinking and maybe quick moves and knowing when to apply which. If there were bats to be swung, bullets to be ducked, a tow to hook up followed by a chase, that wasn't her; the boys could get into those free-for-alls. No reason, if she kept her brain lit up, why she shouldn't do all right. It was just that you could never tell. You had to get used to upset people and not knowing what would happen next. It was a contradiction—you had to get comfortable with all that uncertainty.

This devastating past year, she could say it had been part of her job training. Losing, humbling, adjusting, withstanding the onslaught of the new, persisting. Appreciating what there was to appreciate, even if it was unfamiliar or unexpected. All the book learning. Personal learning. She hadn't been able to use young Mr. Henney's advice to forgive, had she? Not with Robert breaking into her moments of peace or enjoyment. But that was learning too. And she saw now that the kind of sympathy that had always been her part was useful. Sort of a tool, and it came naturally. Apparently, so did the bits of acting that proved helpful from time to time. The acting had been a spur-of-the-moment surprise. A surprise Eliza liked.

Uncertainty it was, and uncertainty it was going to be.

Her next out-of-the-shop job was with Byron Barker at a scaled-down, rust-red ranch house at the end of a cul-de-sac. The place was locked up tight. The doorbell rang to no response. The curtains stayed put. The garage, which allegedly housed a Harley-Davidson Electra Glide, bore a padlock. Byron walked over to check inside, but the four glass panes of the garage door were blocked by tar paper. Barking snarled from the backyard, and Byron turned down his thumb, so Eliza tacked a Paley and Associates card to the front door. The remaining out-of-the-shop jobs were night work, requiring muscle and tows, strictly for the men. As Red hooked up a Chevy Impala Super Sport painted Evening Orchid, he had to hold off a debtor wielding a golf club while Byron twisted and dodged to avoid the aim of the spitting wife. Watching them act out that repo in the office the next day, Eliza was relieved she would never be called on for those jobs.

But Red motioned to her for an appliance repo with him and Freddie. A thin young woman with a fussing toddler apologized as Freddie loaded her Frigidaire onto the dolly. The contents of the refrigerator had to be hastily piled on an old linoleum countertop and on the floor; Eliza helped. The girl trailed them out, saying, "I thought we could pay for it. I'm sorry y'all had to come out here. I'm so sorry." Freddie, fleeing the reedy voice, hauled as fast as he could with the huge Harvest Gold box while Eliza recommended the *Green Sheet,* where a used refrigerator could likely be located for twenty dollars. Eliza caught the girl's shamed hands. "Listen, it's just a icebox. It's not your immortal soul."

Watching as the young woman buried her face against her child's downy head, Eliza too was relieved when the truck pulled away.

XXIX

April's azaleas were blazing bright, deep pink, the dogwoods drifting white. An unusual neighborhood for a collection. Red and Eliza found themselves driving past pillared brick mansions, horseshoe drives, clipped lawns. Red followed the numbers to the end of the street and turned in past a wild hedge. A tiny, gabled house, out of scale with the rest of the grand neighborhood, sat on a vast plot of land. An old, black, lozenge-shaped sedan was planted in the drive by the house, a dandelion family growing out from a flat back tire. The wide backyard faded into woods. They had come to inquire of its owner, a Mrs. Mavis Jordan, about the nonpayment of an emerald cocktail ring.

The doorbell failed to buzz, so Eliza knocked on the door. She heard footsteps. After maybe a minute, she raised her fist to knock again, but the door opened.

"Callie!" said a pleased older woman, welcoming her in. "I looked out through the little"—she tapped the door's peephole—"thing and there you were."

"Mrs. Mavis Jordan?"

"Oh, Callie, how good to see you. Come in!"

Red stepped back, gesturing toward the car; Eliza stepped inside, introduced herself, and stated her mission. This caused only a moment's confusion. The woman seemed to blink away Eliza's name, then the pleasure returned to her face.

Mavis Jordan, who had forgotten the ring's payments, as she was forgetting her charge accounts and her checkbook, her faraway son and her own name, simply unclasped a soft leather purse and handed over four hundred dollars. Not a common occurrence for Paley and Associates. The woman urged her to sit, so Eliza removed a stack of *Harper's Bazaar* magazines from a chair and began to sit down. She breathed in sharply. Fleeing from the pages of the magazines were herds of bugs. They flowed across Eliza's skirt like water and rippled down to the floor, where they disappeared.

Mrs. Jordan waved a hand and assured her guest, "Oh, those don't bite."

Eliza nodded slowly. The small house was a jumble of knickknacks, boxes, and piles. A laundry basket of mail sat on a console table by the door; a clothes rack on wheels situated by a window was crammed tight with dresses— prints, velvet, on the end a lady's tweed suit. Dusty mahogany furniture a mite too large for the scale of the room.

Mrs. Jordan looked on her with such an open face. They chatted. They were not so far apart in age, Mrs. Jordan maybe a dozen years older but not looking older, Eliza speculated, due to years of face creams, hand lotions, manicures, and permanent waves, not an upkeep she herself could have indulged in. The routines had lapsed, though; Mrs. Jordan's ash-blond hair was silver to her ears and straight, crinkling only at the ends that brushed her neck. She seemed to relish its length, tossed back her hair as if she were a girl at a dance. Eliza admired Mrs. Jordan's hands. They were slim-knuckled, white, and spotless, the curved nails tipped with the remnants of a creamy peach polish. Her fingers were slim as well and adorned with gleaming rings, three on each hand.

Mrs. Jordan understood that Eliza was some kind of a merchant here to collect a payment and, further, that Eliza had done her the service of coming personally to her home in order to save her a trip. Again she addressed her as Callie. Since Mrs. Jordan had become more animated, Eliza did not correct her. She knew from experience with her own late father that it was only disruptive to argue, as others had, that it was not Christmas, my goodness, Mr. Brock, take a gander out the window at the sprinklers, or to tell him that his son, Roy, was not shooting marbles in the barnyard, that Roy was, in fact, lost in the Pacific. Why call that up? Who did that correctness accommodate? Much easier to join the speaker in his own world, a world Eliza had shared, and live there again for a while.

Eliza had never liked clutter, so it was disorienting to realize that she was enjoying herself in Mrs. Jordan's crowded house. Enjoying Mrs. Jordan. It rushed in on her that the last visit she'd made to a friend simply for pleasure, simply to talk idly, had been that day she saw Velma Fitzwalter. The day Robert died. Louise and Terry had come to see her, and while she enjoyed their company in different ways, their visits had a motive. The visits from the other young people at the Vidalia did too. They came to borrow items or for a mother's ear, though the ones who came for that didn't understand that's why they'd knocked on her door. They just knew they had to tell something.

"Excuse me a minute, Mrs. Jordan, I'll be right back." She had the four hundred dollars already, but she went out to the car and told Red to return in an hour while she talked the woman inside out of the price of the ring.

Mrs. Jordan wanted to talk. And they did, as readily as young matrons do on a park bench or at a swimming pool as their playing or splashing children leave them the luxury of uninterrupted conversation. Mrs. Jordan also had a gift for listening. She focused intently on Eliza's face; she did not break in; she murmured, "And then?" It was the end of the day for Eliza, and though her hands throbbed too,

Mrs. Jordan had an ottoman, two, actually, if she wanted to choose, on which Eliza could rest her feet.

On a whim—that's what she told herself—she visited Mrs. Jordan a second time, in the evening about ten days later. At the door, she repeated her name, Eliza Brock; when that brought no response, she mentioned her previous visit concerning the ring. Mrs. Jordan's gaze fell to her glittering hand. "Oh, the ring." She nodded. "I see." Her brow contracted. "Which one must I give you, dear?"

"I've just come to visit you," Eliza said.

"To visit." Mrs. Jordan nodded again, businesslike. Her head tilted as she studied Eliza for her next cue.

"Why don't we have a cup of coffee?"

"Coffee, of course!" Mrs. Jordan beamed and welcomed her as a friend. She clattered out a kettle and a jar of instant, some thin china cups, then forgot to serve the coffee. Eliza got up and turned off the boiling kettle, then slipped into her chair and raised her tired feet again to the ottoman. She didn't care for that stimulant in the evenings anyway. She had brought a paper bag with two cherry buns, bought in the day-old section at the bakery. They talked about times during the war, not the one that was on television these days but the war that had been in the newspapers and on the radio. The one that had consumed the world they both knew.

They ate, and they talked. It was like a picture show to hear of USO dances, the songs the bandleaders played, the dresses Mrs. Jordan wore. Sweetheart necklines, peplums, piqué, dotted swiss, linen—"That wrinkles so bad," Eliza put in. "Oh, awfully," Mrs. Jordan agreed. "Sitting between the dances made me look like an accordion!"

Yes, indeed, she was married then, but Ralph didn't mind. He was so often out of town during the war, and here was a little thing she could do for the boys. "I didn't really look my age at *that* time, and then—the soldiers and sailors would have danced with broomsticks. All trying to get your name, a promise to write." The glow on her face allowed Eliza to see the woman she had been then, the hair completely ash blond and rolled back from the forehead, a willowy type who never had to relinquish her dancing posture, simply placed her hands onto the shoulders of the next soldier.

"Did you write any of them?"

"Five! All came home but one. How I cried for that boy. I didn't remember his face, but I cried for him all the same. Did you lose anyone, Mrs. Brock?"

"Yes, I did, my younger brother, Roy. In August of '42."

"Oh no."

"Roy joined up in '37. No farming for him; he meant to make himself a career in the military. But then the war came, and they sent him to Tulagi, one of those little bitty islands by Guadalcanal. The fighting there wasn't a bloodbath like Guadalcanal—only about forty of our boys were killed. But my little brother was one of them."

Mrs. Jordan teared up. "Oh, I am so sorry, Mrs. Brock.

So very sorry. What a horrible loss for you. And your mother, my goodness, your poor mother, bless her. How your family must have hurt."

It had been more than twenty years, but Eliza didn't remember any condolences given to her as sincerely as this one.

"We did," she said, "we did."

Mrs. Jordan nodded, patted Eliza's hand. Again she mentioned the young soldier who hadn't come home. "I put a gold star in my window upstairs, under the curtain, for him. I mean, I hardly knew him. I only talked to him once. My room faces the garden, so no one saw it but me and the maid."

The star. Eliza sat for a few moments, but Mrs. Jordan tipped her head expectantly. She so clearly wanted a reply, more conversation, for Eliza to join in with her. So Eliza told of Robert's enlistment and the quick trip she and Robert had made to his parents when he came home on his first leave before shipping out overseas. How Eliza had wanted them to stay home together, but no. He'd brought his mother a blue star for her window, to announce to the neighbors that her family had a fighting son.

"They must have been proud." Mrs. Jordan, having long finished her cherry bun, kept leaning toward Eliza. Her starving face reflected Eliza's own loneliness, something she had not wanted to see. "Weren't they? Proud?"

Mrs. Jordan was a rare one, Eliza thought, contrasting her with two of her former classmates at Carlton, Maxine and Hilda. Inviting her to share. Inviting Eliza to lay her own life beside Mrs. Jordan's so they might build common ground.

"Well." So she was going to tell it. "My husband's folks were deaf, and they had three other deaf sons, and I think Robert saw himself as somehow fighting for all of them. But my mother-in-law worried about appearing partial." Eliza found herself recounting all of it—how Mother Kratke had taken the star, a shadow flying over her expressive face. Eliza had always believed that she'd read in the shadow not fear for Robert or pride in him but concern for the feelings of the three sons the army would never accept. Though they hadn't spoken of it, she believed that Robert had read that too; the little military luster he'd gathered in training had dimmed.

"He'd known his mother wouldn't have starred the window herself. That's why he brought it. But I think— no, I know he wanted to see them proud of him."

Mrs. Jordan said, "They all wanted that, every one of them! I said that to them—'We're proud of you'—and they melted, every soldier and sailor I danced with. Your poor husband."

"Poor Robert..." Eliza said, trailing off. Abruptly, she stood and collected the plates. Mrs. Jordan followed every move, her brow furrowed, as if trying to locate a magic word to make Eliza stay, be still again and talk and listen. Noticing how she had devoured the bun, Eliza peeked into Mrs. Jordan's icebox. Bare except for a saucepan of congealed soup, an expired carton of cream, and a corked bottle of port wine.

At the end of the week, she brought a casserole. "Oh, Callie, dinner, how sweet of you!" Mrs. Jordan exclaimed. Eliza found two salad plates in the cupboard, which she had opened carefully lest there were bugs to be startled. She found two forks of heavy, tarnished silver and served herself and Mrs. Jordan. They ate on their laps, not bothering with table or settings. The less to wash the better, that was her credo now, though the hot water over her hands was a nice relief. Mrs. Jordan was talking of marriage. How Ralph had spoiled her with jewelry. Some long time away, occupied by important clients, with late meetings, with weekend business conventions, then filling the doorway, producing from his jacket pocket a velvet jeweler's box. Sapphire and diamonds. Gruffly affectionate. Attending to the house, making plans again for the addition they never built, cutting back the pesky vine, clipping down the wild hedge. A touch at her elbow as she served his morning coffee.

"Of course I knew," she said. Her eyes, direct, sober, glimmering with water, held Eliza's. "I knew, Mrs. Brock."

Not Callie. Mrs. Brock. It was not only being called by her real name that made the confidence intimate; it was the familiar formality of last names. Comfortable to Eliza. For years, her mother and her mother's friends had addressed each other that way, in a circle snapping beans, during staccato telephone conversations: *Hello, that you, Miz Willard? It's Miz Brock. Come at two.* Clunk.

Eliza returned her sober gaze and resorted to a platitude. "They do say the wife always knows about the other woman." Thinking, *Not me. I missed it all.*

Mrs. Jordan smiled sadly. "Woman? I'm afraid not. Gentlemen, Mrs. Brock. Young ones. And me such a..." She winced. "Such a *spaniel* for the jewels."

A film came over Mrs. Jordan's eyes. Eliza watched it lower like carefully let-down blinds. Mrs. Jordan complimented Callie on the delicious chicken casserole. "Oh, it's simple," Eliza said. "An old recipe of my mother's."

At last she slid her feet from the ottoman, washed the salad plates with very hot water, dried them, and put them away. Thanked Mrs. Jordan, who hovered behind her at the door, her face creased with reluctance, her clasped hands flashing brilliance.

It was late. Eliza waited for the bus in the dark, appreciating the fragrant air of the neighborhood, eyeing the half-moon. She went home to the Vidalia's flimsy walls, loud record players, barks, and shouts, the parking-lot view obscured by the stiff plastic drapes. She made her concoction as the smells of frying onions and ground meat penetrated the walls. She performed her hand exercises to squabbles and thumping rock and roll.

XXX

In May, anticipating the summer, Eliza bought herself a second fan—she could do that now, buy things—and Mrs. Poston, the manager of the Vidalia, tapped on Eliza's door to call her to the pay phone as she was enjoying the two streams of air pouring toward her and Percy. Eliza expected Hugh or Ellen, but Earl Fitzwalter was on the line.

"Some lady named Vidalia answering your phone, Eliza. Who's that?"

"Oh, just a friend, Earl. How are you today?"

"Got some good news," he said. "When you gonna be in Bayard next?" He had papers he could mail, but he thought if she visited the old hometown often, Eliza could pick them up herself. He'd be glad to see her when she did.

Eliza heard how upbeat Earl Fitzwalter sounded, and excitement flushed her face. Hopes rose. "You got the quitclaim, Earl? You got that woman to sign it? Earl, I—"

"Wait a minute, wait a minute. Haven't got hold of that woman yet. She must spend an awful lotta time outta her house. I got your name-change papers, Eliza." While he spoke, the happy note in his voice had dipped, then returned in full force.

Disappointment folded Eliza a little at the waist. Her hand pressed against her stomach. But she composed herself; it was necessary to rise to the occasion. And she was glad about the name change. "That's wonderful, Earl. That's really good. I am indebted to you."

"Aw, you're welcome. Velma sure likes that breakfront you gave us. She's got it filled up with dishes and wanting to buy more!"

"I bet it looks nice in your dining room."

"I guess so. Come by the office anytime, Eliza. I'd like to be there, but if I'm not, my secretary can hand over your papers."

"Sure thing, Earl, thank you." She wanted to but didn't mention the quitclaim a second time. Receiving favors from somebody you needed more favors from required a strategically shut mouth.

Almost immediately, Eliza reconsidered that thought.

For such an easy job, as Earl claimed it was, the name change had taken quite a while. The obvious conclusion was that Earl Fitzwalter took his own sweet time. And water had run under the bridge. She was supporting herself now. She felt more at home in the outside world. As she was fixing stamps to a set of letters containing invoices, having already checked the addresses on a list, she heard her father's tired voice: *You want something done right, you got to God-dang do it yourself.*

So here she was, with lipstick on and a wave in her hair she'd used curlers to set. She trod the sidewalk carefully, feeling as if she might turn around any minute. The neighborhood was all right, nice enough, though not nearly as nice as Eliza's old one had been. Still, it was on a different side of the tracks from the Vidalia. There were a few large trees and some shrubs, one late-model car parked in a driveway. She had come prepared but her breath was short.

The door opened to a small, square-jawed woman with a blank face, all over it the uniform pink-orange color that came liquid in little drugstore bottles. Her eyebrows were darkly marked, and her mouth wide. The brown irises of her eyes were surrounded by white, even above the sagging bottom lids, what people called puppy-dog eyes. When the woman saw Eliza, her forehead contracted into worry wrinkles. Then Eliza recognized her: the pitiful woman from the funeral.

Eliza knew her name but did not want to use it. "Can we please talk?" she asked through the screen door.

"I have my marriage papers," the woman said menacingly, as though the papers were a gun or a savage dog.

"I've heard you say that." Eliza had imagined they might sit down and talk, but the screen door stayed put. All right, it would be that way.

"I told you on the phone. All I want is for you to let go of my house," she said. "Just let your claim go. I need to sell that house. I see you have one."

The woman looked away. Her hand, with its gold ring like Eliza's, was still on the door as though she would dearly love to shut it. But she didn't—and that gave Eliza the will to go on.

"I reckon that Robert bought it?"

A sullen nod.

"He put a mortgage on my paid-off house to do that."

The whites of the woman's eyes seemed to swell until her brown irises were swimming in them. Her voice rose: "He told me it was savings. I can't pay that off!"

Eliza unsnapped her purse and held out the quitclaim. "I'm not asking you to pay it off. I'm just asking you to take back your claim on mine. To sign this. If this has to go in front of a judge, and he looks at both the marriage licenses, you know what's going to happen. Don't you?"

"No, he'll see that...he'll see..."

"Junie, who you talking to?" A large man appeared behind her, a wrench in his hand. His fair hair was grayed at the temples, and his eyes had the same rim of white around them, but he didn't look frightened; he looked irritable and discouraged. June slipped back from the door until she was standing by the man, and she took hold of his arm. "It's her," she said. "Oh, Ben, make her go away."

Eliza wanted to go away. This was who Robert had loved, this furtive creature, this helplessness. Loved. Made love to.

The man transferred the wrench to his left hand and hardened his face. "You Mrs. Kratke?"

"The first one," Eliza said. June placed herself behind him.

The brother—he must be a brother, Eliza decided—hesitated, then put a protective arm in front of the cowering woman. "You got gall to darken our door. Listen, my sister's been put through hell. Hell! I don't know what you mean by coming here, but she doesn't need any more."

"Mister, all I'm asking is that she sign this quitclaim."

"What claim? Bob bought her this house outright. It belongs to her. I'll be damned, you have no—"

Bob. They called Robert Bob.

Eliza took a step to the side to steady herself. "Not this house. My house. Across town, the one I lived in for thirty years. I need to sell it now, and I can't do that with your sister's lien on it."

"Lien? What? My sister hasn't—she wouldn't..." The brother stopped for a few moments, head sinking down as though he were listening. Then he closed his eyes. Resignation sagged in his face. He held open the screen door.

Eliza forced herself to step in, next to the wall. "It's

this," she said, handing him the paper. "All I want is for her to sign it. So the lien gets taken off my house." Terrified she would find a framed picture of Robert and June, him in a town-hall suit and her with a corsage—surely not a wedding dress, surely not—Eliza did not go farther into the room. It was small, anyway, with a thin tan carpet, a sofa upholstered in early American fabric, and a coffee table with an ashtray on top. On the wall, a landscape with old-timey people and a sleigh piled with boxes. Photographs on a television too far away for Eliza to make out the details—one large person, one small.

"Come here, June. Junie, come on out of there." The man was leaning into a doorway that the woman had passed through. "What's she talking about, quitclaim? You're not trying to take something from her. Come tell her. Come on out, damn it."

The brother turned to Eliza, said, blustering, "I don't know anything about a lien. And after a year! More than a year—God A'mighty, it's May! We're still trying to sort this out, get my sister calmed down and set up again, so we can all go on with our lives after this...this thing." He went into the room and came out with his sister by the elbow.

"Tell me what you did, Junie. Now."

June's mouth was clenched tight. Her jaw was sharp.

"Junie!"

She flinched. "I just showed my marriage license and told...the county clerk that my husband died and didn't leave any will. That I didn't get my due. She said that very thing had happened to her mother, and she entered it into a record."

"Wait. The county clerk—you mean Roseann? Junie, are you talking 'bout Roseann?"

June's mouth closed again. Pink crept up her neck.

"Roseann's mama's husband had a will, Junie, he just didn't put her in it. The money went to his son. You telling me Roseann set a lien on the house without you having any papers to prove it?"

The pink deepened.

"Excuse me," Eliza said. "Why is my house your due?"

The woman didn't answer her, but it seemed she was working up to it. Her mouth skewed strangely. It was like a landslide that started with a single dislodged rock, then pebbles rolling, then the land lurching, a hillside falling.

June opened her mouth and screamed until she ran out of breath. Eliza, her face averted, suffered every second of the scream. She knew it deeply. During her months of hibernation, alone in the house so no one could hear, she'd screamed. Out of pure fury. Out of loss and grating shame and hurt and a desire to hurt Robert, to hurt him back— while he was forever unreachable.

"Bob was my husband! For nineteen months, he was my husband! Oh God, my only-only-only! Then he went and died. He would want me to have some money. I know he would, I know it!" She turned to Eliza. "You're old, you've got grown kids you can go live with. I don't have that." Spittle flecked the corners of her lips.

"Junie, Junie." The brother caught hold of June. He suddenly turned to Eliza. "You see what it's been like? You see?"

Did he expect sympathy? Eliza looked the big man, Ben, in the face. She saw pity, impatience, frustration, and none of it moved her. To June, she said, "So you knew about me?"

"No!" The puppy-dog eyes squeezed shut; her hands were fists. "Not for a long time. Then you know what?" Her teeth were showing now. "I didn't care. Because Bob loved me. He loved me!"

The words had the effect June intended. They rained blows on Eliza. Because blows could not be rained on Robert.

June's brother made glancing, unwilling eye contact with Eliza. He couldn't have missed the pain. He dropped his arms from his sister and roughly pushed back his fair hair.

"Listen, Junie, I'm just through," he told her. His voice had lowered to barely more than a whisper. "So's Melvin. If he didn't tell you already, I'm telling you. You got to get yourself all right. So let's be done with this, hear? Sign the woman's paper. Let her be on her way. Please."

Melvin had to be June's other brother, one of the two men who'd supported her at Robert's funeral. They were tired, Ben said. Eliza understood that. She looked at the woman to see how she felt about her brother's plea.

Little fists. A wail that began, "But I deserve...I deserrrrve—"

A back door banged. A towheaded boy ran into the room and flung himself at the man, who caught him awkwardly. "Hey, Stevie," he said. He shot his sister a hard look and raised his hand near his face. He made a sign that, even after all these years, Eliza recognized. The fingers spread and thumb touched twice to his chin. *Mother.* Something about Mother. The joy in the boy's eyes checked when he saw his mother's twisted face, lit again as he looked toward the man. It faded as he signed something and walked toward the back room. The brother, ushering June too, followed the boy.

What was Eliza supposed to do? She held her head still in order to slow the dizzying circles. She heard talking but couldn't make out the words. The house smelled of laundry detergent. The boy was deaf. Not Robert's boy, too old for that, ten or eleven, and too fair. June's boy.

The large man returned from the back room, his face wretched.

"This is just an awful mess. I—near as I understand it, you have a house you want a lien off of, that right? And June put it on."

"Awful," Eliza said. And "That's what I want."

"You got a pen?"

Eliza fetched one from her purse. He took it back to the bedroom. There was talking, whimpering. One exclamation.

Eliza, unsteady, needed to sit down but that would have been wrong. She moved to feel a wall behind her, next to a bookcase whose top shelf held an assortment of figurines. The lower shelves held magazines and toys—a yo-yo, coloring books, tiny cars. Noise from the back room grew louder as she saw it on the top shelf, next to a pair of frolicking dogs—a china shepherdess, the twin of the one she had broken on the bricks of her patio. Pastel, delicate, still. Forever silent.

June's boy was deaf.

He spoke the first language Robert had ever learned. His native language. Like Robert's family. Like the brothers he'd grown up with.

June's brother strode from the back room, thrust the paper at Eliza. He did not meet her eyes. She stared down at a tangled signature and thanked him.

The bus stop was in view of June's house. There, Eliza stood erect while she folded the quitclaim into her purse. Once in the privacy of the bus's last row, she pressed her cheek into the seat back like it was someone's strong shoulder.

At the Vidalia, she stood under the awning by the garland of onions and called the real estate lady, who was happy to hear from her. Sales in Eliza's neighborhood were strong, she said, since a new elementary school was due to open in the fall. She'd go by the house tomorrow, she promised cheerily, to polish up that dusty sign.

XXXI

A loud sputter of exhaust and Red strutted into Paley and Associates Collection Services. The new guy trailed him. Red flipped back his maroon plaid sports coat, licked his thumb, set it dead center of his puffed chest, and hissed, "Sssssssssst."

Eliza recognized the pantomime from her Vidalia neighbors. It meant that he was so hot, steam was coming off him. Byron Barker took a doughnut out of his mouth. "Whatcha got, big boy?" As he, Ray, and Eliza watched, Red opened the door wide to show the Harley-Davidson Electra Glide parked out front, gleaming like Elizabeth Taylor in a Tiffany jewelry store.

"Couldn't help polishing it," Red said.

"I'd polish that baby with my tongue." Byron punched Red's shoulder.

"Way to go." Ray lifted his thumb in the air. At this praise, Red glanced at Eliza, who added her part to the chorus. "Nice work, Red."

"Thank you, Eliza," Red said with a mock bow.

He launched into the story of how smart he was to come up with a way to bring it in—it included a pound of ground round laced with Benadryl and an A1 padlock popper—as Eliza tapped her fingers soundlessly, thinking. She waited till a half hour before lunch, then approached Red at his desk.

"You reckon you could cut this off?" She held out her left hand with the gold wedding band.

Red blinked. He stared at her hand. "Your fingers ain't fat. You oughta could pull that off. Get you some Crisco."

"It's the knuckle," she told him, pointing out the prominent bulge. "Crisco's not gonna help that."

Red studied her hand awhile, darted a glance at her, and studied it some more. Then he got up and went to a side room that housed tools and supplies. He came back carrying a medium-long tool with a biting end. "Bolt cutter," he said. "Can you hold steady?"

"I think I can."

Byron Barker and the new guy moseyed over to watch. Red waved them back, then inserted one jaw of the cutter between Eliza's finger and the ring, saying, "Gimme room. Okay, don't move a inch, Eliza."

Snap.

It took the both of them to pry open the severed ends and separate the ring from her finger. The men looked on curiously. They didn't ask, and she didn't explain.

Robert had left her, and now she had left him. The ache still lived in her; she believed it always would. Her hand, though — it was lighter.

Of course I knew, Mrs. Jordan had said. Well, Eliza had not known, about Robert, his other wife, or herself. One time, recalling young Mr. Henney's textbook advice about anger and acid and c-corrosion, Eliza tried to feel what the predicament of bigamy had been like for Robert. She succeeded once, receiving inside herself a disturbing torrent of longing and fear. He'd been afraid but unable to stop himself from going ahead anyway. Lies tumbling over lies, the guilt that followed. A soaring freshness with the new woman. Different from the June she'd recently seen, of course. She had to have been. Robert's June smiled, sought his company, laughed and flirted for it. Alongside her, a needy boy he knew like he'd known himself.

Eliza allowed herself to feel what Robert had felt, allowed tendrils of pity to come. The comprehension helped her somewhat, softened her, but did not heal.

She continued to visit Mrs. Jordan, though as the weeks went on, Eliza was Mrs. Brock less often and Callie more. Mrs. Jordan's face became gaunt; sometimes her long hair was not brushed. Eliza visited more frequently and always brought suppers. One July day when she knocked on the door, it was not her friend who answered but a man. A middle-aged man in a double-breasted gray suit and a black shirt, its collar spread wide. Hair that covered his ears. "Who are you?" he asked.

"Eliza Brock. I'm a friend of Mrs. Jordan."

The man grimaced at the foil package in her hands. It contained tuna fish sandwiches and deviled eggs, perhaps not the best choice for a scorching summer day.

"Really? I didn't know she had any. I mean, besides the cleaning lady I send." He glanced around the crowded room—the boxes, the magazine and clothing piles, the mail in the laundry basket—the corners of his lips down-turned. "Not that the bitch does anything." There was dust on his gray suit.

"Is she all right? Mrs. Jordan? You must be her son?"

"Yeah. Come in for a minute. When did you meet my mother? She hardly goes anywhere."

"In the spring. I came here on business. And, well, we just enjoyed each other's company. I've been coming ever since."

"Okay." He did not inquire about the business. "I guess...I guess I'm glad to hear that. Poor Mother. Oh, I'm Blaise Jordan. You are?"

"Eliza Brock."

"Oh, right, you said. Sorry."

"Is your mother all right?"

"Well, no. I mean, yes, she's all right, but she's moved. I mean, I've moved her. Temporarily, until I can find her a place in LA. I can't keep running back to Texas all the time."

Eliza wondered how many times he'd run back here. "She won't live with you?"

"No, no, no. And she can't handle this"—he turned in a half-circle, his arm out to indicate the piles and the jumble—"anymore. She isn't safe here. She could trip over something and break her neck."

"I saw that."

"You could have called me. It was kind of shocking to see her."

"I'm sorry. I should have." Eliza felt genuinely sorry. She'd held on to Mrs. Jordan as Mrs. Jordan had held on to her. Friends in a disappeared world, a world they both knew, that hadn't changed. A respite from Eliza's relentless present, learning everything new. "I certainly should have," Eliza repeated, touching her forehead.

"Well, I'm here now." Blaise Jordan sighed. "You know, when I think about it, I'm glad Mother had a friend. I am. Makes me feel better."

They were still standing by the door. "Where...where is your mother, Blaise?" Eliza was hesitant to ask this question.

"Oh, Bending Willow. It's a nursing home." He raised both palms as though Eliza had stated an objection. "Very nice, very nice. Mother has money. You couldn't tell it to look at this dump, my God. How she ever let it get this way..." He was shaking his head.

"Do they allow visitors there?"

"I didn't ask. Well, uh, Mrs. Block"—he squinted at Eliza—"I've got some phone calls to make."

Awkwardly, Eliza and her deviled eggs took their leave.

In the morning she located Bending Willow Nursing Facility in the Yellow Pages. In the afternoon, she helped Red separate a boat from its delinquent owners, a pretty turquoise-painted boat with an outboard motor and white leather seats. The wife had been the one to watch out for, shouting and cursing. She'd grabbed Red by the belly of his short-sleeved shirt and shoved him. The sweaty, sad-faced husband just stood there, hands in his pockets, eyes shining. Eliza told him the delinquent amount and the steps he would need to complete in order to reacquire the boat, should he wish to. That was how she put it. Sometimes formal language added a little distance between the beloved possession and what was happening before the debtors' eyes. It was the husband's elbow Eliza gently brushed.

Bending Willow smelled like Pine-Sol with a whiff of urine. Eliza signed in and asked for Mrs. Jordan. She hadn't brought food—for now her friend would have plenty to eat, thank goodness, something different every day—so instead, Eliza had had the happy idea of bringing curlers with her, as fixing Mrs. Jordan's hair might be something they'd both enjoy. She was looking forward to it.

Eliza was stunned to see her. Mrs. Jordan sat sideways on a single bed, slumped over, her gray hair dragging over her crossed arms. She wore a robe and socks that had not been washed in a day or two. She didn't stir when Eliza entered, so Eliza said, "It's Mrs. Brock to see you. Mrs. Jordan?"

A small television fixed to the wall was tilted down for viewers in their beds. *The Secret Storm* was just giving way to the local news. The window air conditioner puffed out air that could have been a little cooler.

"Mrs. Jordan?"

Eliza set her purse and the curlers aside and sat down beside her friend on the bed. "Mrs. Jordan, it's Mrs. Brock come to see you. What can I do?"

"I want to go home." Mrs. Jordan's voice was thick; she snuffled mucus back into her nose. "Let me go home. Please." She lifted her head. There was no recognition in her eyes, and her head fell back down.

"Oh. Oh, Mrs. Jordan. Mavis." Stricken, Eliza added the unfamiliar name, but nothing changed. She sat with the collapsed woman. They just sat.

After some time with no response, Eliza reached over and put both arms around her friend in an embrace. Swayed in tiny degrees back and forth, the smallest rocking. She told Mrs. Jordan she'd be a regular visitor and her son would too (this might not have been true) until Mrs. Jordan went to live near him. Near her son Blaise. Mrs. Jordan shouldn't think she was alone. Eliza murmured to her for a while, but her friend's posture didn't change. Eliza searched her brain.

She decided to sing. She went naturally to the old songs she knew well. Ballads, swing that she used to sing to herself while Robert was overseas. That everyone sang.

" 'I'll be seeing you, in all the old familiar places.' " And: " 'We'll meet again, don't know where, don't know when...' "

Mrs. Jordan's lips began to move along with the words.

Her head still hung down, but she joined in with Eliza. Weakly, knowing all the words too. When Eliza ran out of band music, she fell back on church songs. She started "This Little Light of Mine" at a slow tempo because she thought Mrs. Jordan would know that song. Because the Staple Singers did that one on the radio.

They rocked and sang.

Eliza happened to look up and caught an aide in a white uniform staring into the room. Snapping her fingers, the aide finished the chorus with them before she went on about her job.

XXXII

She had envied Mrs. Jordan her house but it had not occurred to her to covet it, as it would not have occurred to Eliza to covet the White House or the Taj Mahal. The little house was put up for sale, however, in October of 1965, after Mrs. Jordan was moved to a nursing facility in Los Angeles, one that offered more care. Until then, Eliza had stopped by Bending Willow once a week, just to sit. There'd been no more singing, and Mrs. Jordan did not call her either Mrs. Brock or Callie. They were lonely visits except for when Eliza took Mrs. Jordan's hand and her friend did not pull it away.

Eliza's house, its title cleared, sold in July and closed in August of that year. She paid off the second mortgage.

The balance, loitering in a passbook savings account, she unhesitatingly signed over to Blaise Jordan in exchange for the house. Mrs. Jordan's son, in town again, considered the small, rundown place an eyesore, but he was not blind to location, location, location. The inducement for a middle-aged man burdened with unhappy family memories, overwhelmed by forty years' accumulation of what he considered junk in his childhood home, a man with places to be, was that the deal stood before him in a shirtdress and flat sandals. The deal knew a lawyer who would complete the sale without a task or a dollar bill required from him. Eliza Kratke would no more have bought herself a house—parting with an entire bank balance, leaving only a few hundred dollars to her name—than bought herself a ruby cocktail ring.

Eliza Brock would and did.

The day she moved in! The bed she'd ordered from Sears arrived; the movers' boots boomed on wood floors in empty rooms. Ellen and Hugh and Pam and Betsy had carried into the little house Eliza's few possessions. Eliza spread a sheet on the floor and put out platters of barbecue, beans, and potato salad and they had a picnic, after which Betsy and John ran around exploring. Eliza assured her kids she'd accumulate furniture little by little—she had the *Green Sheet*. Her coworkers at Paley's would help with transporting and lifting, no problem. She'd already cleaned the windows so her family could take in the wild front yard and the woods, copper and gold spangling behind the house. Eliza's house.

She found that she missed Mrs. Jordan more than their short acquaintance could account for. She ranged outward in search of friendships, not easy to forge at this stage of life.

She has met a couple of other widows at church: A Mrs. Kobliska, Eva, who likes to play cards and bakes fancy pies with dough shapes cooked on them. A Mrs. Franco, Maria, who keeps tabs on the Democrats and the Republicans and whose six kids are grown. These women have opinions, and they listen to Eliza's opinions. Once in a blue moon, Eliza invites Morton for a hamburger after work. While not much for conversation, he can let the dogs run on all this land.

Percy doesn't run with them. On a walk down Greavey Street just before Eliza left the Sweet Vidalia, Percy had lain down on the sidewalk. Eliza picked him up, crooning to him, thinking he was too tired to go on. She was almost to their room when she realized Percy was still. A second later it bore down on her what that meant. Instead of entering number 2, she knocked loudly on the door of number 1 and, when her neighbor opened it, stood there, face crumpled, aware, disconsolate. Morton took Percy from her arms, made Eliza sit down. She shouldn't have been surprised that he proved a world of comfort to her because Morton knew Percy's great and true worth.

XXXIII

Eliza is now sixty. The blackout period over, she has filed for widow's benefits from Robert's Social Security. In her three years at Paley's, Freddie and Byron have wandered away to be replaced by Manny and Lester. She and Red trained them. She is a part of the shop, not a family, and that is enough. A part like the baseball bat in the corner by the door, like the piles of letters, like Red, who was kept on, not let go, during a two-month recuperation from back surgery. Like the rare postcard from Louise, sent from somewhere in the free world. She is a part like Ray with his sharkskin suits, like uncertainty. It is a living, now, rather than a job.

Eliza, bare feet propped on an ottoman, sinks one

hand in the bowl on her toweled lap and sighs. In the bowl is a concoction of honey, fenugreek, borage oil, turmeric, piperine, and hot water, whisked by her mixer into a soup. Every few minutes, she alternates hands. Now and then, with the pad of her thumb, she may tune the radio to stations that play hits from the forties and fifties or gospel. She's learned to be wary of classical. True, she discovered Vivaldi's bright violins, but once a piece by a Polish composer had ambushed her. The bleak music sent her back into the devastation after Robert's death—the bladed curses, the *Whys* and *Did you evers*.

These FM radio stations don't talk much, and when they do, the announcers whisper, as though careful not to wake an audience that has slipped off to dreamland. The gospel station shouts sometimes, airing a visiting preacher. Then Eliza wrestles it off.

The evening light is green. The tenacious vine that is slowly swallowing her little house, that Mr. Jordan had cut back every spring, has permission to grow. It has masked her windows. Relieved her of having to draw drapes she doesn't have. Enough light enters through the jagged spaces between leaves; the leaves themselves are translucent. Birds call and answer, settling in the hedge. Their evening conference will begin soon, a mass twittering as each tells its day at once.

Eliza's arthritis mixture, already combined in its bowl, waits on the stove. She adds hot water and creeps with the bowl, her bare feet on cool linoleum. She nudges the door with her hip. It collides with the screen door, which she has not latched all summer. Outside, in a wooden recliner with a small wood stool for an ottoman, she immerses one hand at a time as she listens to the birds.

Sitting out there is a luxury, a dedicated pastime, a taking-in. The mantle of night air, the whiffs of honeysuckle, the shooting stars and the wheeling ones, in no more hurry than she is. She dries her hands and begins her exercises. She unfolds each finger, stretches, holds, trembling. Thirty slow repetitions for each one, forty for the thumbs. Then each hand, stretching backward as far as the inflammation allows.

In the mornings, a brim of light at the hedge. The stars step backward, the day steps forward. Birds peel off their hedge beds to search for breakfast. Eliza Brock carries her bowl inside, gripping it now, a towel draped over her shoulder. She washes this bowl and the one from the night before, hot water caressing her hands, which she presses triumphantly flat against her kitchen counter. Then an aspirin from the bottle she never caps, and a piece of bread for the toaster so the aspirin will not churn her stomach.

This house is a vast satisfaction to her, a haven. The tall, wild hedge closing in on the driveway thankfully hides it from the stately neighborhood. Thankfully, because if it were not hidden, if the avenue did not appear to trail off at Eliza's hedge, the neighbors would be after her to improve the house, in keeping with the general status. Eliza has neither the means nor the desire to improve it.

Its eastern boundary joins the plot of woods, not yet seized by developers, and a tribe of wild turkeys occasionally visits, pecking and doing funny jumps in the air. Deer leap the hedge in the evenings and early mornings, astounding, standing leaps she loves to see, and graze on the corn she has scattered for them. If she moves, they freeze, and she must freeze herself then, so that her breathing sculpture garden will drift across the grass, reconfiguring itself into different beauties. As evening deepens, the deer fade into it as the stars into the day, their bodies erased. But Eliza has learned to feel their presence still, to watch for a whisk of white tail, quick as a firefly's signal, that tells her they are leaping the hedge, leaving her to herself again.

They will return tomorrow.

Eliza has not returned to the church in her old neighborhood. Or to the neighbors, though she occasionally talks to Velma Fitzwalter on the phone. She's heard that Reverend Olsen has passed, and she hasn't seen the young minister with his unruly hair again. Once in a while, she thinks of saying to him: *Well, Mr. Henney, it turns out the advice you gave me was not wrong.*

Not so much the part about anger being an acid that corrodes, though she concedes that is true, very true; she'd seen it with Louise. Eliza reckons she herself is toting a fair amount of corrosion. The part about silence and stillness—that's where Mr. Henney was right, and helpful. She has considered dropping in on him and telling him that. After all, she'd been rude to a young man just trying his best. Embarrassed him, made him believe he'd failed in a spiritual encounter.

But...no.

Eliza has decided to let him figure it all out for himself.

Acknowledgments

Thanks from the heart to my writing colleagues Lynda Madison, Suzanne Kehm, Barbara Schmitz, Greg Kosmicki, and Shelly Geiser, who read passages in this book and gave solid advice, and to dear friends Celia Ludi, Catherine Ferguson, Laura Davis Hays, and Dr. Jackie Kelly, who added thoughtful points of view. I'm grateful to Josh Kendall for generously communicating his invaluable knowledge and experience and to editor-wizard Helen O'Hare, whose probing questions and comments turned a novella into a novel. A bow to virtuoso copyeditor Tracy Roe and a big *abrazo* to my smart, gracious agent, Jennifer Thompson. Last, I'm indebted to my grandmother Nannie B. Miles for the spirit of this book. Her perseverance through dire circumstances provided a foundational example of strength and ingenuity.

About the Author

LISA SANDLIN graduated from Rice University in Houston and earned an MFA in writing at Vermont College. She taught at CMU; SMU; Wayne State College; the University of Texas; and Kadir Has University in Istanbul, Turkey, and she finished her career as professor emerita at the University of Nebraska Omaha. Sandlin has written four story collections and four novels, two of which will be published in 2024. She has received an NEA Fellowship and a Dobie Paisano Fellowship, and her work has won the Pushcart Prize, the Violet Crown Award, and the Jesse H. Jones Award. Sandlin's noir mystery *The Do-Right* won both the Shamus Award and the Hammett Prize. Its sequel, *The Bird Boys,* was chosen by the *New York Times* as one of the ten best crime books of 2019. She lives in Santa Fe, New Mexico.